GLASS HOURS

Cathy Richard Dodson

BooksForABuck.com

2008

GLASS HOURS

Cathy Richard Dodson

Published by BooksForABuck.com
April 2008

ISBN: 978-1-60215-076-8

CHAPTER 1

To everything there is a season
A time to mourn.
Ecclesiastes 3:1-8

Lyndfield Estate, upstate New York
March 4, 1890

A light mist coated the air and hung lazily over the lush green of the estate. Caroline Lyndfield pushed a strand of damp hair away from her forehead then leaned down to touch the cold gray slate. 'Francis Delafield Monroe', the stone read. 'Beloved teacher and friend.'

Caroline drew a heart into the beads of moisture gathered on the stone. No one had known he was more to her than just a teacher and a friend. Indeed, he *was* beloved. If things had turned out the way they planned, he would have been her husband—her lover. Mist gathered in her eyes and flowed into tears. She remembered the final time she'd spoken with him. That fated last day...

They had stood just inside the conservatory, surrounded by the promise of spring roses. Hadn't it been raining that day too? But of course she wouldn't have noticed. The days always seemed sunny when he was with her.

"Caroline, we must speak to your father soon," Francis said, pressing in his gentle manner, but managing never to push. Just one of the many things she loved about him.

"I know," she nodded. "I know...but Father is so preoccupied with his work right now. I want it to be the right time, my love."

Francis took a step back from her, pulling his warmth with him. "You mean he's preoccupied arranging your marriage to Evan Ludington."

"Tisn't fair, Francis. You know I've told Father I do not want to marry Evan." Caroline reached out to him, but uncharacteristically, he drew away.

"It's time I took this matter into my own hands," he responded with quiet determination.

"Francis," she pleaded. "Not yet. Give me another day. I'm afraid."

"Afraid of what?"

She shook her head, not really certain of the answer to his question. "My father can be very determined to have his own way. You know that."

He sighed. "Yes, I know. I do know that. But no more days, Caroline. It's now, or it will never be." He reached out and touched her

3

cheek, giving her a tender look as he'd spun on his heel and walked silently away.

Caroline remembered the tears held in check as she'd watched the gray and green of the woods close around him. Suddenly, the heaviness and chill of the day had hit her hard. That was the last time they'd been together—and they'd parted in anger.

Caroline fought back a moan of grief and despair. Only babies cried and she wasn't a baby. William Lyndfield had always demanded courage from his only child. Of all the things she'd learned from her father, that was probably the most valuable. Though he himself might beg to differ. With his tremendous wealth, he could buy her any prize, and Caroline knew her father's fortune was his greatest treasure. Not his daughter. Her brave heart had been instilled only to serve his own purposes; she recognized her father for the selfish man he was. Perhaps it took that kind of egocentricity to build a financial empire, but Caroline would have been happy to settle for less money and more love.

But courage her father had bequeathed her nonetheless, and she called on it to serve her now. '*A grown woman who loved a grown man*' Caroline reminded herself, ' *With all my heart*.'

Francis Monroe had been her teacher since she was fourteen years old. He'd come the year after Aunt Jess had died, another tragedy of Caroline's youth. But thankfully, her father hadn't tried to replace Aunt Jess with another female "None of those namby-pamby governesses for my girl," he'd said. "You'll have the best, a male instructor. And you'll learn like a lad. So some day, my dear, you can barter business with the best of 'em."

So had come the beginning of her time with Francis, and in many ways he had filled the gap left by the death of her aunt. She met him on a summer's day when the roses still bloomed fresh on the vine and her heart was bursting with impressionable youth. Caroline had fallen in love with him instantly. With his fair curls and pale blue eyes which made him appear almost too angelic to be a man—his graceful slender form and long sturdy hands. And of course he was every bit as intelligent as her father thought him to be. He'd taught Caroline mathematics and Latin and English grammar and history with the wit and insight of a genius, yet had made it all seem fun somehow. They became the best of friends; their days, and their years, had flown by.

Until finally the year came when they'd at last acknowledged their love for one another. Francis had taken his own sweet time noticing his pupil was no longer a child but a lovely young woman with her heart in her eyes. But since the day he had, they'd stolen moments away from lessons for kisses, and had pledged their troth. They had dreamed of a future together: a dream that seemed real and possible enough, until Caroline's father casually announced his plan for her life over dinner one night. That he wanted her to spend some time—"getting acquainted on a more intimate level"—his words had been—with his friend and colleague, Evan Ludington.

"A fine man," her father informed her between bites of lamb and sips of wine. "A man of wealth and stature. A scientist like myself." He patted Caroline's hand as she looked from him to Francis, who sat across from her, head down and eating his own meal in silent desperation. "I'd like to see our futures united, my dear. With his intelligence and my fortune, a man like Ludington could conquer the world."

How well she remembered the ominous silence that filled the dining room, and she found herself wishing her aunt had been there with her delightful laughter to lighten the mood. Perhaps, as Aunt Jess had been wont to do, she'd have made a stand for her. But only the clink of her father's fork against his china plate, clinging to the air like an echo, broke the quiet of her shock. Through dim gaslight she noticed Francis' gaze trained to his own plate, and it seemed to her they all moved as if in a slow nightmare.

She sought words to question her father's request, but none came to mind or voice. Her only thought— outrageously—was that Evan Ludington must be nearly three times her age. But such trivial information made no matter to her father. William Lyndfield had decided and that was that. Caroline knew better than to argue with him over dinner. When she and Francis spoke of it at last, she'd promised to confront her father. But the time had never seemed right somehow. He was either away on business, caught up in one of his many experiments with Evan, in the wrong frame of mind—or something.

All she ever managed was a feeble, "I'm not sure I want to marry Evan, Father."

To which her he merely replied, "Women never know what they want at your age. You'll be happy enough when you get to know the man better.'

'Besides," he'd gone on, heedless of her downcast eyes and forlorn expression, "The empire I've built must be kept intact, and who better to continue your education than my dearest friend and business associate, Evan Ludington."

Caroline thought her heart would break at such an alliance, yet she had protested not more.

So of course Francis had every right to be upset with her, to take the matter into his own hands. She loved him for being a man who would not sit by and let others deal with his problems. Still, as she'd watched him walk into the rain that terrible day, she'd had an odd sense of foreboding, and she had wished he would wait.

Now, he was gone forever. Caroline wiped the remainder of the moisture off the face of the stone. Cold, so cold and touched with the icy chill of death. Cold as Francis had been when they found him in the river. Why had he gone to its banks on a day as rainy and drear as that one had been? Surely he would have gone straight away to talk to her father after they'd parted? He had seemed so determined. What could have happened to make him change his mind?

Yet when she'd returned to the house, her father and Evan had been deep into a chess game; so much so, they hadn't even noticed her damp arrival. There was no sign Francis had been there or was anywhere nearby. She wondered briefly at the time, but assumed he went to change into drier clothes before speaking with her father.

The storm had grown worse as the evening progressed. Thunder and lightening alternately shook the walls and lit the corridors of the house. Caroline waited all evening for some word from Francis, but none came. The next morning, when breakfast time arrived but he did not, she knew something was wrong.

It had taken four days to find his body, far down the Hudson River. No longer was he the Francis they knew and loved, her father said, wanting to spare her the agony of seeing her teacher and friend so ravaged. That Francis had gone beyond the confines of this world, he told her sadly.

But Caroline would have none of that. She must see him. She must be sure it was her Francis who had gone, and not some stranger mistaken by others for her heart's love. And so she herself laid back the dirty brown blanket and saw the blotched white skin and the filthy matted curls of the man she loved. She saw the long sturdy hands with their torn nails and bloodied palms. The head and heart now vacant of all he'd ever thought and felt. With pain too deep for tears, she turned away from him, knowing he whom she loved was forever gone.

"It's raining, my dear. I think you should come out of the wet."

Not so much startled as disgusted by the voice, Caroline turned to find Evan Ludington standing over her. Despite not having heard him approach, she wasn't surprised to find him there. He seemed to be everywhere she was these days, so much so that sometimes she found herself slipping quietly in a different direction with a direct goal of avoiding him. Evan frightened her with his piercing stares and fathomless dark eyes.

Gazing up and up at his tall form now, she noted his height lacked the lean slender grace which had been Francis'. The dreary wet of the day had pressed his dark graying hair as well as his somber clothes against his body, making him look even older and duller than usual. The lined face had a hard cold look about it that his smile didn't brighten and the day itself did nothing further to light. Caroline knew instinctively Evan was a harsh man, and would bring no joy into the lives of those he loved. If indeed, he had the least idea what love was. Which she doubted.

"Caroline..." Evan addressed her again, and this time she knew she must respond.

Rising from the damp earth, she took the hand he offered and forced herself to hold back a shiver at the touch of his hand. '*Cold. Like death,*' she thought.

"He was a wonderful teacher to you, your father says." Evan drew her arm through his and led her back toward the gray outlines of the house in the distance. "But you must let him go now."

Caroline tried not to turn back but couldn't resist a final glance. His grave seemed so lonely out here under the sprawling beech where she'd insisted he be buried. Francis had had no family, so Caroline's wishes had been carried out, but only she knew the secret of his resting place. He'd first kissed her there, under the breadth and fullness of that tree. There, they'd pledged their love. There, they would have been married. Some day. If cruel fate had not intervened as it did. Now, Francis would sleep there forever. Alone.

"Are you quite all right, Caroline?"

"What?"

Their steps brought them close to the green frame playhouse now, beneath the shadows of the elms. Caroline had never liked this place; even as a child she had never strayed too close, though her father had once built the little house for her. Had she loved it then, she wondered, and simply forgotten the good times spent there having dolls' birthday parties and afternoon teas?

Evan bent his head close to hers and put his icy palm beneath her chin, drawing her attention to him. "I said, 'are you all right'?"

"Yes, of course."

"I know you must miss Francis, my dear. But he would have been going soon anyway. He was only your tutor, and now you have your future to think of now. Our future...the lessons of life await you now, Caroline, and I will be your teacher."

This wasn't the first time Evan had spoken of "their" future. She felt his eyes on her, assessing her, studying with calculation, but something else as well. Some dark lust she had no desire to understand. He had pressed her about a betrothal at every opportunity since Francis' death. As if he thought their marriage might drive away her sadness. Make her want to live again. Ironic, that all she wanted to do

7

was die at the thought of marrying him.

Often she wondered how Evan had come to be part of their lives. He seemed to have always been there, and from her youngest days she could remember both him and her father, scheming together. She remembered how sometimes she'd wanted him gone so desperately, for once she could have her father to herself; but it seemed that was never to be, and here he was now, left with her, while Francis was dead.

She felt anger welling up inside her. Anger at his presumption that she would—could—forget Francis, be he teacher or lover, at a moment's whim. Impulsively, she spun on him. "How dare you? How dare you speak of his leaving and his dying in the same breath? Would to God he could have walked away from here alive. I would give my own life that he might have that day. What kind of callous unfeeling man are you?"

Evan's right eye twitched, but beyond that Caroline had little preparation for what was to come. He grasped her wrist tightly and pulled her so close to his face that his hot breath struck her skin like flames from an open fire.

"Callous and unfeeling, am I?" With those words his mouth came down hard on hers; his tongue probed and pushed against her teeth. As she struggled against an iron hold, his free hand found her breast and fondled the skin clinging to the thin fabric of her dress. His black eyes locked hers into a hypnotic trance, yet all the while her mind screamed to escape from his hold.

Finally he stepped back and released her, so suddenly she would have fallen had he not reached out again to steady her swaying form. "Not so unfeeling, dearest Caroline," he whispered, his voice against her ear sending a renewed surge of fear through her. "Perhaps feeling too much...but you'll understand this better after we're married."

Caroline blanched and stepped away from him. She drew herself up and met his eyes directly. "I will never marry you, Evan Ludington," she yelled through the rain, beginning to fall in earnest now. "I would rather die first."

She left him then, and was soaked through by the time she made it back to her room. Her gown had torn during a struggle with a shrub as she'd hurried away from Evan, toward home and, perhaps irrationally, a sense of safety. She felt sick. Sick with fear, sick with love, sick with grief, sick with loathing. How could her own dear father wish for her to marry such a despicable man? Why hadn't she been courageous enough to say no when Francis had asked her to? If she'd only done that, he might be alive today.

"Oh God," she whispered. "Forgive me."

"Are you all right, miss?"

The voice came from the doorway she'd left barely open. It was Nan, her young maid. Houses like Lyndfield Manor didn't run without a staff, and while Caroline had no pretensions about how she looked or what she wore, her father insisted she have a ladies maid to help with her basic necessities. Aunt Jess had done all that when she was alive—Caroline's mother and her sister had come from parents who simple country folk, and while they had owned a respectable farm in upstate New York, the girls had grown up knowing nothing of the kind of luxury life at Lyndfield would bring. When Caroline's mother had died in childbirth, Aunt Jess had taken over and tried to teach her niece the difference between respecting her place in society and being able to take care of herself. Now that she was gone, though Caroline would have preferred to be alone, her father insisted on keeping up appearances.

Caroline brushed away a tear. Not even Nan knew the truth about her love for Francis, and Aunt Jess had taught her it didn't do to gossip with the servants, no matter how much you might like them. But now, with both Francis and Aunt Jess gone, there wasn't even one person she could talk to about her feelings, and the pain was killing her. She felt certain her aunt would have understood her love for Francis: she, too, had been a romantic at heart. Caroline remembered how they'd read Jane Austen together, giggling like schoolgirls over their favorite parts. But Aunt Jess had changed, in the end. Something had weighed heavy on her mind, and Caroline had never been able to pry out of her what it was. She shook it off now, not wanting to dwell on that older grief.

"It's nothing, Nan. I'll be fine." Her eyes searched the room as the younger girl entered. "Where's the dog?" Shannon had been her one comfort on these lonely evenings—he'd been Francis' Irish setter, but she'd taken him in since the death of her love. Normally he'd be waiting at the foot of her bed, but tonight he was nowhere in sight.

"I think he's out in the barn, miss. I saw him chasing down a cat earlier. He musta' got caught there by the storm." Nan went to the bureau and opened a drawer. From it she took a flannel gown and shook it open. "You're soaked, Miss Caroline. Let's get you into something dry. Then you'll feel better."

Caroline gave Nan a weak smile, desperately wishing for a friend with whom she could share her feelings. "You're probably right."

Maybe the girl sensed as much, because Nan winked conspiratorially and began to help Caroline remove the wet clothes. "Course I'm right, miss. Then I'll bring you a cuppa and you'll feel well in no time a'tall."

By the time Nan returned with the steamy tea, Caroline's nausea had begun to dissipate. While she sipped it, Nan fluttered about, drawing curtains and lighting the lamps.

"You been out to his grave again, haven't you miss?"

Caroline nodded with silent despair, biting back the words she so wanted to share.

Nan looked at her then seeming to make a decision, crossed the room and pulled up a chair beside the bed. She leaned close to Caroline and took her hands. "I know about loss, Miss Caroline. My beau was killed in a carriage accident last spring."

Caroline leaned toward the girl, at last recognizing a sympathetic soul and realizing even if she didn't share, at least she could listen. "He was? You hardly seem old enough to have a beau."

"Dickie and I were pledged when we were ten. We always knew, you know? Now, maybe it twasn't the same for you and Master Francis, but you were still the best of friends and that's a great loss too, ain't it?"

"Oh, yes, Nan, a very great loss. I miss him so much."

Nan, for all her youth, patted Caroline's arm like a grownup and rose from the chair. "I think it's best to grieve and let it go, Miss Caroline. He woulda wanted it that way, don't you think?"

"Yes," Caroline said, sadness filling her voice at the thought she couldn't let the conversation go further. "I believe he would have."

"I'm here if you need to talk," Nan said over her shoulder as she whisked out the door but Caroline knew it wasn't to be.

"Thank you, Nan," she whispered softly, laying her head against the pillow and allowing the promising peace of sleep to come upon her. "Thank you."

* * * *

Thunder shook her awake from a fitful sleep. Caroline sat up, disoriented, and tried to focus her sight in the darkened room. She'd been dreaming again, about Francis. Always the same dream. He called out to her. Begged her to help him—to save him.

She tried to run toward his voice, but was always swallowed in a cloud of black emptiness. "Oh Francis!" She bit her lip and sobbed with despair. "What can I do? What didn't I do for you?"

Staring at the outline of the long French windows opposite her bed, she shuddered as lightening flashed again and lit the night. Movement caught her eye. Was it only her imagination or had something crossed the lawn? She rose and crossed the room, ignoring the feel of the cold wood beneath her bare feet. Yes, there it was again.

Someone—something— was out there! Straining to see into the darkness, Caroline caught a glimpse of the playhouse, then another image flashed through her mind. A man, and a child. A struggle. Something terrible was about to happen.

"Go now!" her mind screamed out to her. Without another thought, her rescuing spirit came to call. Fearless and with purpose, she threw on her heavy woolen robe and lurched into the night.

CHAPTER 2
A time to kill.
Ecclesiastes 3:1-8

Lyndfield Estate
March 4, 2006

Rain fell steadily, saturating the late afternoon with a dull gloom. Shadows shrouded the drawing room walls, adding their own dismal conclusions to the day's gray atmosphere. Their depth gathered heavily round, so much so that Jake Stanton could barely see to write. He should get up and turn on the lights, but his words were flowing well and he couldn't bear the thought of even the slightest interruption. Lightning flashed, followed by a quick crack of thunder. Jake's eyes strayed up, focusing as usual on the monstrosity over the fireplace: an almost life-size, gilt framed painting of Caroline Lyndfield, mysterious lady of the manor, and present subject of his research.

He couldn't quite decide what it was about the picture that kept drawing his eyes again and again. She wasn't beautiful, or even pretty for that matter. Her mouth was too big for her small round face; long and unruly brown hair fell in haphazard curls from beneath a bonnet slightly askew. The loose-fitting dress she wore was, he felt, unsuitable, and more than that even, unfashionable for the day. Arms laden with an assortment of flowers, a few had fallen near her feet, which were bare. Her light green eyes had a direct inquisitive look about them—a look completely out of character in a mild-mannered Victorian woman.

Maybe that was it. She didn't fit the mold of her times. Jake knew Caroline had been known for her skill with plants; she had evidently developed several new varieties of roses, and had even come up several still-used flower remedies. Whether or not her father, the rich banking tycoon William Lyndfield had supported his daughter's odd endeavors, Jakes had no idea. When it came to Caroline, his research had led him down dead-end roads.

Jake chewed on the nub of his pen and continued to stare, irritated that a lifeless painting had interrupted his words when a shadowed room could not. After a moment he tossed the pen down and approached the mantle. The eyes of the woman followed him, curious and somehow commanding. He stopped before the picture and sighed. "Ah, Miss Lyndfield, if only you could talk."

The slight curve of her mouth seemed to taunt him, and Jake laughed aloud. "What?" he asked. "What do you want?"

"Don't you know, Jake?"

He turned to find May Whatley standing in the doorway, a serious expression on her face. May had been Jake's guardian since he was ten years old, and though some twenty plus years had elapsed, she still sought every possible opportunity to mother him, and today was no different.

"Ah, May," he said, smiling and ignoring her question, "come to check my progress?"

She shook her head as if clearing misty cobwebs of her own. "I'd rather find out why you're writing in the dark? Where's your computer?"

Jake laughed. "Good questions, my dear May. I only wish I had simple answers. I'm not sure why I was working in the dark or without the wonders of modern technology." When she raised a quizzical eyebrow, he continued, "Seems like I work better with a pen than a keyboard these days."

May's eyes held skepticism as she entered the room, flicking on the light switch as she did. "So how's the book coming along?"

"It would be coming along a lot better if your mysterious lady here gave up a few of her secrets." Jake walked back to the desk, resisting the urge to cast an eye back at the painting, now two-dimensional with light.

Of course May had every reason to be curious about his work. She'd been part of the administrative staff on the Lyndfield Estate for over twenty years, managing the main house and an entourage of volunteers. Through her position, she was largely responsible for Jake's present employment, the project he'd been hard at work on for the past three months: a history of the Lyndfield family. She knew he was between books and had recommended him to the estate board of directors, who'd given him the job of chronicling the family history. The research had been going well until he'd gotten to this generation.

"I don't suppose we'll ever know about her," May sighed. "Poor dear. I'll never believe what they say of her though." She stopped before the painting and stared up at it for a long moment. "A girl like that doesn't have it in her to kill anyone, especially her father and why would she steal her own money... She disappeared for some other reason; I'd stake my life on it..."

"Ghosts been talking to you again, May?" Jake asked, sarcasm evident in his voice. As much as he loved his guardian, he didn't buy into her hocus-pocus about spirits from the past communicating with people in the present.

May ignored his skeptical tone. "'Bout as much as they have to you, I reckon." The woman moved closer and peered at him intently. "You look tired."

He shrugged and laid down his pen. "I am a little. But frustrated more than anything, I think. How can someone just disappear like that? I mean, well-brought-up young women in her day didn't simply walk away from a home in the middle of the night. Not to mention she left behind a rich prospective husband."

A crash of thunder filled the air and the lights in the room flickered. Jake turned accusingly back to Caroline's picture. "I feel like she wants me to do something, May." He tried to laugh, feeling more than a little foolish. "It's ridiculous, isn't it? What on earth could I do for a woman who's been dead a hundred years?"

"Maybe clear her name?"

Turning to the window, Jake glared into the storm, in full force of its own fury now. May remained close behind him, and he could feel her gentle wisdom gathering round, permeating him as it always had since he'd lost his parents. Most of the time he fought it, wanting to shut out her love. To shut it out as he had shut out anything and everything that made him feel. He hadn't wanted to feel since...since he couldn't remember when. Today though, he let her love envelop him. Better May's warmth than the obsession he felt for a dead woman.

He turned and met her gaze directly. "So how exactly am I supposed to do that, May? It's useless. She disappeared in 1890 and that's the end of it. I don't know where else to look."

"Haven't you found out anything else about her fiancé?"

"Ludington?" Jake shook his head. "Nothing but the obvious, which you know. He's a dead end. Literally. He stayed here, managing the estate and working on the scientific experiments he and William had started, until one of them went up in smoke and took him and half the lab along with it." Jake took another bite off the tip of his pen. "That's another weird thing...I can't even figure out what kind of experiments they were working on, though all the news clippings refer to his being killed in a lab accident. You'd think someone like William Lyndfield, with that much prestige, would have talked more about his work."

"Maybe he was afraid of someone stealing his ideas?"

"Maybe so, though I sure wish those 19th century reporters had done a bit more investigative journalism."

May smiled as she reached out and touched his arm. "I think you're going to have to go a bit deeper into your soul to solve this one. Approach it from a gut level."

"Jesus, May, what's that supposed to mean?" Jake moved angrily beyond her reach. "Don't start your mumbo jumbo with me now."

He walked back to the desk and began to gather up his notes and papers. His work for today, it seemed, was finished.

"Why do you refuse to believe in the supernatural? Souls are timeless, Jake. You, of all people, should know the things I can see and feel. And I know what I know you can see and feel them too. We both know that. Reach out to Caroline with your soul and see if she doesn't answer."

Though she hadn't moved a step closer, he suddenly felt oppressed by her presence. His head had started to throb, as it always did when she broached this subject. May was always trying to take him back, make him remember—remember things he had no desire to remember. Jake knew if he didn't get away from her now, they would both be sorry. These conversations always ended badly.

"Enough, May." He mustered as much calm as he could in his response. Turning, he left her quickly, and with her, the ghost-like painting of Caroline Lyndfield.

* * * *

From behind the beveled glass windows of his office at the Lyndfield manor, Mitchell Johnston watched the slender light-headed young man crossing the lawn from the gatehouse. He seemed heedless of the rain, and something about that irritated Mitchell. He hadn't wanted Jake Stanton here. This was his domain, and Stanton intruded. Mitchell had been the curator of the Lyndfield Estate for fifteen years. He'd always been certain it would be he who wrote the history of Lyndfield. Yet when it came time to discuss the project, it quickly became apparent the board of trustees wanted more than just a historian: they wanted a published author with a well-known name to chronicle the family. When May suggested Jake, they'd jumped at the chance of having him work on the project.

Arrogant young bastard, Mitchell snorted to himself. *A successful writer indeed.* Maybe, if one considered trite murder mysteries and one little-known historical saga, authorship. Jake Stanton was better known for his philandering, if truth were told. Mitchell had heard the stories from May, how she wished he'd settle down but he just seemed to go from one woman to the next, from one project to the next, with no real direction for his life, or his career. Of course the board had little interest in Mitchell's "unreasonable" protestations, so here was Stanton, doing the work he himself had always expected to undertake.

Mitchell backed away from the window and gazed down at the open volume on his desk. Smiling, he ran his hand tenderly across the rough leather volume. Well, here was one treasure Stanton would never get his grimy hands on. He might be writing the family history, but only Mitchell knew their real secrets. And he would never divulge a word of it. Not to anyone. Especially not to Jake Stanton.

* * * *

Jake's sleep was restless, as it had been since he'd come here. He tossed and turned in the bed, twisting and wrapping the heavy dark bedclothes around until they gripped and encased him like a death shroud. Her eyes haunted him even in the dark of night, where in sleep he sought release from her ghostly image. He saw her bending tenderly over the place where he lay, stretched out in his nocturnal tomb. His view of her was shrouded, as if she—or perhaps he—were hidden behind a misty veil.

She reached out to touch him but her hand stopped short of the actual contact, and he watched with helpless curiosity as she traced the shape of a heart onto the flat invisible surface over his head.

He could tell her hand was cold. The slender fingertips were blue with the chill. With unfathomable sadness, he wondered how long she'd been standing there in the storm.

Jake saw tears in her eyes. "Why are you sad?" he tried to ask, but no words came forth from his frozen mouth. All was silent except for the sound of the rain falling in gentle splatters around his resting place.

Someone came and led her away. He watched her go, wanting to cry out and beg her to stay. "Caroline!" his heart screamed again and again, but the words only echoed and bounced off the walls of his phantom sepulcher.

She turned back once, as if she knew he was calling her, and in that instant he understood that her heart, too, was breaking. When he woke, his eyes were filled with tears and his mind with the horrible comprehension of her grief: Caroline wept for him. And he was dead.

* * * *

Lyndfield Estate
March 4, 1890

The wind whipped and whirled around her as Caroline silently slipped out the front door and pressed her way into the arms of the storm. Flashes rose and fell across the sky, crashing into the night like a symphony of angry musicians. The rain lulled, but the heavy clouds threatened to explode again with the force of their fury.

Some inner force compelled Caroline toward the small grove of elms not far from the house. Where was the dog, she wondered? She'd have liked his company now.

She was drawn inexplicably to the same spot that had sent shivers across her spine earlier in the day. There, she must go. She somehow knew it was there she would find whatever purpose the darkness held in store. She drew her robe close, wanting to cringe and hold back, yet moving forward with a will stronger than her own.

The playhouse loomed in the distance, eerily quiet in the midst of nature's rage. Caroline lingered for a moment, checking herself, then quickly shook her fear aside and moved on. She tried to call out her presence, but the wind swept up her words and carried them beyond hearing.

The small building beckoned like a fairy tale, but for Caroline it was a Hansel and Gretel facade.

Don't be silly, she admonished herself, forging on.

As she approached the place cautiously, moonlight caught something in a bright glint on the ground, and Caroline stooped for a closer examination. It was a miniature hourglass, one she'd seen on her father's desk many times. Briefly she wondered why it would be out here. She tucked it in her pocket then proceeded toward the window. Then she peered inside, allowing her eyes a moment to adjust to the deeper darkness of the small space.

Someone was in there. She could barely make out a small figure hovering in the corner, then suddenly, another, larger, advancing. Advancing, horribly, with grasping hands and a body grotesque in its nudity. A woman's scream split the night, leaving Caroline uncertain if it was herself or someone else whose voice pierced the air. She shrank away from the anguished sight in front of her. She drew in her breath in short unsteady gasps. Fleetingly, she prayed for Francis to appear. Why did she have to be alone in this? Why? But it was only for an instant, and then she knew she must act.

Caroline raised a fist and shattered the glass, drawing back a blood-red hand that seemed not to be her own. She forced her gaze back to the room and realized with despair that the commotion had been drowned in a deafening clap of thunder.

Abruptly, something yanked Caroline back, and in the next second she stared up into an angry face. Evan Ludington.

"What are you doing here?" She thought he snarled at her, but still another crash confused the words.

She struggled against his firm grip and somehow managed to break his hold. Without further ado, she ran around the corner of the playhouse and in the door. The room hid itself so heavily in darkness, at first she believed she'd been mistaken about its occupants. Then light flooded the black and she saw the horror.

Nan's limp body sprawled across the floor, garments askew and bodice torn open to reveal youthful white breasts. Her hands crossed her face as if she'd sought to block out some the terrible truth about her attacker.

Trembling, Caroline forced her eyes up to the place where the man stood, still recovering from the throes of his lust. A burst of primal rage rose in her throat, but it died on her lips at the sight of the villain. The villain, whose face she knew as well as her own

"My God!" she whispered in a cry that broke in two. *How could it be?*

The image reverberated inside her brain and fell through to her heart, where it struck her with a blow so staggering she almost fell to the ground. She backed away from the image, groping for something to hold on to and finding only the hourglass in her pocket. She drew it out, wishing the sand inside could somehow transport her away from the terrible truth she'd found this night.

While light fought with darkness for possession of the playhouse, Caroline searched her mind for something...something...another image she had shut out long ago.

This had happened before.

Suddenly Evan was leaning over her, reaching for the glass in her hand, telling her she must forget, that he could help her forget this night. She grasped the hourglass, struggling against him, as if this small instrument might save her from all she had come to know.

In the next instant the air splintered and hissed with the static of electricity, causing every nerve in Caroline's body to crackle in spasmodic agony. The space around her turned white with piercing illumination and she shut her eyes against unbearable brightness. Her being seemed to fragment itself into a million tiny pieces of pain. Light, lightening, a terrible pounding in her head. Thunder? Something hot yanked at her, sucking her deeper and deeper into its depths, and surrounding her, smothering her, was the burning agony.

Then the pain stopped as abruptly as it had started, and there was nothing more.

CHAPTER 3

A time to be born.
Ecclesiastes 3:1-8

Lyndfield Manor
March 5, 2006

From her upstairs bedroom in the gatehouse, May gazed out on a morning washed fresh by the night's storm. The wide expanse of green lawn glistened before her like a sparkling array of raindrop diamonds. Nearby, the oval pond basked in a sunlit glow of angels' kisses, while the last of the wild winter roses danced playfully beside its bank. May was happy—happier than she'd been in a long time. Today promised to be a very good day. She knew it. Something wonderful was going to happen. She left her window and wandered leisurely downstairs. No point in hurrying over to the manor house this morning. The grounds didn't open until two o'clock on Sunday and from experience, May knew Mitchell would be sleeping at his own house on the outskirts of the estate.

In the kitchen, she set the percolator to work then stepped out the back door, inhaling deeply of the crisp air. *Nothing like the fresh warmth of a new morning,* she thought and was glad. She wasn't getting any younger and the damp cold played havoc with her bones. Smiling, she strolled back into the cottage. The coffee gurgled merrily in its pot. May poured herself a cup and headed for the living room. Since she'd taken this job so many years ago, this had been her home. The gatehouse, small but comfortable had once been the place where the estate managers lived, not so different from what she was today. Truthfully, she couldn't imagine living anywhere else. Lyndfield seemed to be ingrained into the very fabric of her being: life before and life after were blank slates.

She drew the front drapes and looked out, over the vast green lawn and beckoning forest of the estate. Once again watched the day with envy, yearning to be a part of nature's scene playing out before her.

And why shouldn't I? she chided herself. Normally, she spent her Sundays pouring over the newspaper or catching up on her reading. But today, she felt a need to commune with nature's beauty, to be at one with the universe.

So go then, she told herself. It was early and Jake, even if he woke, probably wouldn't want to be disturbed. He wasn't a big one for breakfast anyway. She definitely had time for a nice long walk.

Resolved, she put down her cup and reached into the closet for a jacket. Pulling the light tweed on over her sweats, she cheerfully sought the outdoors once again.

A thick grove of birches beckoned like old friends as May set off for her favorite place: a secluded bench near the old playhouse. The past always seemed closer in that spot, as if some slender thread held just taut enough to tug at her, a gentle reminder of the patchwork circles of time. May liked to be reminded. To her, life was a tapestry whose yesterdays and tomorrows were all interwoven. Sometimes, she thought if she could only reach behind the very thin veil, she would easily—and eagerly—touch the other side of today.

Humming as she went, May forgot about past and future and gave herself up to the moment, enjoying the peace and solitude that seemed so rare. Even at Lyndfield—remote as it was from the hustle-bustle of city life—the pace of living often tired her. Always something or someone to attend to: tours to guide, questions to answer, bills to pay. Moments such as this were a treasure indeed. But here too, tranquility could not reign for long as attested by a vociferous argument between two sparrows. May laughed. The natural world had its little skirmishes to contend with too.

May rounded the corner of the playhouse, running her hand across the smooth green wood. *Was this place Caroline's*, she wondered? She could imagine the little girl playing here, surrounded by dolls dressed in their Sunday best. Yet there was a sense of danger about the place, of something slightly askew in its energy. May always came back though, an inexplicable something drawing her again and again.

Without warning, she almost stumbled over a shape on the ground.

"My goodness!" she gasped in astonishment. Before her—lying on the still-damp earth—was the body of a woman.

After a brief instant of shock, May knelt and touched the girl's brow. She was feverish, but alive, a young woman, dressed in a long white nightgown, covered by a heavy woolen robe. Bare feet peeked like pale shy twins from beneath its length and dark hair spilled in a tangled web about her head. May saw nothing to give any clue as to who the girl might be, but something about her struck an old chord. Reaching out to try and gently awaken her, May saw that the girl's right hand bled badly.

"What on earth happened to you, love?" she said aloud, and then, though she wasn't usually an excitable person, she screamed for Jake.

* * * *

"Damn it, May! You yelled loud enough to wake the dead."

In other circumstances Jake might have been amused by the irony of his humor, but after the night he'd just spent, he wasn't. He'd just come down to the kitchen for a cup of coffee when he's heard his aunt's scream and ran out to find her.

Jake cut his admonishment short at the sight of the limp female body. May, busily putting the finishing touches on a tourniquet torn from the bottom of the girl's gown, appeared oblivious to his remark anyway.

"Jesus Christ! What happened here?"

"I don't know," came her matter-of-fact reply. "But could you help me get her inside?"

"Don't you think we should call an ambulance, or the police?"

"We'll call the police from the house, but it's damp and I want to get her inside. She's okay, just seems to be in a faint."

Jake took her at her word, knowing May had study nursing once upon a time, until she realized she working so close to people who were dying didn't suit her sensitive nature.

"Yeah. Of course." He bent down, noting briefly that the woman was young and fairly attractive despite her present bedraggled appearance then he swept her light form into his arms without further thought.

A few minutes later he and May eased her gently into his bed, mainly because the room he was using while he worked on his project happened to be the guest room in the gatehouse cottage. While May fluttered about getting supplies to dress the girl's hand, Jake stood silently by the bed, unable to speak. He felt short of breath, body clammy and cold, and he wasn't sure why.

After a moment, he found his voice. "So she was just lying there?"

Now that he'd managed to regain his composure a bit, Jake became incredulous. What on earth was a woman dressed in a nightgown and robe doing wandering about the Lyndfield estate? How did she get through the gate, which was locked every night?

Unable to take his eyes from her, he took in the fragile features carefully. Her curly hair was auburn, deep brown with burnished red, the face not exactly attractive, but in sleep looked vulnerable...and frightened. But it was more than the features. Something about her appearance bothered him, he wasn't sure what.

"Yes," he realized May had replied to his question. "She was just lying there. I stumbled over her."

May acted like a mother cat whose littlest kitten wasn't eating properly. Jake had to smile in spite of himself. After some minutes of seeing to the hand, and the bedding, and the lighting in the room, she finally spoke. "I'm going down to phone the doctor about that hand, and she seems to have a fever. Can you dry her off a little while I call

Henry and the police?"

Jake nodded absentmindedly, still trying to figure out why he felt like he knew this girl.

"I think I should call Mitchell too." She hesitated. "Don't you?"

"Sure," he replied, never looking up. "...whatever you think."

* * * *

Mitchell hadn't slept all night. He'd been waiting. He wasn't sure for what exactly, but he knew he would know when it happened. From the moment he'd come to work at Lyndfield, all those years ago, he knew he had come for a reason. He felt as if this entire scenario had been created for him, and his presence meant the fulfillment of a destiny. The past had gripped him and never let go.

Today, he sat before his living room window in a dark leather chair, staring out on a scene much similar to that May had witnessed earlier. As curator, Mitchell had been allowed to live in a small cottage near the outskirts of the estate. Where normally, he cherished this privacy, today he wished he were closer to the big house. He longed to know what was happening there. A large deep-red journal lay open on the table beside Mitchell's chair. He'd read all night—as he did on this same night of every year—trying desperately to understand what might have happened so long ago. Ludington had written of his shock, his lack of comprehension. 'The girl simply disappeared....' went his words and the pen strokes sprawled across the page as if the man's hand had quivered as he wrote. '...and I—who had studied and dreamed of just such an event—was left to deal with the horror left behind.'

His tale went on to tell of her disappearance, which had been anything but simple. How much of it had Evan really understood? He must have spent the rest of his life trying to understand what exactly had happened, to piece together a puzzle of bizarre proportions—to cover up his crime and to try and figure out what had happened to Caroline. Yet he too had disappeared shortly after.

Where did you go and what did you find out, Mitchell wondered? *Did you ever learn the truth?* The diary was no help there. Gently, he reached out and caressed the timeworn volume. He felt so close to her when he read it. As if she were right here in this room with him. So near, if he just reached out he could—

The ring of the phone pierced his reverie. Startled, he watched it for a moment. Could this be the answer—after all this time? With shaking hands, he lifted the receiver to his ear. Even before May started talking, a clamoring started in the back of his head, and little by little words began to form inside its ominous tumult.

* * * *

May opened the back door of the gatehouse to Mitchell, just as a patrol car was pulling away. May raised her eyebrows, surprised that he seemed breathless and agitated, even though it had taken him much longer to get here than she would have expected. The police had come and gone, for Pete's sake!

"You phoned the doctor?" he asked after he'd caught his breath. "He said he would come?"

May nodded. "When I explained the situation, he said he'd get here as quick as he could. I've bandaged the girl's hand—she cut it somehow—but except for a slight fever, she seems to be okay. There's no sign of head trauma, so I'm not worried about a concussion."

"What did the police have to say?"

"Not much. They said they'll come back and talk with her when she's awake, but they don't have reports of any missing persons."

Nervously, Mitchell paced back and forth as if he were alone in the room, muttering to himself, then finally to May. "Who's with her?"

"Jake. I asked him to look after her while I made the calls."

"For God's sake, May. Not Stanton. That imbecile pup."

May stared at him for a brief moment; she'd never seem the man so uncharacteristically emotional. She reached out a hand to pause his flight up the stairs. "Might I remind you you're speaking of my nephew?"

He looked somewhat contrite but May knew better than to press an argument with him about Jake. "Besides," she continued, "the girl's resting. I don't think we should disturb her. Henry should be here any minute. She'll be fine with Jake."

For reasons she couldn't fathom, May did not want to take Mitchell Johnston to the bedroom. She did not want his avaricious eyes feasting upon the innocent young woman as she slept. She did not want him— as she somehow felt certain he would—to claim possession of this girl.

* * * *

Jake returned from the bathroom, towel in hand. What was it about this girl that troubled him so much? He still had the strangest feeling he'd seen her somewhere, but where? He leaned over her and pushed a damp strand of hair away from her face. May was right—her forehead was hot. But as his hand slid down to her arm, he noted that the rest of her body was like ice—like death itself—as if she herself had come back from the dead.

Jake drew back his hand quickly but evidently not quickly enough. His touch seemed to have struck a nerve in her. Suddenly she rose straight up in the bed, eyes wide and frightened. "Francis!" she cried out, looking around the room wildly. "Francis!"

Then her wide eyes turned to him, and she stared, shock evident on her face. "Francis?" she whispered tearfully, squeezing his arm with an iron grip. "Is it really you?"

Her voice had an odd intonation; stilted, almost as if she were English—or educated in an incredibly old-fashioned manner. He pondered this but briefly, then looked down at his arm—blood-covered—both from her freshly bleeding hand and from the damage done by her nails, which had plunged in clinging desperation. He started to draw back at the sight of so much red but before he could pull away from her, another vision of crimson flashed before his eyes. A dark-headed shadowy young woman clothed all in black, expression downcast and arms— overflowing—with wild red roses. Stung with an unexpected cold-hearted fear of his own, he thrust her aside, and then she screamed again and slipped from his arms, like silk flowing into a sea of white silence.

CHAPTER 4

A time to break down.
Ecclesiastes 3:1-8

Lyndfield Estate
March 6, 2006

Shadows gathered about the room in dark folds. Through half-opened eyes, Caroline saw them hover over her. Francis, a woman...could it really be Aunt Jess, gone from her life for so long, but never from her heart? A kind looking older man with a black leather bag—the doctor, perhaps? And Evan. Why was Evan here and not her father? But her father, the thought of him made her cold, there was something she needed to remember, but could not. Voices surrounded her now though. Whispering among themselves like conspirators. About her? Didn't they know she was awake? Or was she dead? Had she come to this place with all these people who were gone, because she was dead? She tried to speak but no words came. Then someone moaned and Caroline sensed the sound came from her own lips.

"There, there, dear." This came from the woman who seemed to be Aunt Jess yet wasn't. "You're going to be fine."

Why was Francis standing so far away? She wanted him to come closer and hold her hand. Death could have no better gift for her than bringing her to the man she loved. If only he would come closer

Instead, the doctor reached down and touched it himself. She winced in pain. If she was truly dead, how could she be experiencing something so real? Was that why she was here in bed? None of this made any sense. What had happened to put her here in this strange bed? And before all this...something...something terrible had happened, something the very thought of started her head pounding in agony. She pushed it aside.

On the bed, she saw the white gauze bandages wrapped around her hand, stained with her own blood. *Why?* From there, her eyes drifted to the other man, the man who was Evan, and the connection they made sent sparks across her body. She knew without a doubt it was she who started to scream then.

She screamed and screamed, until the doctor drew a long needle from his bag and plunged it deep into her arm. Then, she tumbled toward darkness once again—but not before she saw Evan Ludington's malevolent face bending close to hers, obsessive evil ever-present in his eyes.

* * * *

Dr. Henry McWilliams, at the kitchen table with May and Mitchell, jotted specific instructions on a notepad for care of the girl's hand. Jake stood silently next to the counter, nursing a cup of cold coffee, while his mind remained locked on the girl in his room upstairs. He couldn't stop thinking about her bloodcurdling scream. Or the terror he himself had experienced in his vision of her rose-laden form. May and Mitchell had stormed the bedroom when they heard the first scream, quickly followed by May's friend, Dr. McWilliams, who'd just arrived on the scene.

While May and the doctor had seen to the girl, Mitchell spent an inordinate amount of time staring at her. He couldn't seem to turn away, and his face had the strangest expression, as if he were seeing a ghost. When he finally managed to pull his gaze from the pale form on the bed, the full force of his angry attention moved to Jake.

"What did you do to her?" he demanded as Jake stood by sheepishly, wondering himself.

May raised her hand, warning them to keep their voices low.

Jake shook his head. "Nothing," he whispered. "She woke up for a minute. I believe she thought she knew me."

Mitchell gave him a sharp look. "Do you know her?"

"No."

Mitchell had left him and gone closer to the bed, listening as Henry asked May for soap and water then bent to examine the girl's hand. Her eyes had fluttered open, and that was when she'd screamed for the second time. Screamed even more horribly than she had the time before, as if the very devil himself had come upon her.

"She'll sleep the night," Henry informed them now, "and I'll look in on her in a day or so. If you want her to stay here, that is. We could call an ambulance, you know."

May shook her head. "No. She was found here. There must be a reason." She looked to Mitchell for confirmation.

"Of course she'll stay here," he said. "At least for the time being."

"Any ideas at all who she might be?" Henry rolled down his sleeves.

"None," May said as she helped him into his jacket a moment later.

"Well, I'd say she's been through some trauma," the doctor continued. "She's got a nasty cut on her right hand, and a low grade fever. But the aspirin should help the fever by morning. I don't see evidence of a head injury. Once she's recovered from the shock, she should be fine. Might even be able to walk out of here before I come back."

May responded with an absent-minded nod, then seemed to see

Jake standing silent by the back door. "Are you all right?"

He hadn't said a word since they'd left the bedroom, and she was worried. Had something happened before she and Mitchell entered the room?

Jake shrugged. "Yeah, I'm fine. Think I'll go out for a breath of fresh air though."

She watched, puzzled, as he left the kitchen. Mitchell rose a moment later and walked with Henry toward the front door, speaking with him quietly. May had the odd feeling he was up to something, but what it was she had no idea.

"Call if you need me, May," Henry said over his shoulder and she waved her reply. Slowly, she rose and headed back upstairs.

The girl was sleeping, a peaceful expression on her pale face. May reached out and stroked her brow, which was much cooler now.

Who are you? May wondered then turned to fold the woolen robe that had slipped to the floor.

As she picked it up, something fell from the pocket. Bending again, May retrieved it, a miniature hourglass, sand half emptied from one side into the other. She stared at it curiously. It appeared quite old, and May felt certain she had seen it somewhere before. Making a mental note to ask the girl about it later, she turned to tuck it back into the pocket of her robe.

"What have you got there?"

May let out a startled gasp. Mitchell's voice came from out of nowhere. "For heaven's sake, Mitchell, you scared me to death."

"Sorry," the man said with irritation then repeated his question. "What did you find?"

"I'm not sure." She held out the small hourglass, much to small to hold the sands of an entire hour, its shimmering sand sparkled inside all the same. "This was in the girl's robe."

Mitchell glowered at the glass like it was a living object. He sucked in his breath heavily then reached out with a quivering hand.

"What is it, Mitchell?"

He crossed the room without answering and held the piece up to the light, studying it.

"Mitchell?"

"It's nothing."

Did she imagine it, or did his voice shake as he spoke?

"Mitchell!"

He spun back to her, seemingly back to normal. "It's nothing, May, really. It just looks very much like one I've seen before, in a portrait of William Lyndfield—but it isn't."

May laughed with sudden understanding. "That explains it then."

"Explains what?"

"Why I thought it looked familiar."

Mitchell handed the glass back to her. "Yes. That's why I was so surprised. The hourglass wasn't discovered with any of the estate property, so locating it would be a major find. But this isn't even a good copy."

"Do you think that's why the girl came here? To try and convince us this is part of the estate property? That she's some sort of relative?" May studied the sleeping figure, doubtful even as she spoke. She couldn't imagine this girl being some kind of fortune hunter, she appeared far too frail and innocent for that.

"I suppose we'll find out tomorrow." Mitchell took a seat next to the bed as if he planned to stay. "Why don't you get some rest now? I'll sit with her for a while. Perhaps you should check in at the Manor, as well."

Surprised at his interest, May felt reluctant to leave the room. No one needed her at the big house. The volunteers normally handled the tours themselves on Sunday. She searched for some excuse to remain here. "Jake may need some things from here. After all, this is his room."

"Then he can come and get whatever it is when he returns." Mitchell gave her a reassuring glance. "I promise you I won't snap at him again."

Still not convinced, May moved to the door, reluctant to argue with this man who was in essence her boss. Every fiber of her being told her something wasn't right, but she couldn't put her finger on what it might be. Maybe the walk up to the Manor would clear her head and give her some sense about all this. One thing May knew for certain, if you listened to your inner voice, you'd more than likely find answers there.

As she left, she looked back for an instant and saw Mitchell lean toward the sleeping girl, a look of rapture evident on his face, and for the second time that day, May felt afraid.

* * * *

The sun peeked over the horizon as Jake reentered the house quietly, a day and a half after the strange young woman had appeared. He wondered if May had gone to bed or still sat vigil upstairs with the girl. He remembered a vigil years ago, when he had been the recipient of her attentions, and abruptly felt guilty for abandoning his guardian to Mitchell.

Still, he'd had to get away and hadn't been able to return until now. The kitchen had become close and stifling, and Jake had thought he'd suffocate if he didn't get out. He'd gone up to the manor with his laptop, intending to try and get some work done, but the girl's face kept swimming before him like a phantom, making all attempts at any productive completely futile. Not to mention that working wasn't so easy with tourists coming and going, and while Sunday wasn't a particularly busy day, Lyndfield Manor still drew its share of tourists. Jake suspected people who came to see the place weren't particularly interested in William Lyndfield himself, but rather the magnificent Gothic manor house where he'd lived, and the cloud of suspicion that had come over the family after his tragic death. Still, come they did, and today Jake couldn't shut out the distraction they provided. Finally he powered down his computer and gave up trying.

The previous mid-afternoon had found him by the river, staring into the murky depths of the Hudson. He'd never particularly liked the water, but this day he'd found himself drawn there to the bank against his will. It was spooky: standing there on the water's edge, he'd experienced the eeriest feeling—something surrounding him, pulling, threatening to suck him down into a black sea. Gasping for air, he'd staggered back, away from the fear of whatever it was, knowing he needed to put as much distance between himself and the water as possible.

He'd headed back to the gatehouse, back not seeing anyone around, he grabbed what he needed, then jumped in the car with his tent and his dog Sam, and headed for the hills. Hopefully an afternoon of hiking, would exhaust him to the point that nothing would keep him awake once night arrived.

Unfortunately, the fresh air and exercise hadn't proven the tonic he thought they'd be, and once the sun had set, sleep still wouldn't come, so he packed up the car shortly before dawn and headed back to the estate.

May, used to his odd habits, hopefully hadn't waited up for him. Entering by the kitchen door, he flicked on the light switch and had his answer. She sat slumped, head in her arms, at the table.

"May?" He rustled her gently. Dazed and heavy-eyed, she looked up. "You should go to bed," he whispered.

"What time is it?" she asked groggily.

"Almost six a.m. Go to bed."

"I wanted to talk to you," she said, her eyes meeting his with concern. "Something is wrong."

Jake shook his head. "Nothing is wrong, May. We'll talk later. How's our patient?"

May jerked to full alertness. "Dear Lord, I don't know. Mitchell's been with her for most of the time since you left. I had to go up and check on the volunteers. When I got back, I...I couldn't get him to go home, so I came down and waited up for you. Thank God we're closed on Mondays. I need a rest?"

"I'm sorry I disappeared. I just needed to get away. Mitchell's been with her all day and all night? Did she wake up again?"

May frowned as she shook her head. "I'm not sure. I don't think so. I took meals up to him. But he wouldn't let me take over. Besides, someone had to see to things at the big house. I just glad there aren't any tours today. I need a rest." She paused for a long moment, as if searching for the right words. "He seems rather obsessed with her."

Jake laughed sarcastically. "I always knew he was a dirty old man."

"Be serious, Jake. I have a bad feeling about this."

"For Christ's sake, May. Give the intuition a rest, will you?" He sunk into a chair next to her.

"Don't you sense something?" she asked. "And don't lie to me. I know you do."

Jake dropped his head into his hands. "Leave it alone, May. I mean it."

She rose, proudly. "Fine. I will leave it. And you. For now."

She turned toward the door the room, then abruptly back to him. "By the way, if you don't mind, I'd like you to stay with her for thirty minutes or so. One way or another, I'm determined to get Mitchell out of here. I'll take care of her today, but first I need a shower."

Did Jake imagine it, or did his heart beat just a trifle faster at her request? "No problem," he replied, and followed her up the stairs. "If she wakes up, I'll be the one to scream for help."

They nearly had to drag him, but Mitchell did leave the room. May convinced him Jake would call him the instant the girl showed any indication of waking.

"The instant..." Mitchell said insistently and Jake promised with weary resignation. Did the man actually think Jake wanted another scene with her like the one that occurred before? No chance of that.

Before they'd been gone less than five minutes however, the young woman stirred. Jake, who'd been staring out the window at the colors of the sunrise, turned back to at the sound of movement in the bed. *Let her be okay,* he prayed silently. *And let me be okay, too.*

The girl stretched then raised her head, taking in the room and finally stopping at Jake. When her eyes focused on him at last, she smiled. "I had the most terrible dream," she said softly. "I dreamed you were dead."

Jake shuddered, but crossed closer to her anyway. "Hi. How are you this morning?"

The girl studied him for a long moment, then closed her eyes as if to clear some confusion. "I...I'm so sorry. I...for a moment...I thought you were someone else."

Thank, God, Jake thought. *She's going to be okay.* "Hey, that's all right. People are always mistaking me for someone else. The mystery today is who you are."

He should go downstairs and let May know she was awake, but he couldn't move. The young woman fascinated him. Her light eyes had a way of catching and holding on, and her voice, so tender, when she'd thought she knew him; he found himself wishing those soft words had been for him.

She smiled a little, then let her gaze rove uncertainly around the room. It stopped on the radio next to her bed, softly serenading with strains of James Taylor. Jake couldn't abide the sleepy classical station Mitchell had been listening to, and had changed it immediately to something more suited to his taste.

"Where is the music coming from?"

He wanted to laugh, but something held him back. After all, she had just hit her head. But unless her eyes weren't working properly, he didn't understand why she couldn't see the radio right across from the bed.

"From the radio, of course," he replied as casually as possible.

"The what?"

"The radio. Right there." He walked over and laid his hand on top of the stereo. "Is it bothering you?"

Her eyes grew wide with amazement as he adjusted the volume. "I've never seen such an instrument. How does it work?"

He reached over and flicked it off with a sharp touch. "Like that. Let's talk about you, why don't we?"

With an arrogant toss of her head, she ignored his question. "Where am I?"

"Well...you're in my room right now. This was the closest place to bring you after we found you."

"Found me?"

"Yesterday morning. May found you actually. Clean out."

"Clean out?" She stared at him, bewildered.

"Yeah, you know." He point to his head. "Unconscious. Now what we'd like to know is who you are. So we can get you home."

"Home?"

Why the hell is she acting so weird, Jake wondered?

She struggled to sit up, a surprised expression crossing her face when she saw her bandaged hand. Jake helped her adjust a pillow behind her back, his heart pounding like a drum at her nearness. She smelled of roses, just faintly, but roses all the same.

"Does it hurt much?" he asked, trying to keep his voice steady.

"A little. How did I hurt myself?"

31

"You don't remember how?"

"No," she said quietly, "the last thing I remember was going to bed."

"And where might that have been?" Jake's effort at teasing disappeared after a sharp look of disapproval from her. He took several steps away from the bed, willing calm. "Okay, then, let's get back to who you are." He was growing impatient and wanted some answers. "What's your name?"

She drew herself up almost haughtily. "Caroline Lyndfield. Daughter of William Stanton Lyndfield. Surely you know who *he* is?"

Jake's heart fell in his chest. She was definitely not okay. When he finally found his voice, he did the only thing anyone could possibly do in such a circumstance. He laughed. "That's about as likely as my being George Washington."

Now she stared at him as if it he was the crazy one. "It most certainly is not. I quite assure you I am who I say I am. And if you don't believe me, you can ask my father." She looked around again. "Where is my father?"

"Your father—if you were *the* Caroline Lyndfield—is dead and buried, and has been for well over a hundred years," Jake said in exasperation.

Her eyes widened and she bit her bottom lip. "Do not speak of such," she whispered. "Not even in jest. I have lost so much of late."

Jake decided to let it rest there for the time being, and as he watched her, wondering what to say now. Her eyes searched the room, frightened, and she attempted to rise from the bed. "Hey, where do you think you're going?"

The girl turned to answer, then stopped abruptly. "Sir, are there no women in this house?"

"Well, May's downstairs. But let's see if I can't help you first. She's been up all night."

"But...I...I need to..." her voice trailed off as eyes searched for something.

Suddenly, it dawned on Jake what she wanted. "Oh, it's right here." He pointed to an open door then went to help her from the bed.

Reluctantly, she accepted his arm and they moved toward a smaller room. His arm about her waist felt so warm, so familiar; it was all Caroline could do not to turn and cling to him with all her might. Where...where had this man who was so like her Francis come from? Was this a dream? If so, she prayed she would never wake up. Amazed, she watched as he pressed something on the wall and flooded the little room with light. What kind of place was this? Her gaze explored the tiled room with its strange white fixtures.

She gave her thought voice. "What is this place?"

He dropped his arm from her waist and stepped back. "Oh for Christ's sake, woman. It's the bathroom."

Caroline turned what she hoped was her haughtiest stare on Jake. "You needn't be profane, sir." She turned toward the toilet and peered into it. "An indoor well? This isn't what I required, I'm afraid."

Jake, completely at a loss, knew he needed help for this one. "I'll be right back."

After he'd gone, Caroline decided the bathroom must be the equivalent of her water closet. She took care of her most pressing business first, then tried out the switch on the wall that made light go on and off. *Amazing,* she thought, wondering if this might be some new invention of Evan and her father. They were always up to some mischief in their laboratory, and she wondered if this was one of their results. But how long must she have been out to miss a development of this magnitude?

Finally, after washing her hands carefully to avoid disturbing the bandages, she returned to the other room, making her way on shaky feet to the window. She must find out where she was. Outside, the sun was just slipping up over the horizon. Across the lawn she could see the stark outline of Lyndfield Manor. With surprise, she recognized now her dwelling place. *I'm in the gatehouse, where Francis lived.*

Then her gaze slid to the conservatory and she clutched the windowsill in shock and dismay. Yesterday, the conservatory had been flooded with a wild array of green and red and orange and pink, the very last of the summer roses. She should know its flowers and greenery by heart, since she spent most of her days there. She remembered how what seemed like only moments earlier, she had stood inside and wept again for the death of Francis.

Today, it seemed her weeping would be for more than her lost love. For on this day, the conservatory was little more than an empty hull, its glass broken out and ironwork covered with the rust of years of misuse. With disbelieving horror, Caroline knew all was most definitely not as it had been yesterday. With growing alarm, she wondered if anything would ever be the same again?

CHAPTER 5

...A time to tear.
Ecclesiastes 3:1-8

Lyndfield Estate
March 6, 2006

Caroline was leaning against the windowsill, her hands clutched across its smooth frame, when Jake reentered the room followed closely by Mitchell and by May, still dripping from her shower.

Something about Caroline's stance tore at his heart. The shadowy silhouette of her face was just visible, its stark whiteness forming a sharp contrast against the blue backdrop of sky beyond. Instinctively, Jake knew she was fighting a battle, though he couldn't have said *how* he came by this knowledge.

"You shouldn't be up, my dear."

Mitchell's words struck an odd chord somewhere deep within Jake's breast. *Why was he taking such an intimate tone with this girl he didn't even know?*

As the sound of Mitchell's words resonated across the open space between them, she turned slowly, but rather than look to the older man, her eyes sought Jake, questioning. He wished he had answers to give her.

Mitchell went to her, slipped an arm about her waist, and assisted her back to bed as May pulled to straighten the tousled bedclothes. Jake watched. Could he be imagining the slight drawing back of the girl at Mitchell's touch?

He stayed safely to one side, watching without words. His feelings were jumbled; again the walls felt close around him. She'd seemed so strange and eccentric when he was alone with her. Now she appeared little more than a fragile and uncertain young woman.

She allowed the two older people to help her, but her eyes remained trained on Jake. Her gaze had taken on a new sharpness. She's trying to tell me something, he thought, and wondered why the thought seemed familiar.

"Are you all right, honey?" Concern was evident in May's voice.

Jake was glad she was here. One thing about May, she always seemed to know the best thing to do no matter what the circumstance.

"I do not know. I think something is not right." The girl replied in the same precise voice she'd used with him earlier. So he hadn't imagined her behavior after all. Now he was sure he detected a wavering note in her words though she appeared to be trying very hard to remain outwardly calm.

"Did he do something to upset you?" Mitchell jerked his head in Jake's direction.

"Just what do you think I might have done, Mitchell?" The familiar irritation rose up in Jake. "Threatened her life?"

Caroline watched the interaction between them, apparently puzzled, while May continued to fuss around the bed, straightening covers and plumping pillows.

"I don't presume to know what you've done, but every time you've come near her, she gets upset." Mitchell paced the floor, his heavy shoes tapping a steady rhythm on the bare wood. This, Jake had noted, was his habit when upset.

"You come downstairs telling us you think there's something wrong with her...mentally," Mitchell continued, "How could you know—or even suspect—such a thing? You've only spent a few minutes with her. That kind of accusation is enough to upset anyone."

Jake relaxed against the papered wall, tracing the outline of a flat flowery bouquet, sure his nonchalance would irritate Mitchell more than any outburst. "Well, Mitchell, what would you have done if someone just told you she was the missing Caroline Lyndfield? Missing, of course, for over a hundred years?"

Abruptly, Mitchell halted his pacing. Jake watched as he turned a sharp and penetrating eye toward the woman in the bed. But apparently May had had enough of their sparring. She positioned herself between the bed and the two of them. Folding her arms across her chest like a field sergeant, she said sternly, "This young woman has a shock, and has just had stitches in her hand. She needs her rest, whoever she may be. Out with the two of you. Now!"

Something in her military-like command took charge of the situation. Even Mitchell couldn't find any words to argue with her force.

A surge of relief swept through Jake. May would stay with the girl. May would talk to her. Talk some sense into her. Just as she'd promised earlier, 'everything was going to be fine.'

He followed the older man from the room, with a last look back at this beautiful girl whose mysterious appearance in his life would, he suspected, change everything that happened from that moment on.

* * * *

"I'm sorry," May said. "Those two can be a real headache at times. And since Jake is my godson, I'm often caught in the middle."

May collected a glass of water from the bathroom. After handing it to Caroline along with a pill from the bottle on the table, she sat down in a chair beside the bed. "How are you feeling?"

"Afraid," Caroline replied in a soft voice, looking at the pill several moments before putting it in her mouth.

"Why, my dear? You're safe here. Jake and Mitchell are completely harmless. I can promise you that. And you'll be home in no time." May patted her hand in a motherly fashion.

"But this *is* my home." She spoke so quietly that May was sure she'd misunderstood the words.

"What's that?" She leaned closer.

The girl sighed heavily then looked toward the window without answering. May knew it wouldn't be too long before weariness and the medication took effect.

"This...is...my...home," she said again. "It is...but it isn't."

"What is your name, then?" May asked, feeling a shiver creep up from nowhere. "Did you really tell Jake your name was Caroline Lyndfield?"

"It is Caroline Lyndfield," she replied, laying her head back against the pillow as if the thought of who she was somehow tired her even more.

"A relative, then." May said her thought aloud but noticed that before her eyes slid shut, the girl shook her head and barely whispered one word.

"No."

* * * *

"That is absolutely ridiculous, May, and you know it." Jake had brought May's lunch. They sat side by side on the small tapestried sofa across from the four-poster bed where Caroline slept.

"I'm not so sure. I have a strange feeling about this."

Jake rose and walked toward the bed, visually tracing the outline of the girl, harmless to him in her slumbers. "God damn it, May. You and your feelings. Sometimes I get so tired of them. And this time...what you're suggesting is impossible!"

May shook her head adamantly, and then took a bite of her sandwich. After a moment, she spoke again. "Odd things happen, don't they, Jake? Let's wait and see, shall we?"

"Jesus Christ!"

"Where's Mitchell?" May asked, changing the subject.

"He said he had some things to take care of at home. He told me in no uncertain terms that I was not upset our patient here again. And since when does he come off telling me to stay out of my own room, for Christ's sake?"

"It's odd, isn't it? His reaction to her?" May studied the figure in the bed. "There's a resemblance, isn't there? You saw it too."

Jake stopped what he was about to say and faced Caroline once again. Yes, he had seen the resemblance to the painting of the real Caroline Lyndfield. There certainly was a resemblance, except this girl was far more lovely than anything the artist had captured.

"It's not possible, May. People don't travel through time in real life. That only happens in the movies."

May put down her plate and crossed the room. Reaching across the motionless form, she pulled the girl's woolen robe toward her. Jake watched as she searched around in the pocket, finally retrieving the small hourglass. She handed it to him.

"Caroline had this."

He took the slender cylinder and held it up to the light, noting the way sun shimmered against the light of the white sand. "So?"

"It's exactly like the one in the painting, Jake. Remember, it sits on William's desk, near the spot where his hand is resting. It's the same one. I know it is. Mitchell tried to deny it. But I'm sure it is."

"So what if it is, May? Maybe she has one like it in her house?" Jake gave the glass back to her, suddenly burned by its cold touch against his palm.

"There isn't another one like it. Tiffany made this one especially for William. Look, the signature is right here. It's one of a kind." May put the glass back in the pocket of the robe. "I tell you, there is something very odd happening here. Whether you or Mitchell choose to acknowledge it, or ignore it, is of no consequence to me." She spun around, surprising Jake with the fire in her normally tranquil eyes. "But I will tell you one thing. This girl has suffered enough, and while there's breath in my body, I intend to see that she suffers no more. Is that clear?"

Jake nodded like a chastised schoolboy. It was clear all right. And he was glad—glad, and relieved. Again. He didn't want anything else to do with this girl. It was bad enough that he was obsessed by a dead woman—but believing that woman might have come back to life in the 21st century, well, that was taking things a bit too far. As far as Jake Stanton was concerned, this woman—whoever she was—could confide all her fabrications to May and Mitchell. He intended to have no more of such nonsense.

* * * *

Mitchell Johnston could scarcely contain himself. She'd finally come, just as he'd known she would. His mind raced with the impossibility of it. And yet, somehow, someway, he knew the impossible had happened: Caroline Lyndfield had traveled through more than a hundred years of time to the present day.

So much to be done. He had to prepare the house for her, and there was further work to do, to make sure only he knew the secret of her time travel, so no one could ever take her away from him. How on earth was he ever going to accomplish it all?

Hurrying across the grounds toward his house, he hardly noticed that the clouds had cleared and the day was now sunny and crisp. His step felt lighter, lighter than it had in years. It wasn't too late. It wasn't too late for him and Caroline. First, he needed to hire a nurse. Caroline would need someone to watch her during the days of her recovery. Not to mention the fact that having someone there while he was working would prevent unwanted visitors.

Damn that Stanton! Just the thought of the younger man made Mitchell's blood boil. How dare he upset her? How dare he speak of her in such jaded terms? She was *his*, and she needed *his* care and attention.

Pushing open the heavy oak door to his house, Mitchell looked around the place. Luckily, he'd always enjoyed antiques. As the years had passed and he waited for Caroline, Mitchell had managed to acquire quite a collection of late 19th century furnishings. The gilt mirror next to the claw-footed hat rack, the hand embroidered screen, the floral-print chaise across from the fireplace. All things a young woman from that period was sure to love. He could picture her sitting here, reading Dickens or Hardy, who were almost her contemporaries. How much she'd be able to tell him. The books he would write! Elated, Mitchell headed toward his study. Was it really possible? What else could it be?

The heavy journal lay open on the table, exactly as he had left it yesterday morning. He ran his finger down the page. He almost knew the words by heart. Year after year he'd read them. How many now? He wasn't sure any more, at least thirty. He'd been here that long and had found this book not long after his arrival. Found it right in the dusty and neglected attic of this house. This was the house where Evan Ludington had intended to bring young Caroline as his bride. There was even a rusty old trunk filled to overflowing with pale and lacy clothes that surely Evan had meant for his intended. These were probably too moth-eaten for use, but Mitchell could have them copied. Another task to complete before she became his. How long then? How long before she fell in love with him? How long before he was able to hold her in his arms and speak words of love?

Mitchell shook his head, trying to clear away such titillating thoughts, while at the back of his mind the quieted voice leapt to life once more, whispering of wonderful things to come for both of them. Maybe he was getting a little ahead of himself. But he felt he knew her so well. Evan had written so much about her in his journal and now his words slipped into Mitchell's mind like old friends. He'd written of her favorite meals, the way she liked to read in the garden on Sunday afternoons, of the clothes she wore, her beauty.

Mitchell knew that green was her favorite color, which was the reason he'd had the upstairs bedroom painted that color five years ago. He knew that lilacs were her flower of choice, and that she pinned a little sprig to her blouse whenever they were in season. Mitchell knew all this and so much more. But now, she was here to share these things with him—these things, and other as well. So of course she would love him. She would love him as she'd loved Evan. Evan had written much of Caroline's love for him. Mitchell knew what he must do to ensure that love.

Reaching for the phone, he smiled to himself. After all these years of waiting, his life was about to begin.

* * * *

She was dreaming of home and Francis. Of course he was there. Where else would he be? They were reclining beneath the beech, where they'd sat so many times before. She was attempting to paint a watercolor of the river but kept missing brushstrokes because Francis was braiding clover blossoms into her hair.

"Stop it," she told him with a playful swat. "You're spoiling the picture."

"What's more important," he asked, placing a kiss upon her nose, "your painting, or me?"

She met his eyes, those dreamy blue pools, so light, so deep, she feared she might float away and melt in their depths like a misty cloud stretched thin across an almost cloudless summer sky. Putting down her pad and paintbrush, she cupped his chin. "You're my tutor...don't you know the answer to such a simple question?"

He laughed and the lilting music of his laughter filled her with such sweet delight. How could she be so happy? How could she have ever believed she was happy before?

"Oh, Francis..." She reached out her arms, wanting desperately to draw him toward her, to hold him tighter than she ever had before. But in that instant, he was snapped back, away from her.

"Francis!" She screamed, and her voice echoed round about her as his face became dimmer and dimmer. She clutched at the space before her, but caught nothing. Nothing but the white sheets twisted in her hands as she struggled against them. Cloudy-headed, she shook herself firmly from the effects of her dream. She guessed it must be early morning. Her thoughts were tangled. She tired to remember back to the last thing that had happened before she awoke in this room for the first time, but the effort only made her head ache all the more. Later.

All that would have to wait till later.

Caroline leaned back against the pillow and tried to relax. She stared down at her hand, and wondered again what she had done to it. She remembered going to bed after Nan had brought the tea, but nothing beyond.

The woman she'd spoken with earlier was in the chair next to her, dozing, which gave Caroline ample opportunity to study her. Small boned, and attractive for her age, which Caroline guessed to be around sixty, her dark hair was barely touched with gray and formed a wavy cap around her bent head. One slender hand lay still on the mattress next to Caroline, palm down, its pale skin lined with life.

So much like my aunt, Caroline thought sadly, once more missing the woman who'd been like a mother to her after her own had died. Caroline had confided her deepest secrets to Aunt Jess, and when she'd lost her, she'd also lost her best friend. Not to mention that her death had been so sudden and unexpected. Even after all these years, the pain of it still stung.

The older woman stirred and opened her eyes. "Hello there," she said sleepily. "You should have woke me up." She stretched and gave Caroline a long look. "You look better this morning. How are you feeling?"

"Well, I think," Caroline said. "My head hurts. And my hand a little."

"Probably because it's about time for your medicine. But at least you got plenty of sleep. You've been out since yesterday morning. Henry came by to check on you and said since your fever was down to let you rest." She laughed. "It's about time I had some of that, myself. I'm too old for sleeping in chairs."

Caroline toyed with the lace on the sheet. There was so much she needed to know. But she hardly knew where to begin her questions.

"When...when may I go home?"

The woman hesitated. "Let's not rush things, my dear. Henry says you've had a shock and should take it easy."

"But I think my father should be informed. I feel sure he will come for me."

Without replying, the woman rose from her chair and glided over to open the curtained window. It was then that Caroline noticed, for the first time, her attire. *How strange,* she thought, *and quite inappropriate.* The woman wore a very strange suit of baggy pants and a matching blouse. The fabric had an unusual pattern of some kind of geometric shapes across the blouse. Caroline rarely wore pants herself, except when riding—she could not imagine a woman Aunt Jess's age doing so, ever.

"What is it?" the woman asked.

"I was just admiring your clothing," Caroline said with Victorian tact, mixed with only a tad of guilt. She'd been taught it was rude to stare, and here she was doing it anyway.

"Do you like it?" The woman seemed oblivious to any breach of etiquette and ran her hands across the slacks. "I'm afraid after two days of wear, it's more than a little crumpled."

"Why don't you ask your maid to iron it then?" Caroline asked.

This brought a resounding laugh from the woman. "My maid. Oh dear! I'm afraid a maid will never see the likes of this house. Besides, you don't iron knit like this. It's wash and wear."

"Wash and wear?"

"Yep, I just toss it in the washer then throw it in the dryer and I'm ready to go." The woman swept up a quilt from the floor and began folding it.

Caroline eyes widened in amazement. What on earth was this woman talking about with her strange expressions, she wondered?

"Washer and dryer? These are things I have never heard of." She pulled herself further into a sitting position, ignoring the woman's questioning eyes. "What is your name?"

"Oh, dear me. I have been remiss, haven't I? Of course you were so out of it before." She crossed to the bed and extended a hand. "I'm May Whatley. I live here. Well, actually I work here too. Which entitles me to live here."

"But I don't know you. You're not one of the staff, are you?"

There was a long moment of silence as a gap of unspoken questions passed between the two women. Finally May broke the uncomfortable spell. "I think you need some fresh air. If it's not too cool outside, you could sit in the garden for a spell. We'll work out all these problems a bit later. What do you say?"

Caroline was actually rather glad for an opportunity not to pursue this subject further. Her head was beginning to ache even worse. "That would be nice," she replied as the odd woman May Whatley held out her robe.

Some time later, as she reclined in a lounge chair just outside the gatehouse, Caroline had another chance to inspect the grounds of her home. Except for the empty and abandoned conservatory, they seemed the same. Or did they? The lawns had their normally well-cared appearance; but the trees looked fuller, taller than they had yesterday. The house stood like an oddly placed turreted castle, just as she had left it a few days before. But there was some kind of sign in front of it, which Caroline could not read from where she sat. She had hoped to have the strength to slip up there after the woman May went inside to get something, but one woozy attempt to rise from her chair told her she wasn't as well as she wished. For now, Caroline would have to be happy knowing she could call for help if she needed to.

She couldn't understand why her father didn't come for her. Why someone didn't come. Though she hated to admit it, she'd even be happy to see Evan right now. The thought of Evan reminded her of the man who was so much like him. Who was he with his obsessive eyes and concerned demeanor? *That man...and Francis.* She knew she must stop calling him Francis. He'd acted as frightened as a titmouse when she had said his name before. And truth be told, he wasn't exactly the same as her love. For one thing, he wore horrible loose and tattered clothes that were nothing like Francis' attire. And he lacked the grace and self-confidence of the man she loved.

She smiled. Francis would have thought her ridiculous for even imagining him in such clothing.

Startled by a noise, she turned to see none other than the man himself heading in her direction now. And, wonder of wonders, Shannon was with him. Here, at long last, was someone she knew!

CHAPTER 6

...A time to keep silence.
Ecclesiastes 3:1-8

The big Irish setter bounded across the lawn like an oversized rabbit straight out of *Alice in Wonderland*. He plowed onto the center of Caroline's lounge chair, nearly tumbling her off with his frisky enthusiasm. She leaned into his red neck, laughing. Shannon had belonged to Francis, but since his death the dog had been Caroline's almost constant companion. Now here he was, a welcoming friend at long last.

"Sam!" Jake yelled as he approached the happy duo. "Get down!"

Caroline turned an inquisitive eye up to the man as she fought to keep her seat and continue to embrace Shannon at the same time. "I beg your pardon. This dog's name is Shannon."

Close to her now, the man shook his head firmly. "And I beg *your* pardon. His name is Sam." He grabbed the dog's black leather collar and ushered him down. "Sit. Now." Shannon obeyed, but his low whine indicated obvious displeasure.

"So you're up and about today?"

He seemed to be making an effort at polite conversation as well as to change the subject. What was his name again? Well, Caroline intended to have no part of it. She wanted to clarify the preceding issue.

"What are you doing with my dog?" She called forth her most authoritative tone while inside her body shuddered with uncertainty.

Though a solemn frown tugged at the corners of the man's mouth, his pale eyes teased her with their light intensity. Fair hair fell casually across his forehead, lacking the tousled curl that Francis' had had, and burnt with a deeper shade of brown highlight. Again, she felt the familiar ache to reach out and take him in her arms. But his attitude, his behavior—these were nothing like the man she had loved, a man full of warmth and sensitivity.

He shook his head again at her words, abruptly laughing aloud. The laugh disturbed her. Was he mocking her, she wondered?

"Let's start over, why don't we? I'm Jake Stanton, in case you don't remember... and you are? Wait, don't tell me. I bet you're the renowned Miss Caroline Lyndfield of Lyndfield Manor." He extended a hand, which she did not take. "I'm very happy to make your acquaintance, Miss Lyndfield. Or may I call you Caroline?"

"You may not," she replied haughtily, drawing her body up to its

43

fullest and what she hoped was its most daunting height. "I doubt I will ever be more than Miss Lyndfield to you, sir. Now about my dog?"

"Jesus, woman. This happens to be my dog. He's been my dog since I was eleven years old and my father—." Jake broke off suddenly, leaning down to scratch behind Shannon's—her Shannon's—ears. Kinder then, he continued, "I'm sorry if he reminds you of your dog. But he isn't. He's not. *Comprendez?*"

"*Pardon moi, monsieur. Je ne savais pas que vous êtes français? Preferez-vous parler français...ou anglais?*"

Apparently, the fact that she was well-versed in French really annoyed him. "What the hell, woman? Can we speak English here?" He stomped a few feet away, knelt down, and picked up a stick, reminding Caroline of some military commander preparing to plot his next strategy.

While he proceeded to draw some type of pattern on the ground, she attempted to hide a smile. "Of course. If you prefer."

"I prefer. Now then, how are you feeling today? Obviously better...but I see you still haven't found your marbles."

Her eyes sought the grass below her chair. She could see no marbles. She did not remember bringing any with her either. Now he thought she had lost them? This man was very odd indeed.

"Never mind," he said sarcastically as he continued to watch her and shake his head. "Where's May?"

"Ah, Mrs. Whatley. She said she must dress for her work. Does she work in the kitchen or is she a maid? I forgot to ask. I am surprised not to have seen her before."

Jake laughed. "She's neither cook nor maid. She does administrative work and gives tours up at the big house. You know, your house...."

A strange shiver crept around Caroline's heart.

"I can see that surprises you a little, Miss Lyndfield. Didn't they give tours in your day?" Jake knew he was being unkind, but he couldn't stop himself. "By the way," he went on, "as long as I'm talking to you, I wouldn't mind having answers to a few questions for this little project I'm working on. Such as, where'd you run off to and what did you do with your father's money? And what really happened to your father that night? I'm sure you can fill in all these gaps for me. Or have those things slipped your mind in the last one hundred years?"

"Your jesting pains me." Caroline lowered her eyes and held out a hand to the dog, who had quietly managed to inch his way nearer the spot where she sat. He licked her fingers with fervor.

Ignoring Sam's treachery, Jake paced nervously around her. Before him sat a woman with whom he had no idea how to deal—and normally, dealing with women provided him with no problem. Normally, he didn't let them get that close. Intimidation and chauvinism—not to mention sarcasm—rarely failed to hold them at bay. This woman who claimed to be Caroline Lyndfield was quite a case. She appeared unintimidated, oblivious to chauvinism, and sarcasm was definitely lost on her. He was completely baffled.

While she played with the dog—his dog—he watched the sunlight mingle its rays with the golden highlights in her auburn hair. Funny, the way it frothed about her face like cresting waves in a storm. Yet, somehow, it managed to look perfect at the same time. Most women he knew spent hours in perm rollers trying to get their hair to look like that. Hers, however, was natural. At least he thought it was. He leaned a little closer to her and inhaled. Sometimes you couldn't be sure by looking, but smell was a sure giveaway. Her hair smelled only of fresh air and sunshine.

"I didn't mean to upset you," Jake said softly, only to curse himself the next instant for admitting it.

She raised eyes clear and fresh as a summer meadow to meet his. "I know. I know you did not."

How could she do that? How did she manage make tingles pulse through his veins like tiny electrical currents? Just by speaking to him?

Jake backed away, needing even the smallest distance to regain his composure. He drew slow deep breaths like May had taught him years ago when they practiced meditation. After a moment, he felt better.

"So what's on your agenda for today?" He tried to make his voice sound casual.

"Excuse me? Is there a meeting?"

He wanted to scream. To take hold of her and throttle her. She was taking this act entirely too far. Where the hell was May?

* * * *

They do make a pair, May thought as she pulled on her red turtleneck sweater. From her bedroom window, she saw Jake's slender form as he leaned against a tree, talking to Caroline. Before moving toward the stairs, something in the scene caught her attention, and she paused for a moment longer, watching the two young people and the dog. Her eyes clouded over, and it suddenly seemed as if she'd watched them this way before. The girl was laughing at something he said, then she picked up a ball and threw it across the lawn, clapping happily as the dog chased after it. Jake bent close to her head, whispering, and she laughed again and looked up at him with loving eyes. Loving eyes...

The mist cleared and May realized it was only Jake and Caroline: the girl looked uncomfortable, Jake merely irritated. *What's going on between them now,* she wondered?

A few minutes later she joined them, smiling. "I see you two have found each other again." For some reason, she felt that funny shiver again as she said the words. She shook it off, promising herself she'd deal with the subject more fully at another time.

Caroline lifted concerned eyes to May's approach. "Mrs. Whatley," she asked, "do you know this dog?"

May gave a jolly hoot. "Do I know this dog? Of course I do, my dear. I helped Jake's father pick him out. Runt of the litter, he was, but we liked him all the same. Jake was a pretty scrawny boy himself at that time...if you can imagine that."

"I cannot," Caroline replied in a cool tone.

The roar of an airplane overhead drowned any further response Caroline might have wanted to make. She jerked her head up and away from the two at her side.

"Oh my, God!" She realized she had spoken aloud without intending to. She had never seen such a sight in her entire life. A gigantic flying vision or monster. An entity with bright shiny wings that looked very much like steel. Soaring through the clouds at an incredible speed. It was impossible.

Caroline clutched the quilt across her lap as if it were a shield of armor. Where did such a being live? What did it eat? Did it eat people? She crouched low in her seat.

"I...I," she found herself unable to formulate any reasonable question.

"Oh, May, for God's sake. She's acting like she's never seen an airplane. This is ridiculous." Jake spun around to leave, but a single gesture from the woman paused his retreat.

Their obvious lack of fear calmed Caroline. As the noise faded into the distance, she relaxed a little. Whatever it was, they had been spared any harm. But how often did these creatures appear? Why had she never seen such a thing before?

"What's wrong, my dear?" May asked gently. "Are you afraid of airplanes?"

"Airplanes? Airplanes..." Caroline had never heard this word. It flew in the air. But what was a plane?

"May, I have to get to work. I told you yesterday I've got no desire to hear this nonsense. I'm going."

The older woman stomped her foot like an adamant child. "If you take one step from this spot you can just pack your bags and find somewhere else to live. I mean it, Jake."

"Well, hell, May," he returned angrily, "I'm gonna have to do that anyway. Someone's living in my bedroom. If you recall."

May laughed, and the unexpected injection of humor seemed to break the tension between them. Again Caroline wondered at Jake, so unlike Francis who was always so polite in the company of women. What would Francis have made of this man who so resembled him, she wondered? But she must try to cease thinking of her love. She must let him go. She obviously had other more pressing problems to concern her right now. Still, even giant metallic birds in the sky and Mr. Stanton's incredible accusations seemed of little importance next to the loss of the man she had loved.

"I do not know these airplanes," she told May. "When did they first appear?"

Baffled, May appealed to Jake. "Hell, May, I don't know," he told her. "I'm no authority on early aviation history. My specialty's weird late-Victorian families."

May shot him a warning gaze then turned back to Caroline. "They've been around for some years, honey. Most people like to fly, you know?"

"People?" Caroline shook her heard in disbelief. "People fly in them?"

Just as she felt she was completely over her scare, an odd square-shaped vehicle with strange wheels rounded the corner of the drive and slowly wound its way up to the house.

"My God!" Caroline breathed, again pulling the quilt close. What had happened in the day or two she'd been asleep? First, a though she had seen the boxes that played music, this one was made of some strange material, and then there was the strange plumbing, the steel in the sky, and vehicles that moved under some amazing power of their own.

"Please," she turned to May with pleading eyes. "You must tell me what this is all about. Is this a dream? It must be a dream. Or perhaps Evan has had a breakthrough with his experiments? Yes, that must be it."

Jake knocked his head against the tree as May knelt at the girl's side. "You mustn't be afraid, my dear. It's just a car. You've ridden in a car."

Caroline shook her head. Watching as the vehicle stopped, she saw that two people did indeed emerge from it safely. People flew in the air and rode without horses. It was too much indeed.

"Mrs. Whatley," she said with quiet firmness, "You must get my father. I must speak with him."

In her mothering manner, the woman patted Caroline's arm. "I'm afraid I can't do that. You see, your father isn't here."

Knowledge dawned anew within her breast. *He must be away on business with Evan.*

"I see," she said brightly, "then when will they return? I really must speak with him."

"When are you going to get it, woman?" Jake's words sliced angrily through the air, and she could not fathom his anger. But the words he spoke next were more than harsh, they were cruel.

"Like I told you yesterday, they aren't coming back. "They're dead, and if you really are who you claim, then so are you."

After that, Caroline heard no more.

* * * *

She woke to the sound of raised voices, slightly surprised to find herself back in bed again, and wishing at least Shannon was here. The pounding in both her head and her hand had merged in to one aching throb, so she couldn't concentrate on the words at first. After a moment however, they began to take shape.

"Call off this bastard, May," Jake warned. "Tell him I am not responsible for her fainting."

"I'm sorry, Jake," came the woman's response. "I'm afraid I agree with Mitchell. Regardless of what we think about that young woman's mental state, she obviously believes she is *who* she says. For you to tell her that her father and her fiancé were dead, in such a cruel way, well...it was just plain insensitive. That's all I can say."

"Great. Nice to have your support."

Caroline heard a door slam, then another man continued, "I told you to keep him away from her."

May's voice again took a stern stance. "Mitchell, Jake may be a thoughtless young man, but he is not a dangerous one. I need his help with her. For the moment anyway, until we find out who she is and where she's come from."

"I'm looking into that," Mitchell replied. "In the meantime, I want her to come and stay with me, at least until she's better. I have much more room for her, and my housekeeper has agreed to come in every day."

Their voices had moved closer, and a moment later they entered the room. At first glance Caroline was again struck by the man's resemblance to Evan and the woman's to her Aunt Jess. Why did everyone here look like someone in her family? It was almost as if she'd crossed some line in time where people she knew were living a completely different existence. But that wasn't possible, was it?

"So...you're awake again."

The man approached the bed almost cautiously, and suddenly she realized that while he did have a certain look of Evan, it was in features only: the tall gaunt form, and steely gray hair. His soft cultured voice was much kinder and his eyes in no way as penetrating. This man seemed to genuinely care about what happened to her.

"You fainted, honey." May reached over and felt Caroline's forehead. "I think the exertion was just too much. Jake helped me bring you back inside. Are you feeling any stronger now?"

"I am not inclined to vapors."

They turned, raised eyebrows to each other.

"Of course you're not," Mitchell said kindly. "It's the shock."

"Precisely," Caroline replied, accepting this logical reasoning. Finally, someone was beginning to make some sense. "Waking up in a strange place, then seeing the new inventions, not knowing my father was away. And...you...you all remind me of people I know. But, I realize now, it must be shock. I will recover soon. I have never been ill in my life."

"May," the man called Mitchell addressed Mrs. Whatley, "why don't you make us some tea before you head up to the office? I'll stay here with Caroline for the rest of the afternoon."

"But..." May protested.

He held up a hand, refusing further argument. "No buts. I want to stay and read to Caroline for a bit. And you need to check on the staff and volunteers—you've already been away from your desk for two days."

He gave what Caroline suspected he meant to be a reassuring smile. "You know they can't run things without you."

Caroline listened to the interchange, wondering again why Jake had told her that Mrs. Whatley gave tours at the big house. Her home had never been open for tours.

May turned to Caroline, her eyes still full of understanding and concern. "Is there anything else I can get you before I go?"

"No," Caroline replied. "But please...if my father returns..." She broke off, dreading any reply she might receive.

May frowned as she patted Caroline's arm, then turned to leave the room, shaking her head.

* * * *

Afternoon shadows curtained the room as Mitchell came to the close of a he'd been reading aloud from Dickens. Caroline had remained silent as he read, and now she had fallen asleep.

When she'd spoken earlier, it had been with kindness, and her eyes meeting his had been warm and friendly. She hadn't pressed him with any further questions, evidently preferring to let her concerns rest for the time being. He was thankful for this, for he hadn't had to lie. Now, if he could only get her away from here before she found out that this really was the 21st century. If things progressed as he planned, she might never need to know at all. She might come to think all this had only been a bad dream, once he had her alone and in his carefully created 19th century environment.

He remembered the way she'd thanked him for staying to read to her. "This is what I needed," she said softly, pressing his hand as if they were already old friends. "There is no one like Dickens for creating a diversion. And you have helped...with your kind words."

She's warming to me, he thought happily, feeling the murmur of another voice at the back of his mind, this time a happy voice as well.

The girl shifted in her sleep, and he reached out and timidly touched an errant curl. She was so lovely. Evan had described her loveliness: golden hair, full lips, light green eyes, an enticing womanly figure. But neither he nor the portrait at the manor had done her justice. This girl was a timeless beauty.

The drawing-room painting mocked her beauty, with hair in a wild array and clothing drab and oversized. The artist who'd done the portrait may have been popular at the time for his unusual representations, but he'd certainly done the girl no justice in his portrayal.

Mitchell could imagine her in formal attire—her full bosom spilling from a low-cut and flowing dress; tendrils of hair escaping from her coiffure—her halo as it was—entwined with roses and baby's breath. In his mind's eye, he saw himself, sweeping her into his arms and out to an open dance floor—the dining room at Lyndfield, cleared of its furniture and prepared for a summer's ball. They would waltz across the room, eyes locked, hearts in tune, lovers in love. It would happen. He knew it was only a matter of time.

Mitchell sighed. Time. The time would come for that—soon, soon, soon enough.

* * * *

The sun slipped beyond the horizon like a graceful dancer clothed in a misty haze of purple and orange. Jake strode slowly back toward the gatehouse with half a mind to accept May's challenge and move out. After only one night he was damned sick of sleeping on the sofa. His nights were restless enough without such irritating complications. *Why the hell is this woman haunting me,* he grumbled to himself.

Opening the back door, he flicked on the kitchen light switch. "Great," he said aloud, "I'm supposed to stay out of her room, but that's where all my clothes are, and damned if I don't need a shower. Guess I'll have to wash under the kitchen facet."

"You needn't take things that far," a voice replied as May entered the kitchen. "She's sleeping. You can get your clothes."

"Some godmother you are," he said with as much anger as he could muster. "Taking Mitchell's side against me." Much as she irritated him, at the heart of it he cared about May deeply, as deeply as he would allow himself to care about anyone.

"Well quite frankly, my dear boy, I've never been ashamed of your being my godson until today." May peered inside the refrigerator, then pulled out a carton of milk. "Whoever that young woman is, Jake, there's no need for you to deliberately upset her."

Jake tucked his chin down to his chest, sufficiently chastised. "What about me?" he asked, refusing her offer of a glass of milk. "She's moved into my space, slowed down my work, screwed up my sleep, and...and..."

"And what?"

May had that certain look in her eye now, and past experience told Jake she was about to get around to something. She didn't let him down. "And what?" she prodded.

He shrugged and sat down at the table. "I don't know. She disturbs me."

Milk and cookies in hand, May approached the table and sat down next to him, offering the plate. "In what way?"

Jake picked up a chocolate chip cookie and toyed with it. "I'm not sure. She just does. I don't trust her, May."

He knew May's penetrating eyes were trying to read him from the inside out. That was her way. But he couldn't let her in just yet. He had to sort some of this out for himself.

"Are you sure it's her you don't trust? Maybe it's yourself."

"May, please don't do this to me. Why do you have to make everything into so much more than it is? She's a woman who showed up here claiming to be 100 years old. She's a nut case. Plain and simple."

"When is life ever so simple, Jake? I think you know better."

He tossed the cookie back on the plate and rose. Enough of this. "Did Jolly Johnston have a pleasant afternoon with his patient?" he asked.

May, ever patient, ignored his sarcasm. "Mitchell read to her. He said she seemed calmer when he left. He's hired a nurse, you know?"

"Oh really...his sustained interest in a woman he just met is impressive. I never pictured Mitchell for a philanthropist."

"You could do with a little of his compassion, you know?"

"I'll work on it." Jake started for the stairs, having heard enough lecturing for one day. "I'm going up now. Do you think she'll be leaving soon?"

"She'll go when she's ready. And you should apologize tomorrow," May said, dipping a fat cookie into the glass. "First thing."

"Whatever you say, ma'am," he said, saluting her over his shoulder.

Once in his bedroom, he crouched on his knees by the bed, watching her. She was beautiful in a way that normally didn't appeal to him. Pale skin, large tender eyes, tiny mouth, a particularly feminine example of womanhood. What a shame she wasn't a bit more right in the noggin.

She tormented his thoughts. He'd dreamed of her all night. Of times with her. Other times: laughing happy times when her eyes had lulled him to a peacefulness he'd never known in the light of day.

Jake knew why he was so cool with her. She scared the hell out of him. One touch, he thought, and he would lose his sanity too. Still, his fingers shyly strayed to the place where she lay, wanting, needing to know if her pale skin was really as soft as it had felt in his dream. He barely stroked her cheek.

"Ahh..." he breathed into the dark. It was.

Suddenly a great sadness welled up within him and Jake's heart throbbed like an aching wound. There was so much...so much...it seemed so close, this understanding. But he couldn't seem to grasp it, no matter how he tried. The sadness...he'd felt it once before, he thought.

Images crept round him dimly, and he strained to reel one in as it struggled against his pull like a slippery fish on a line. Then suddenly, he caught one. *No*, groaned inwardly, *not this*. It was a fine spring day and he was nine, and spending the weekend at his godmother's. They were working in the garden, and his new dog Sam was tugging playfully at his pants leg, when it happened. Right before his eyes as he plucked an ugly weed from its bed—the vision, the horror. He saw the car as clearly as if it were only a few feet away, when in actually it was hundreds of miles. His parents...taking the curve too fast....plunging over the rim of the canyon...soaring through the air...striking earth at last...exploding into a fiery ball of death.

He had screamed. Screamed for May. Clutched wildly at her when she ran to him. Muttered nonsense until she calmed him enough to hear his story. Then she'd run to the house, the phone. But it was too late. They'd already gone. Less than an hour later the police called with the news. It had happened as he'd seen it. Exactly.

Jake's cheeks were wet. He'd fought this memory for years. The sadness. The pain. The love lost.

He rose now, needing to leave her. To deal with his own grief. To put it back in the compartment where he kept it safely contained. He sensed May was right. This girl too had suffered terrible tragedy, and his words to her had been too harsh. And unfair.

Tomorrow, not only would he apologize to her, he vowed he would find a way to make up for his poor behavior. He would try to find a way to help her back to herself. Then she'd go back to wherever it was she came from. And he would be himself once more.

CHAPTER 7

…A time to mourn.
Ecclesiastes 3:1-8

The next morning, returning from an early walk with Sam, Jake found them together in the garden. For an instant, he thought it was he who'd stepped back in time. At the old wrought-iron table under the apple tree, a festive array of croissants, jams, and tea lay spread before them like a queen's feast. May had the somewhat prim appearance of a watchful aunt with her wavy gray hair swept away from her face and attired in a dark navy sweater with a high-collared white blouse underneath. Caroline, still sheathed in her heavy woolen robe, with the frilly Victorian nightgown May had provided peeking out from beneath, had her hair drawn back with a white ribbon, creating the illusion of an innocent schoolgirl. Heads bent together, as if sharing some sweet secret, their lighthearted laughter danced in the air as he entered the scene. Sam, the traitor, had beaten him back and now lay napping at Caroline's feet.

"Good morning, Jake," May called out, noticing him. "Isn't it a fine warm morning for early March? We decided to give the fresh air a try again, didn't we, Caroline?"

The girl nodded a silent assent, obviously, still upset with him. Not that he blamed her after his earlier behavior.

"How 'bout some hot coffee?" Jake cast an accusing eye at Sam before he sat down, and was rewarded with a low whine. *Traitorous dog,* he thought.

May emptied the carafe into his cup.

Before he opened his newspaper, he quickly caught May's unspoken warning. *I'll behave,* was his silent reply.

"I'll get some fresh," she replied and rose from the table.

After he heard the kitchen door slam behind her, Jake refolded his paper and drew a deep breath, then turned to meet Caroline's level gaze. He couldn't remember ever having this much difficulty talking to a woman. Not that he'd really tried to all that much.

"Look," he said, deciding to dive directly into the problem. "I owe you an apology. I'm sorry for my behavior—for upsetting you. It was thoughtless of me."

She didn't speak. As he watched her eyes filled, then slowly brimmed with tears. *Now I've done it,* he thought. *Made her cry again!*

"Please don't cry," he said when he found his voice at last. "Please.

54

I feel bad enough. I want to help you."

She wanted to respond to him, but found she could not. At this moment, Caroline felt nearer to Francis than she had at any time since his death. She trembled as Jake's hand reached out to brush her arm, not expecting the shocking warmth of his touch. An eerie breathless silence passed between them before he spoke again.

"So...will you forgive me?"

She continued to study his hand. Slender veins running like lovers to meet his long fingers. The deep burnished olive of his skin, lines crossing lines at his knuckles. She thought she might watch his hand, utterly fascinated, forever. If only she could keep feeling this close to him. To Francis...

"Hey, are you in there?"

The old irritation had come back into his voice, breaking the spell. He wasn't her Francis, with his sweet words and gentle murmurs.

She raised her eyes to his. "I..." She almost felt she would die with the pain of it. "I accept your apology."

Jake withdrew his hand quickly. Had he really felt nothing, she wondered?

"Good," he responded, "Now that that's settled... What's on your... What do you plan to do today?"

"She plans to rest and get well, and not much more, I'd say." Dr. Henry McWilliams marched toward them like a field marshal, followed close on the heel by May. "How are you today, pretty lady?"

"Hi, Henry." Jake smiled. If there was ever such a thing as an old-fashioned country doctor, Henry McWilliams was it. Not only did he still make house calls, he had a gentlemanly manner that should make Caroline feel right at home.

"Henry," he said, "I don't think you've been formally introduced to your patient." May shot Jake another warning look that he ignored. "This is Henry McWilliams, and this, doctor, is Miss Caroline Lyndfield." He thought he did a rather good job of keeping the sarcasm from his voice.

Henry didn't bat an eyelash. "How do you do, Miss Lyndfield?" He took Caroline's hand and bent low to brush a kiss across it.

Rather over the top, Jake thought with irritation.

"So, how is my patient today?" the doctor asked.

"Much better, thank you."

"Have the police been back to talk with you, about your accident," Henry asked.

Caroline looked to May, uncertain.

"They'll probably come later today, Henry. I wasn't sure how Caroline would be feeling, but she seems much better, aren't you, dear?"

Caroline nodded again. "But I really would like to go home." She paused and studied the three of them for a moment. "And, well, since I'm already home, in a manner, might I not just walk up to the house? To my room?" She stopped as she caught their bewildered expressions.

"Hey, I've got an idea." Jake rose from his chair and came to stand between her and the doctor. "Why don't you check Caroline out this morning, then if she's feeling better later, we'll take a slow and easy walk up to the house." He faced her once more. "Maybe it'll trigger something in your memory."

"Why do you persist in this belief that I do not remember?" she asked impatiently. "I am who I say. At least I was until I woke up here."

Henry patted her arm in fatherly fashion. "Now, now, pretty lady. Don't you go getting yourself all upset. That's the last thing you need to do."

"I'm sorry...I just want to help." Jake wondered if he would ever say the right thing when he was around this woman.

"Well, 'course you do, Jake, my boy. 'Course you do." Henry considered for a moment. I think that might be a good idea. If...this young lady really is feeling better. Slow and easy," Henry said with a meaningful look. "Why don't you just see how it goes?"

Jake breathed a sigh of relief that another scene had been averted.

"If you don't mind bringing me some warm water and towels, May, I'd like to have a look at these stitches. Jake, you can be off doing whatever you do, and let's see..." he checked his watch, "why don't you come back for Miss Lyndfield around twelve-thirty. I'll be done well before then and she'll have a chance to get dressed. All agree?"

As everyone left in response to his commands, Henry drew up a chair next to his patient then, taking her hand, he set about his work.

Jake followed May, irrationally happier than he'd been in days.

* * * *

A short time later, with Henry had gone and Jake safely ensconced in the study at the manor, May returned to relax with Caroline in the garden. The girl was stretched out in a chaise lounge with the newspaper open on her lap and Sam at her feet. She appeared to be a million miles away.

Glad for a chance to talk to with the girl, May pushed away any guilt she might have felt about being away from the office so much lately—the staff could just manage without her for a change. Everything had been fine when she looked in this morning. Once a system was set up, it worked pretty well with or without you, and May prided herself on the organization she'd managed to accomplish with the Lyndfield Trust. The books were in order; volunteers helped with the tours on a regular basis; the household property had been inventoried and cataloged. Besides, she hadn't taken a day off in years: she deserved a little time away. Mitchell was there if someone needed to be in charge. At least she hoped he was. Mitchell was being awfully mysterious these days.

Moving closer, May realized that Caroline held something in her hand, staring at it intently—the little hourglass. Without warning, unreasonable panic gripped May. Her heart pattered like a sparrow's, and she clutched at a nearby tree, afraid she might black out. Something pressed at her mind, trying to force its way into her thoughts, something dark, shadowy. Some dim memory, poised on the verge of a becoming a thought. It tugged at her, dank and musty...evil. May shut her eyes against the suddenly over-bright sunlight and gulped for air, breathing in and out, in and out; and with each out breath she fought for repossession of her mind.

Then, as quickly as it had come, the fear disappeared. When she reopened her eyes, Caroline was at her side.

"Mrs. Whatley..." Concern filled the girl's face. "I heard you gasp. Are you ill?"

May focused her attention, trying to cast off the last traces of anxiety. She allowed Caroline to help her over to a chair. "That was very odd," May said after a moment. "Very odd indeed."

"Did something happen?"

"I was walking over, watching you, and I noticed the glass. There, yes, that's it. You're holding it now." She reached out and took the hourglass from Caroline. "I suddenly felt the most incredible anxiety. Like something was trying to get at me." She gave a faint laugh. "How silly of me, my dear. I'm just being a fanciful old woman, I'm afraid."

Caroline took her free hand. "I think you are very dear," she said. "For caring about me. When you do not even know me."

"But I do know you, don't I? I've lived and worked here twenty years now. How could I not know you?"

Their eyes met, and a silent understanding was forged between them. May understood, and she believed. For the second time that morning Caroline's eyes misted. May put out her arms and the young woman went into them like a lost child. "Thank you," she whispered. "For believing." She paused. "When belief is not even a viable option."

"Now, there. There's no need to thank me for a thing. For now, you are who you say you are. Right?" May drew back as Caroline wiped at her eyes. "Will you tell me about the hourglass?" she asked carefully.

Caroline sat up straight. "I'm not sure I can tell you. I noticed it in my pocket just a moment ago. I feel I've seen it before. But I'm not sure where. Or for what purpose I had it."

"But it came belonged to William, didn't it?"

Surprised, Caroline took the prism from May and stared at it for a long time. "Of course. That's where I've seen it, on his desk. I remember I always wondered why it was so small—it really couldn't hold the sands of an entire hour, could it?" She smiled at May with nostalgia. "But how did it get in my robe? I never touched anything in my father's office."

"You don't remember ever having it then?"

Caroline shook her head 'no.' "Maybe there are some things I have forgotten." She raised a finger to her mouth and chewed anxiously at a nail.

"Mrs. Whatley..." she continued after a moment, "Before you came, I found this paper," she pointed to the open newspaper on the table. "This man," she indicated a picture on the front page, "George Bush? He is President of the United States? And the date...the date is 2006?"

"That's right."

"But how can this be? How could such a thing happen? Before..." She seemed reluctant to continue. "Before I went to bed two nights ago, it was 1890. Francis had been dead for a month, and I had gone to see his grave that day." May did not fail to notice the way her chin quivered when she mentioned Francis Monroe's name. *Could there have been something between the two of them,* she wondered?

"I heard something in the night," Caroline continued, "at least I think I did...beyond that, I do not remember anything."

May stared, open-mouthed. The girl herself made further comment unnecessary. "Those things Mr. Stanton said...about my father...they are true, aren't they? Somehow, in this time, they are true. He's dead, isn't he?"

May recognized the distress rising in Caroline once again. "I tell you what," she said, linking her arm with the girl's, "we have a few hours before lunch and Jake comes to take you on your walk. And you can't go in your nightgown, now can you? Let's put all this aside for a while and go shopping. Do you feel up to it, just for an hour?"

Caroline smiled a weak little smile. "I think so."

"Well my wardrobe's not much, and we're surely not built anything alike, so what do you say we make a quick trip out to get you a few new things. There's nothing like shopping to perk you up, right?"

The girl gave May another brief smile. "Will we ride in a car?"

May grinned. "You betcha. Now, let's see if we can find something suitable enough for you to wear into town." She eyed Caroline critically. "Maybe a sweatshirt and skirt will do." Patting Caroline, she linked her arm in the girl's. "We'll deal with all these uncertainties when you're stronger. What do you say?"

"Thank you," Caroline replied softly. "Thank you."

* * * *

Tarleton, like almost everything else she had seen in the past few days, was quite changed. Oh, there were places she recognized—a place May called a "supermarket" where the old butcher shop use to be; a few rows of little townhouses still neatly stacked, their windows smiling with bright boxes of flowers and dainty curtains; a card shop where the printer once housed. But so much was different. Busy streets crowded with vehicles directed by strange lighting devices signaling when the cars should stop and go. Painted signs announced more businesses than Caroline could imagine any one town needed.

The little dress shop where she and May stopped reminded Caroline of Mrs. Pettit's Dress Shop—she always went there when she hadn't the time to travel into New York City. Situated between an attorney's office and card shop, its cheery display boasted a crowded display of goods for sale. But all resemblance to Mrs. Pettit's ended there. The garments in the window—Caroline had never seen anything like them in her life. And she had always believed her tastes in fashion to be just a daring. But these...these outfits were hardly outfits at all. Skirts sewn of the most bizarre printed fabrics boasted tops made of material such as she had never seen—it hardly looked as if it would fit over one's head, but they stretched miraculously to a shape that fit the body snugly. Though May had assured Caroline this was a woman's clothing store, pants adorned the long legs several models. Pants, it seemed, were now considered common feminine attire. In spite of it all, Caroline had to smile. To be so very comfortable in dress was enviable indeed.

The ride in the car had been wonderful as well! May opened the windows in the vehicle, and Caroline had loved the feel of the wind as it caught her hair and tossed it about her face like a full-blown flag catching on the breeze. It had taken them less than ten minutes to leave the estate and arrive at the store. With no timetable or other passengers as the train would have had. *Incomparable*, she'd thought as the scenery whizzed by.

As she and May perused the racks of garments now, however, concern began to well up in her. May had taken several dresses and held them up to determine the size, and Caroline had not failed to note their length. While she had always considered herself a 'modern' woman, these clothes were beyond anything she would ever have considered appropriate. Finally she stopped and stared, not certain how to tell her benefactress of her dilemma.

Eventually the older woman, turning to show Caroline her latest consideration, realized she stood alone on the row. "Caroline," she asked, "What's wrong?"

Caroline hesitated. "These...these garments...are..."

May chuckled. "I know they're a little mod. But I think these will look better on you than something from the store where I normally shop." Noticing that Caroline still wasn't responding, she came back to stand next to her. "You're not worried about the money, are you? It's my treat."

"Oh, no," the girl replied. "Of course I know my father will..." She broke off, apparently uncertain whether her father would or not.

"It...it is not the money that concerns me. These clothes are not suitable." Caroline took a skirt from May and held it to her waist. "You see?"

This brought a burst of laughter some nearby eavesdropping women. May shot them a look of warning and they went back to their business. "Oh, my dear. I hadn't even considered that. Most young women these days wear their skirts up to their...." She stopped and pointed to her derriere, causing Caroline to clasp a hand over her mouth and widen her eyes in shocked disbelief.

"It never occurred to me that would bother you," May continued, patting the girl in her motherly fashion. "You have a lovely figure and well, this is what women wear. But...let's try some slacks, what do you say?"

Several minutes later, an enormously relieved Caroline emerged from the dressing room attired as May and the shopkeeper had shown her, the tiny little undergarments— panties and brassiere—May had labeled them—secured and in place. The brassiere, much better than the tight and cumbersome corsets she and Aunt Jess had always worn felt like a Godsend, and the panties, well, shamefully. Caroline blushed as she considered the freedom she felt in them. The brown slacks and printed orange silk blouse—Caroline had insisted she would have none of the clingy stretch fabric—also felt incredible next to her skin. The soft leather shoes they'd found caressed her feet like kid gloves. She could run, or walk, or ride, and never have to worry about changing into anything different. How she wished she had always dressed thus. What would Francis have thought of these carefree garments, she wondered? Would he have admired the way the slacks clung to her derriere and the blouse accentuated her full breasts?

And then, even more curiously, she wondered what Mr. Stanton would think?

* * * *

Jake couldn't believe his eyes. At first, he'd almost wanted to laugh outright. It wasn't that she looked ridiculous—quite the contrary. *She looks good enough to...* he thought outrageously, then mentally reprimanded himself and pushed his teasing aside. With May standing like a sentinel at Caroline's side, he knew he'd better be on his best behavior.

No, Caroline looked great, so great in fact, if he hadn't known what a nut case she was, he might have been tempted to become his normally flirtatious self. But she obviously was incredibly uncomfortable in her new clothes. She stood, self-consciously, slumped, almost as if she were afraid he might notice she had breasts.

Still, he was determined to keep his vow of benevolence. He swept into a low bow at their feet. "Ladies," he said. "You look lovely."

Caroline chewed a nail hesitantly as he rose to make his bow. May had pulled the younger woman's hair up into a ponytail and tied a big orange ribbon around it. With the naive look on her face, she could easily have passed for about sixteen—except for the fact that her body...Jake wiped his brow. It sure seemed hot for March.

"Mrs. Whatley...May..." she said hesitantly. "May helped me with this attire." Jake gave her his best grin. "You both did a great job. You look splendid, Miss Lyndfield."

May, apparently pleased with his behavior, gave him a rewarding smile. "Now then," she said, "I'm going up to the office to prepare Mitchell for your little surprise visit. We wouldn't want him to have a hernia that you're up and about without his permission." She gave Jake a pointed look. "And consorting with the enemy. You two have a nice walk and I'll see you later at the house," she called back to them as she headed up the drive. "And behave!"

Left alone with her, Jake suddenly became shy. Why had all his self-confidence mysteriously evaporated? His palms were actually sweating. How on earth had he gotten himself into this little outing? And why must he act like a fifteen-year-old around this woman?

"So," he said reluctantly, "where would you like to go first? And before you say it, let's save the house for last. That'll give Mitchell a chance to cool off. Okay?"

She acquiesced, and suddenly quite sure of herself, said without a further moment's pause or thought, "His grave then."

Of course he'd known whose grave she meant. Who else but the man she claimed to have loved? Jake watched silently from a safe distance as she knelt by the stone and outlined the name with her finger. There was something oddly reminiscent about her movement, and without reason Jake felt more than a little chilled. She was crying, but he didn't know what to say to ease her mind. So he kept his place and waited.

"I insisted they bury him here." Her voice caught on the breeze and flew to him. "Not in the cemetery. But here. Where we were happy." Jake remained silent, mesmerized, as she continued to trace a pattern on the stone. "You look like him, you know?"

He shivered again as her words crept round him. "Do I?" He moved a little closer despite his reluctance.

"Very much. But you are not so like him in other ways." She sought his eyes and watched him for a moment, then her attention went back to the slate. "I know you don't believe me, but I loved him. With my life. My life has been nothing since his death."

"I thought you—she—loved Evan Ludington. They were engaged, weren't they?" He couldn't believe they were having this conversation. As if she were a dead woman.

She shot him a venomous look. "Who told such a terrible lie?"

"I read it somewhere. Didn't May tell you I'm writing about the Lyndfield family?"

"You'd do well to tell the truth then." Caroline stated then turned to face the slate again. "'Tisn't true. I was not engaged to him. Never officially." Her voice broke and she laid her face against the cold rock beside her. "I loved Francis. I would have married him. I would have." She spoke fiercely, as if to convince herself what she said was true.

"Well," Jake said, in an attempt to lighten the mood, "that was all a long time ago, so why don't we put it behind us and finish this walk. Okay?"

She drew herself up, and Jake could see it was with great effort. He had to admire her, whoever she was. She played this role to the hilt.

Once more, they headed across the lawn toward the big house. Jake was already beginning to regret his decision to help her. He suspected *helping* her might take a lot more patience than he possessed. Which wasn't much to begin with.

Caroline stopped abruptly, directly in front of the playhouse. "It happened here," she whispered.

"What?" Jake leaned toward her, trying to catch the words.

"Here." She shivered suddenly and sensed him move closer; for now she knew she was safe, but for how long? How long before she had to face the darkness again? Something had happened here that she needed to remember. She slipped her hands into the pockets of her slacks as a cold chill crossed her.

"Ouch!" She gasped and drew out her freshly bandaged

"What happened?" Jake asked, then seeing a drop of blood on her fingertip, "You cut yourself."

He took her hand and inspected it. Again, she trembled at his contact and he gave her a curious glance. "Doesn't look too bad. Did you leave a pin in your new pants?"

"No, it was this." She pulled out the hourglass, still dotted with a drop of blood at the sharp point on one end.

"Oh. That keeps turning up, doesn't it? Why don't you let me keep it?"

"No!" The ferocity of her words startled even her. She had no particular attachment to the hourglass, but for some reason she didn't want to let it out of her sight. Why was she so insistent it must be kept on her person? She took a deep breath. "I feel like it keeps me connected to my family," she said.

Jake backed away and took the warmth with him. "Okay. Keep it then. But don't expect me to come running to your rescue every time you cut yourself."

She studied the shape in her palm for a moment more then followed him toward the house.

* * * *

"They're doing what?" Mitchell was even angrier than May had expected. "I told you he was not to be alone with her. Can't you follow even the simplest of instructions?"

May drew herself up haughtily. "You will not talk to me like that, Mitchell Johnston. This young woman is under my care right now, and if she wants to take a walk with my godson, I'll be damned if I'll say no."

"Look what's happened the last two times he's been with her? I don't want a repeat performance."

"And you won't get one," came Jake's reply from the doorway. "Here you are, Ma'am, safe and sound." He ushered a silent and withdrawn Caroline into the room.

She had yet to recover from the eerie sense of being in her home, but not in her home at all. From the moment they stepped inside the heavy oak door, everything had seemed somehow different. The furniture was the same. The paintings were all there, lamps, and knick-knacks, and books in their places. But then she had seen a square window box, suspended from the ceiling, with images of people moving around inside and the sound of voices coming from it.

Catching her bewildered stare, Jake informed her, "It's a videotape," she thought he called it, "for orientation." Neither of those words made one bit of sense to her, but she decided to leave her questions for now, not wanting to irritate her guide any further.

If that wasn't unusual enough, that people needed to be 'oriented' to her home, in addition several strange-looking people milled about— whom Jake slyly referred to as "the tourists." They had seemed so very odd, nothing like visitors who might have come to her home in the past. One tall portly man wore a large cowboy hat that threatened to devour his head, and boots that proclaimed the death of several lizards, but any resemblance to the frontier nomads ended there. His denims appeared clean, and pressed, of all things! The shirt he wore boasted a bright red shade and about his neck hung a black instrument that Jake told her was a camera. Never in her life had she seen one so small. And where, Caroline wondered, had this odd man tethered his horse, since there were no longer any hitching posts in front of the house? Perhaps these 21st century cowboys all traveled about in the "cars" now.

This most unusual man, and the woman next to him—with her outrageously short skirt and a top so tight it outlined her breasts in detail and caused Caroline herself to gape and blush—were conducting the strangest conversation she had ever heard. She could make neither heads or tails of "Ah'm tellin' yew, hon, this ain't the guy yew thought it wuz. This here dude wuz some kinda financial wiz up in the Big Apple."

The woman, her hair like spun gold and somehow puffed up, had something in her mouth, and kept chewing and smacking so loudly Caroline wanted to go over and demand that she stop.

"Yer, right, darling," she drawled, "Ah wuz thinkin' this place wuz some kinda artist's hangout. Like Woodstock or something? I wuz wrong, sugar."

Caroline looked Jake, baffled. He'd laughed and shrugged his shoulders. "They're from Texas, I think."

She attempted to comprehend it all without losing her sanity: the odd people, vehicles she'd never seen before, the house with its cold, unlived-in feeling. The fact that in the short space of a few days, her home and all the people who went with it had disappeared.

When she asked Jake about going upstairs to her own room, he told her that area wasn't open to the public. Rather than protest, she'd merely sighed, wondering what her family had done to make them so interesting to people one hundred years later.

"Are you all right, Caroline?" May was asking her now.

She forced her thoughts back into the moment. What could she say to them? How could she make them believe she was who she said she was? That she came from where she said she came?

A shrill ringing filled the room and Mitchell crossed to a desk and picked what she assumed must be the modern example of Bell's telephone. Caroline had begun to wonder if Evan and her father could updated all these things; if so, there remained a good possibility she was not dreaming. Since dreams normally did not feel so real and rarely continued for more than one night, it seemed there could be no other explanation. Time she accepted that this absurdity had happened, and start to think about what she should do about it.

"That," Mitchell said, replacing the instrument in its holder and crossing to them, "was Miss Henderson, my part-time housekeeper. She's agreed to come in full time for a while, to take care of you until you're completely recovered." As he went on, Caroline noticed that he was studying her attire with something akin to displeasure. "I'm really surprised you're even out and about today, my dear. I'm sure you should be resting. All the more reason to get you settled at my place. You can rest in peace without the coming and going of others." He tossed a pointed look at May, who seemed suddenly at a loss for words.

Caroline looked from one to the other of, wondering that she had not been consulted about any such plans, and unsure herself of what to say. "I really don't think I need a nurse. I'm perfectly all right now, just a little tired at the moment."

"My point exactly," Mitchell replied with a firm tone. "If you don't get enough rest, you're going to be back in bed in no time."

"Actually, Mitchell," May interjected, trying to steer Mitchell away from his plan, "I think it may have been a bit premature to think Caroline needs further bed rest, or even someone to keep an eye on her. She's feeling much better now, aren't you, dear?"

Mitchell's benevolent smile encompassed them both. "I'm sure you are, but either way, you definitely need a place to stay for now, isn't that true, Caroline?"

He took a seat next to Caroline on the sofa and patted her arm. "You're going to need some space of your own, where you can stay until you sort things out. My little house is toward the rear of the estate; it's got an upstairs apartment that's completely private." He beamed at her with a fatherly smile. "I'd love to have you as my guest. This way, Mr. Stanton can have his room *and* get back to his writing, and you'll be much more comfortable. Not to mention that you'll have someone nearby all the time. Just in case there's anything you need."

Caroline could not think of any reason for argument, and she did like Mr. Johnston. Yesterday, when he'd stayed to read to her, she had felt more comfortable than at any point since waking up. Obviously, she could not stay in her old room here in the big house—unless she wished to have strangers coming and going at all hours. Of course, it was terribly inappropriate for her to stay at the home of a man she did not know. But no more so than it had been sleeping in the bedroom of another man she did not know. Which, she wondered, was worse in 2006?

Jake had been remarkably silent throughout this entire exchange, and as she looked to both he and May now for some guidance or reassurance, she found none forthcoming. In fact, Jake appeared visibly irritated. Perhaps everyone hoped she would have recovered her senses by this time. Obviously that hadn't happened.

"I suppose it would be for the best for the time being...I am a nuisance," she said hesitantly. Jake shrugged without comment and May seemed at a loss for words to argue further.

"You're not a nuisance to anyone, my dear. But of course this will be a better arrangement," Mitchell replied, seemingly the happiest person in the room. "Yes, indeed, it will. Until you're back to normal, you'll be my very special guest."

CHAPTER 8

...A time to plant.
Ecclesiastes 3:1-8

For the first time since coming to this time and place, sleep eluded Caroline. Her mind raced with the events of this strangest of days: shopping with May, talking in the cemetery with Jake, her unreasonable fear at the playhouse, the changes in the place she'd once known as home, the seemingly unanimous decision to send her to Mitchell Johnston's home—so much to comprehend—too much. After tossing about for what she was certain must have been several hours, she rose from the bed, threw on her robe, and slipped quietly downstairs.

She crept across the front room toward the door, then paused briefly when she saw Jake's sleeping form stretched out on the couch. Her heart caught in her chest, and she drew her breath in sharply. How like Francis he was. How could life be so unfair, bringing her so close to someone who so resembled her lost love, yet was not? So unfair— that somehow, beyond belief and comprehension, she could cross a century of time, only to find this man who looked so much like Francis, but in reality wasn't like him at all. Cruel fate, to play such a trick.

A chilly burst of air struck Caroline as she stepped into the night, but the cold was a welcome relief from the pain and longing set firm within her heart. When would she be free of this grief? Why did she feel so close to her love here, closer than she'd felt since he died? Like he was only a heartbeat away, and needed her desperately? She would be more than willing to give to him, if only she knew what—and how.

She ambled in the direction of the conservatory and then, approaching the edge of what had once been her garden, sank down on a bench and stared out at the river. The long span of metal that was now the bridge blinked with the lights of crossing motorists. Caroline drew in a short breath and pressed her hand hard against her mouth.

"Oh, Francis. Francis," she whispered into the darkness. "How could this have happened? Why has it happened? What am I to do?"

Then she waited, almost certain in the darkness that the breeze would send an answer.

* * * *

Jake saw her slip out the door, but he waited in silence—until he was sure she was beyond hearing distance—before he got up. *Where is she going in the middle of the night?*

He followed at a careful distance, watching as she drew her robe close against the cool air, then feeling a chill of his own when she shook out her long hair and caught a moonbeam in its tresses. God, he'd been wrong when he'd thought her kind of looks weren't beautiful. In this light, she was stunning. Jake wanted her more than he'd ever wanted anyone in his life. A crazy woman, and him mad with desire for her. But he didn't *want* to want her. He wanted to retain his safe cocoon of protection from this sudden onslaught of feeling.

As she wandered down to the stone bench and took a seat, Jake paused and held his distance. She looked so fragile there alone, a precious jewel, with tangled hair spilling its golden cache about her shoulders like a pirate's treasure and pale skin glowing like priceless porcelain. When she brought her hand to her mouth and uttered an almost silent, strangled cry Jake could take no more. He stepped from his hiding spot and moved into her line of vision, hoping not to frighten her too much with his action.

"Caroline..." he crooned like the lover her wasn't.

She lifted tortured eyes to his, calmer than he might have expected at the interruption to her reverie. An unspoken question seemed to hang in the air between them and against his will, Jake reached out a hand to touch her cheek. She cradled her face against his palm, and something so sincere, so tender, in her movement brought him to kneel on the cold ground at her feet and put his arms around her. She trembled in his light hold and he gathered her to him like a frightened child.

"Shh," he soothed. "It's all right. Everything's going to be all right."

Her tears gushed, making the ache in Jake's breast almost unbearable. He drew back a little and pushed a strand of fallen hair back from her forehead.

"Okay...okay, love. Wanna tell me what's the matter?"

Bravely, she brushed the moisture from her face. "It's very silly, in a way."

Jake gave her a crooked smile and steeled himself for her explanation. He'd never considered how hard it might be, trying to make someone nuts believe you believed them. Still, he planned to give it his best shot. Something about her seemed worth believing.

"If it's silly," he phrased the question with care, "why are you crying?"

She refused to let him break out of their hold completely, and he wasn't sorry she stayed in his arms. Something about having her there felt so comfortable, so right, he couldn't bring himself to set her free.

"I know you don't believe me." She put a timid finger to his mouth as he made to protest. "I understand. Truly, I do. If you told me you had traveled in time across more than a hundred years, I probably would not believe you either."

"Thanks a bunch," Jake teased. "I'll make a mental note to remember that when I get to your century."

Caroline returned his smile tremulously. "But whether you believe it or not, I have come from the 19th century, my whole world has been shattered, and yet I weep...I weep for Francis...my heart..." Her eyes teared up again as she tried to continue. "I feel so close to him. Here..." she indicated her breast, and with reluctance Jake forced his eyes away from their dim outline beneath her gown and back to her face.

"I was planning to marry him," she continued, unaware of his discomfort. "But my father had other plans, you see."

"For you and Evan?"

"Yes. And I delayed confronting him. And then Francis died."

Jake shivered unreasonably. "How'd he die? The records don't say much about him."

"He drowned." She looked to the river beyond. "There."

"An accident?"

"There was a storm. I do not know why he went out that night." She bit her finger, as Jake was learning was her habit. "But we had argued."

"So you blame yourself?"

"If I had not delayed. If I had spoken with my father sooner. I did not love Evan. I should not have let him think I might marry him."

Her eyes filled once more, and Jake raised a finger and touched a tear at one corner. "We have a saying in the 21st century," he told her. "Hindsight is 20/20."

She smiled in spite of herself, but he felt glad for her smile all the same. He took a corner of his tee shirt and dabbed at her eyes.

"So, what are we going to do with you, Miss Lyndfield?"

She shook her head and shrugged. "I'm sure I don't know. I feel there must be some answer—some reason for my being here. But I confess I do not know what it might be."

"Well you've obviously had some pretty heavy stuff going on in your life. Would you be willing to let me try and help you, Caro?"

Jake slipped into the familiar use of her name without notice, but his use of it touched Caroline nonetheless. Francis had often called her that, and spontaneously now, she reached out and stroked Jake's cheek.

"Yes," she said in a low full voice. "I believe I will trust you, Jake Stanton."

Her lips bent to meet his without thought, his kiss gentle against her mouth. His tongue traced a pattern around hers and as his hand cupped her breast beneath the robe, a heat rose in Caroline that she had not felt since... since...

Another time, and another kiss had found them here in this very garden. The garden she put so much love into, the plants that had been such a large part of her life then. They'd been sitting beneath the beech tree and lessons had become mundane. The warmth of such close proximity had reached a point where it was almost unbearable.

"Damn it, woman!" Francis had said, tossing his book angrily to one side. "I cannot tolerate this treatment any longer. We must talk."

Caroline remembered how she'd stifled a little smile. She had known for so long that she loved him. Years, actually. And now that he had realized, he wanted immediate release. So typical of men!

"What would you like to talk about, Francis?" She'd toyed with him, relishing the way he'd risen from the spot and began a nervous pacing.

"Well, I...you...we..."

When he broke off, obviously frustrated with himself, Caroline had laughed outright. How she had cherished those moments when he first tried to confess his love! Then he had come to her, and knelt on the ground beside her, and brought his warm mouth to hers possessively...and gently caressed her breast...

She pulled away, horrified. This was not Francis! She hardly knew this man. And yet he fondled her in the middle of the night.

After the initial movement away from him and Caroline had reclaimed her faculties somewhat, she felt a little silly. That had been long ago. This was another time and place.

But Jake seemed to sense her sudden barrier of propriety, for he rose from the ground and pulled her up with him, teasing. "Time we got you to bed, miss priss. Wouldn't want those Victorian sensibilities to get riled up, now would we?"

She immediately suspected he mocked her, but as he led her back toward the house, Caroline knew she must find a way to put an end to any expectations he might have concerning their brief romantic interlude. A kiss might be one thing, but anything beyond was absolutely prohibited. How did she know what he meant when he said 'time we got you to bed...'"

"I...I..." She didn't know how to continue, yet knew she must find words to convey her meaning.

By this time they'd reached the front door. Jake paused and put two hands on her shoulders, and Caroline dreaded what was to come? Would he really expect her to dally with him further?

"Tomorrow," he said. "We're going into the city. There's someone I want you to see."

"To see?"

"Yep, a doctor."

"But I'm not sick." What on earth was he talking about?"

"I know that. But you said you were willing to trust me, right?

She nodded.

"Then, go with me into the city. We'll see my friend the doctor and then we'll go to the archives."

"Archives?"

"Your family history, my dear. All the original documents from the estate are in the New York Public Library. I want to check a couple of things out. Besides, you'll get a kick out of 21st century New York City, I think. Okay?"

Caroline confused by all the strange language, nodded in uncertain agreement, feeling a little tug of disappoint that he had made no further mention of the kiss.

He's not going to make further advances now? she wondered irrationally.

"Will May chaperon us?" Caroline asked, hoping against hope that the 21st century disallowed such things.

She was rewarded with a quick and quiet laugh from Jake.

"No. We won't be chaperoned. But I'll take good care of you, I promise."

"Do you think I should discuss this with Mr. Johnston? He seems so concerned about my welfare."

Jake frowned and she recognized again that he definitely didn't care for the other man. "Leave him a note if you want too. But you're a big girl. You don't have to ask permission to take a road trip."

She smiled. "I suppose I don't, do I?"

Jake smiled in return, then walked her the rest of the way to her bedroom. Just outside the door, he planted a friendly peck on her forehead. "I'll see you bright and early, then?"

"Yes," came her quick and happy reply. "Bright and early."

* * * *

Mitchell paced angrily back and forth across the Oriental rug stretched across the office floor. He thought he would explode; his head rattled with an angry cacophony of its own. He'd seen them. He'd watched Caroline and that idiot Stanton together. Outdoors, at this hour! Stanton even had the audacity to kiss the girl. Mitchell knew he couldn't get her out of that gatehouse quick enough. Thank God Ruby Henderson would be there to keep an eye on her at his house! If only she'd been available sooner—none of this would have happened. But he'd needed someone he could trust, and Ruby owed him a few favors. So, he'd been forced to wait until she could get here.

How he wished he could have come up with some reason for breaking up the little scene he'd just witnessed. When he had first looked out the window and seen Caroline sitting alone on the garden

71

bench, he'd immediately wanted to go to her. But before he could move to do so, Stanton had appeared out of nowhere. The interchange that followed was more than disgusting—him, forcing her into his arms. Then kissing her like he had—like a lovesick schoolboy in the clutches of his first passion.

Mitchell picked up the first thing his hand encountered a book—and flung it across the room. "Damn him!"

He turned to his desk and stared down at Evan's open journal, which he carried with him always these days. In one violent motion, he swept it to the floor. According to Evan, she'd loved him once—hopelessly so. Why was she so eager then to find love in the arms of another man? If such was the case, Mitchell intended to make certain that man was himself, and not Jake Stanton. Somehow he knew she was his destiny—how he knew he couldn't say, but he knew it with all his being.

He knelt down and retrieved the cumbersome diary from the spot where it had fallen. As he moved to lay it back on the desk, the spidery writing of Evan's hand caught his eye for a long moment, then blurred before him. 'Ah!' he thought and crossed to the tall bookshelf. He reached up and pulled down a faded volume. *Hypnosis and Its Effects*, it read. Evan had had his own little secrets. Now Mitchell would have his. The secret to winning Caroline's love.

"She will be mine," he said, believing completely, and even as he thought it the murmuring in his head subsided at once.

* * * *

Lyndfield Estate, 1889

Evan Ludington held the tiny hourglass up to the window, turning the cylinder about so it caught the light, its glass reflecting a bright array of colors across the walls of the room. He did not particularly care for the task at hand, but William Lyndfield had strange appetites, and like it or not, Evan helped feed his desires.

Of course it would be worth it in the end. Caroline would be his, just like her mother was supposed to have been. Already, he had dreamed and planned for their future when he wrote in his journal. There, she loved him already. He would be ecstatic when he could make his dreams an actuality.

Evan remembered the first time he had seen Caroline's mother. Lila. It had been the same. When he looked at her his heart melted—such a woman—her eyes, the golden brown hair, a young body about to blossom into a Venus. And the daughter was almost an exact replica of the mother.

Unfortunately, it was his friend William who captured Lila's heart. Evan had thought he would die with pain of it, and seriously considered doing bodily harm to his rival. But he had been young then, with his fortune yet to be made, and ambition won over love.

Then, of course, Lila had died in childbirth. Childbirth, of all things. When she was little more than a child herself.

Again, Evan had plotted murder in his heart. But when he stared down at that tiny baby who clutched his finger like a lifeline, he had decided he might wait. There were ways to have what one wanted. Maybe the time had not been right for he and Lila. But somehow, miraculously, he had been given another chance. So he had waited and planned and seen to William's needs, and now the time was almost at hand for all of his own dreams to materialize.

A shadow crossed the room and Evan turned to the window. What he saw was them, Caroline and Francis. His throat tightened as he watched the woman go into the man's open arms—his love, and another man. This time, he would kill if need be. Fate was not going to cheat him again. He would not allow it. This time she would be his.

Evan stared down at his hand, and despite the fact that he was cut and bleeding from his tight clutch on the sharp-edge of the object, he smiled. This time she would be his, all right, and he had the power to make it so.

CHAPTER 9

...A time to dance.
Ecclesiastes 3:1-8

When Jake told Caroline they'd be traveling by train, she thought at last she might be about to re-enter the realm of the familiar. She supposed she should have guessed this was not to be. The train station was a completely modern facility, boasting glass and steel such as anything she'd ever seen, and now the landscape sped by at such an amazing pace that it made her as dizzy as Francis' first kiss had done. She could scarcely make out shapes as they whizzed past, but she was quite certain there would be many things she did not recognize. In fact, she remembered only a mere handful of towns between her summer home and New York whereas now they passed one every few minutes. Times had certainly changed, and Caroline suddenly felt much older than her nineteen years. If truth be told, her age must be somewhere over one hundred by now—not a comfortable assessment.

She turned to find Jake studying her with amusement, as if he could read her very thoughts. After sending him what she hoped was her severest silent retort, she faced the window once more.

Oddly enough, Caroline found that despite his obvious doubt in her authenticity, she felt much happier being with him than she had been since Francis' death. She could still imagine the taste of Jake's mouth on hers, so familiar yet somehow new and exciting; her senses tingled each time she thought about the touch of his warm hand against her breast. Francis wouldn't have dreamed of taking such liberties, though she knew he'd wanted her every bit as much. How times had changed.

Even Jake's ungodly arrival at her door this morning, well before the sun had placed its own good morning kiss upon the day, brought a sigh of delight to her heart. Many times she and Francis had slipped out before lessons to spend the early hours of the day alone together, but those times consisted more of walking, talking, handholding and kissing. Passions rose, but they'd both held them in check, befitting of the times.

"I don't want to give Mitchell a chance to stop our little outing," Jake had told her. "And we can catch the 6:05 train. So get a move on, woman."

"Why would he want to prevent our trip?" Caroline had asked from the bathroom where she had gone to don her new clothes.

"Well," he replied, "in case you haven't noticed, Mitchell Johnston doesn't like me much—and he really seems to dislike my spending time with you."

"Why is that—that he doesn't like you, I mean?"

"Lots of reasons, probably. Right now, the main one being that I'm writing a book he always thought he would write."

"The book about my family?" She came out of the adjoining room, dressed for departure, and they had slipped quietly down the back stairs to avoid waking May before he had a chance to finish answering her question.

"Yeah, that's right," Jake whispered with only a trace of sarcasm. "That book."

Caroline knew even then that his polite behavior was no further indication that he believed her story. She had asked him yesterday if his sudden interest in her wellbeing was such an indication, and he laughed outright.

"I wouldn't go quite far, Miss Lyndfield." He smiled and cheerfully drew her arm securely under his. "Let's just say I'm beginning to see the advantages of your full recovery."

She had wanted to argue that recovery couldn't be an option unless one was ill, which she wasn't. Although perhaps if John considered her returning to her own time an event worth recovery—perhaps he truly was tired of sharing his space with a helpless woman? But she refrained from making any reply. She wanted it to be a good day, and had determined to do whatever she must to see that it was just that.

Drawing her gaze away from the scenery and back to Jake now, she asked, "How do you know this doctor will see me? Did you make an appointment with him?"

He put down the paper he'd been reading. She looked even more lovely in the morning than any woman he'd ever known. Eyes bright and alert and cheeks flushed with color, her unruly hair appeared perfectly natural with its waves and curls tossed about her face. He held back a sigh and stuck the newspaper between their seats.

"It's a 'she,' and she'll see you all right. She owes me a couple of favors." That much was true. He wasn't bothered about Melanie seeing Caroline; it wasn't often she turned down one of his requests. What he worried about more than that was that she'd see too much. Psychologists had a nasty habit of doing that. They also saw things when many times there was nothing to see. He and Melanie Hartford had had a "convenient" relationship for almost five years now. They had a lively and interesting sex life and they didn't interfere with each other on a daily basis. She had her work. He had his. It was comfortable. She wouldn't even mind the fact that Jake was seeing someone else. He was pretty sure she had her own little things going on the other side of the sheets. But how she'd react to Caroline—and her bizarre tale—presented an entirely different matter.

"A female doctor? Is that more common in your 21st century?" She was surprised but not shocked, for female doctors were certainly beginning to appear on the scene during her own time. "She has an office here in the city? Or does she work at a hospital?"

"She has an office. But we're going to catch her before she goes there." He glided over his reply to Caroline. "Because I don't have an appointment."

"Will she approve of such a thing?" Caroline's innocence shown through her question, making Jake feel more than a little guilty. "You and I coming to her home so early in the morning? Unannounced?"

He laughed. "She'll be surprised. But she won't say no."

Jake was right. Nothing had prepared Caroling for New York City in the 21st century. From the moment she saw the sun peeking out from behind the tall needle-like buildings—skyscrapers, he called them—the differences between 1890 and 2006 became vividly apparent. The train slid to a grinding halt in the station and for Caroline, it was like slipping into another world. A bizarre arena packed with a menagerie of people like none she had ever seen, even more bizarre than the strangers she had seen at Lyndfield.

"Are they tourists?" she asked, bringing an explosion of laughter from the man at her side.

"Not hardly." Jake steered her through the crowd like an experienced captain. "Most of these nuts live or at least work here."

She wasn't sure what his use of the word "nuts" meant, but they were indeed quite unusual. Women in bizarre and vulgar clothing—made with so little fabric that she wondered how they managed to keep them on their bodies. Men in everything from three-piece business attire carrying dark square cases and wearing shiny leather shoes to others in ragged denims, loose fitting shirts with strange writing on them, and large oddly-made footwear.

People of all nationalities flocked the station: Africans, Oriental, Latinos—how many others she could not be certain. The number of Negroes amazed her as well—many of them with unusual designs cut or shaped into their frizzy black hair. As Jake led her outside and down the street, she watched in fascination as they passed by people carrying large metal boxes from which terrible noises blared. Scraggly men and women dressed in tattered garments tugged at them and begged for coins. Street vendors had the weirdest assortment of wares: everything from gold watches and rings to brightly dyed clothing—all this, and so much more. Her head spun with disbelief.

Eyeing her, Jake smiled with indulgence. "It's refreshing," he yelled above the loud din of traffic and other noise.

"What?" she asked.

"Watching someone watch all this with new eyes. I can tell you're impressed."

"I'm not certain *impressed* is the word I would choose. New York has always been impressive in its own way. But this? This is something entirely different from anything I ever dreamed of. Your 21st century is...fantastical."

Jake clapped his hands. "Fantastical—what a wonderful Victorian word, Miss Lyndfield. I'll have to remember that one. Could work in a novel somewhere."

Ignoring his remark, she asked, "Where does your friend live? Will we ride there in a car?"

"Nope," he said. "I have a real treat for you." He watched her eyes light up with curiosity. "The subway."

Caroline wasn't sure she'd would call the subway a treat. But then, she was gradually coming to recognize words didn't seem to mean in 2006 what they had meant in 1890, so perhaps she was confused. The subway, a long crowded vehicle similar to a train, jammed its occupants in its silver hull like sardines in a can. No one looked at anyone else, and if one did sneak a peek it was only to find that everyone wore nasty frowns. Only the very lucky could even sit down. Jake told her to do what he did and to keep her mouth shut. After a few minutes she understood why.

Somewhere in front of them an argument broke out, followed by pushing and shoving and the use of the filthiest words Caroline had ever heard, some of which had meanings unknown to her. As Jake and Caroline emerged from the car, she found herself shaking with both relief and amazement. Such frenetic and sensitive emotion filled the city now. The New York she remembered New York had been bustling and thriving with energy and activity, but it left one with a sense of positive feelings. Now, the place seemed tense, anxious and slightly oppressive. As if people lived on the very edge of their fear, and that fear spilled over into the atmosphere.

She remarked as much to Jake as they neared the building where he said his friend lived. He agreed with her, but while he spoke he suddenly found herself wondering what his woman doctor friend would be like, and asked what kind of doctor she was.

He hesitated. "She's, uh, well, a shrink."

Caroline gave him an astonished and open-mouthed stare. "I most certainly will not be shrunk," she replied. "Not even if it is the 21st century."

He bent over with laughter. "No, she's not going to shrink you. She's a psychiatrist. You knew, a psycho-analyst...like Freud. Or was that after you?" Jake pointed to his head in illustration.

"A doctor of the mind?" she asked, dismayed. "You have brought me to see a doctor who will study my mind."

He held up his hands. "Now don't go getting so upset. You said you'd trust me."

She did an about face and headed in the other direction, not sure where she was going but determined not to go any further with him.

"Oh for Christ's sake, Caro, give it a chance. I want her to hypnotize you."

His words sent an eerie quiver down Caroline's spine. She sensed something evil was afoot but stopped in spite of herself. "No!"

Jake ran to catch up with her, a pleading look in his eyes. "Please, Caro. I want to help.

"Just give this a chance, won't you? It might turn something up. We'll never know if you won't try it."

Something in his gaze touched her heart. Here stood this man...who looked so like the man she had loved and lost...and he was asking her to do this thing for him. Surely he would not want to see her harmed. It must be a harmless thing he asked. She suddenly realized that she had it in her power to say 'yes' and to somehow, some way, make up for a tiny bit of what she had done—or not done, as it were—for Francis.

"Yes," she said softly.

He raised her hand to his lips and kissed it with tenderness, a silent thank you written across his face. *So be it*, she thought, recognizing at once she would probably do almost anything for him.

* * * *

While Caroline drank hot tea in the kitchen, Jake lazed across a desk from Melanie behind the closed door of her study. She'd just finished spending the past forty-five minutes alone in this room with Caroline, while he'd spent the time pacing in her living room. After setting the other young woman up with tea, she'd led him back to her office.

"I've never seen anything like it," she told him. "Either she can't be hypnotized, or else she's incredibly easy to hypnotize—I'm still not sure..." She paused and watched Jake for the effect her words had. In the five years she'd known him he'd never done anything impulsive or unexpected. Today, in the space of a few minutes, he'd done both. Showing up at her door, at the crack of dawn, with a woman who sounded like she'd stepped right out of some romance novel—well, it was pretty out of character to say the least.

"Of what?" he demanded.

"If she's pulling the wool over my eyes or not. As best I can tell, she honestly believes she is what she says."

"That's impossible."

"That she believes it is not impossible," Melanie countered. "Of course what she believes is impossible...as you and I both know." She couldn't resist a taunt. "Don't we?"

"Of course we do. I'm not the one who's nuts here. She is."

Melanie clicked her ballpoint pen in and out, and gave her roller-tipped chair a lazy twirl with her foot while she watched his obvious discomfort. "So what's up?" she asked. "And don't tell me it's nothing."

Jake rose from his chair and began to pace back and forth. "I don't know, Mel. I like her. She brings out the heart in me, I guess. She's a nice kid. I want to help her." He turned to her as if for confirmation. "Isn't that enough?"

"This is me, Jake," Melanie retorted. "The person who knows you never do anything without some reason. Are you in love with her?"

His mouth curled up in a smile. "Not intentionally."

"Good. I'd miss our lazy little afternoons upstairs."

"I don't plan on giving them up anytime soon," he assured her, knowing even as he said the words they weren't true. He did plan to give them up. He'd met Melanie has at art opening almost five years back, and there had been an instant attraction. They'd started seeing each other immediately, and their sexual but non-committed relationship had suited them both. But when Melanie had opened the door this morning, still wearing her short teddy, her long legs and full cleavage beckoning like the old companions that they were, he'd suddenly discovered he was no longer attracted to her. He no longer desired Melanie Hartford. The strange and wide-eyed girl who'd been at his side was all he wanted now. She'd filled up his thoughts and senses from the first instant he'd seen her, and when he'd kissed her last night...

"So what do you think I should do?" he asked, pushing both the guilt of his small white lie and the sudden rise of temperature he was beginning to feel to one side.

"About what?"

Melanie could be infuriating at times. "About Caroline?"

"You don't need to do anything. She seems perfectly okay to me. She's grieving—about the loss of her father and the man she loved. But other than that, I think she'd handling all this rather well."

"All this what?"

Melanie laid her pen down on the desk and twirled a strand of straight blonde hair around one finger. "Well, it's not every day you travel forward more than one hundred years in time. She's got a lot of catching up to do." She teased him with a wink and a grin.

"Thanks a hell of a lot, Mel." Jake headed toward the door but her laughter and voice called him to stop.

"Seriously, Jake. Take it one day at a time. She'll come back to the present when she's ready. Maybe she'd just not as interested as you are." He shot her a curt but acknowledging nod and reached to open the door.

"Oh, Jake," she called before he completely made his exit from the room. "*I'm* still interested. Call me soon."

* * * *

The library stood like a king, stately and proud, guarded by a stone lion at each side. The facility had turned out well. Caroline remembered when the old reservoir had been here, and the talk of taking it down to put up a library. Her father had been one of the major donors, and they'd been in the city earlier that month for an event to raise money for the building. A relatively unknown firm called Carrère and Hastings had been selected to design and construct the new library. The result promised to be the largest marble structure ever attempted in the United States, though from the looks of it many others could now make that claim. Their town home wasn't been too far from here, and Caroline wondered if perhaps she and Jake might pass by there later in the day.

She followed Jake quietly through the long tiled halls, marveling at the tall marble columns and the walls of dark mahogany. "The palace for the people" they'd said it could be, and she hoped that it was indeed such a haven. From what she could tell about the people beyond these walls, they truly needed this sanctuary.

"Where are we going?" she whispered.

"To the archives," Jake answered. "That's where the Lyndfield records are kept."

"And what will we look for?"

"I don't know. I thought maybe you might have some ideas. You're the mystery lady."

"But you wouldn't believe anything I told you, would you Mr. Stanton?" She gave him a light smile.

"Let's just say I'm trying to develop a healthy skepticism. Okay? And you never know what might turn up?"

Several minutes later found them across from one another at one of the massive research tables in room with many other such tables, boxes stacked around between them like columns of bricks. Light filtered in from tall skinny windows, highlighting partners of dust that danced through its glow. A stern but attractive librarian approached and added two more books to the pile, then faded without comment into the distance.

Caroline dove into the nearest container and exclaimed with delight as she pulled out a ribbon tied package. "My mother's letters! To my father! I never even realized he had saved them."

"I knew she died young, but none of my research really mentioned how..."

An expression of grief crossed her face. "She died giving birth to me."

"I'm sorry." He stroked her hand with a tender touch.

"Yes, well, I'm sorry I never knew her. But perhaps I shall. Through these letters... Do you think I might take them?"

Jake shook his head. "No, but we'll have them Xeroxed while we go through the rest of this stuff."

"Zee rocks? Is this a new type of writing apparatus?"

Jake, intent on the contents of his own box, looked up with questioning eyes, suddenly realizing his mistake. "Copied."

"But that would take forever."

He let out a frustrated curse. "It's a machine for Christ's sake."

"Dear me," Caroline said. "If only my father and Evan had had even one such invention, they would have been famous indeed."

"What exactly were they trying to invent, do you think? Your father never mentioned anything specific in his writings."

Caroline sighed. "I honestly have no idea. All I know is that they spent hours together in their laboratory, and I was often lucky to see my father at meals."

"Well, I've been through these boxes a couple of times, but maybe there's something I missed that will help us out now. Let's getting to the task at hand, what do you say?"

She nodded in agreement and removed another lid. "What exactly are we looking for?"

"I don't know, really. Some kind of connection, something to jog your memory." He raised a hand as she opened her mouth to protest. "I know. I know. You say the last thing you remember was going to bed in 1890. But whenever you went to bed, something happened between then and the time you woke up at Lyndfield. Some trauma, maybe." He looked pleased, as if he'd suddenly convinced himself there must be some connection here.

"You look like Caroline Lyndfield, there's got to be some link to the family. Maybe you were doing research of your own. Trying to find a relationship or something. And whatever happened is tied to that. Something you found out. That frightened you."

A ghost walked across Caroline's grave as he spoke those words.

Something evil. As if he'd spoken a truth that so close to reality that she should know what it meant. If only she could remember.

"What is it?" he asked, apparently noticing the faraway look in her eyes.

"I don't know. Something. Something. It is so close." She sighed in frustration. "But I can't recall."

"Was it something you knew, or wrote, or saw? Something you were running from."

She frowned in concentration, trying to capture even one of the dim images flitting through her mind. "I think I saw something. But I was young, still a child. Whenever I try to pursue the image, it flees."

"Nothing more concrete."

"It may have something to do with the playhouse. That place always frightened me, for some reason. Even when we passed it yesterday, I felt afraid."

Jake tapped a pencil against the table in concentration then, catching a look of disapproval from a nearby patron, stopped. "Well, that's not much, but it's something. We'll keep looking."

They spent the next hour or so sifting through more contracts and letters and business papers than Caroline had ever realized her father was involved in. Her eyes were beginning to blur when Jake pushed a small volume toward her.

"What's this?" he asked.

She picked up the little book and laughed. "It's my old diary. I lost it years ago. Simply disappeared one day, and the next I'd forgotten it ever existed. Until this very minute actually."

"Do you think it might mention anything about the playhouse?"

Caroline turned the pages with care for several moments. "No, it all appears rather trivial. Wait...here's something." She began to read, "'Papa brought Mr. Luddington home today. I don't like him.'"

She gave Jake a pointed look. "You see, I told you I didn't like him."

"Oh for Pete's sake. Just keep looking, will you?"

Drawing her attention back to the little book, Caroline flipped to the back and began to peel back the lining. "Hey," Jake whispered, anger evident in his voice, "what do you think you're doing?"

Ignoring him, she reached under the fabric and pulled out a faded sheet of paper and began to read, while Jake watched in amazement. *How the hell did she know that was there?*

"What's it say?" he asked after a moment.

She handed the paper to him with a trembling hand. "'Evan did it,'" he read, "'I hate him.' Did what, Caroline? Do you remember?"

He knew he'd spoken as if she were the girl who'd written in this diary. And that was impossible. But he didn't care anymore. Maybe the only way to relate to a crazy woman might be to become a little crazy yourself. "What did Evan do?" he asked again.

Caroline tried to clear the cobwebs from her mind. "I don't remember. I'm sorry."

He shrugged and tried to clear the foggy madness from his mind. "Well, it's weird you knew it was there. But it doesn't prove a thing."

She rose angrily and pushed her chair in hard against the table. "I do not care what it proves or does not prove. I am quite tired of trying to prove something to you, Mr. Stanton. What good will it do if I prove to you I am who I say? Will it take me home? Will it bring back my Francis? Of course not. So why should I bother?"

As she prepared to move away from him, her eyes caught sight of an old newspaper clipping lying at the top of a box. Reaching down, she touched the photo of herself on the page. As her gaze roamed to the headline, she gasped in disbelief.

"This is not true." She moaned. "I swear to God it is not true."

Jake recognized the story detailing her disappearance and the death of her father. "I told you about that. She ran off with a large amount of his fortune, and was suspected of having a hand in his death. It's a bit late to try and prove her innocence."

The girl cast anguished eyes toward him, and absurdly he remembered an earlier conversation with May, something about clearing Caroline Lyndfield's name.

"But I'm innocent," she cried. "I am. My father...he wasn't dead the last time I saw him. He was... he was..." Caroline's face turned a ghostly shade of gray and her hands gripped the back of the chair. Then, without warning, she backed away from him and began to run, slowly at first then faster, as if her very life depended on her escape. She ran down the long dark corridor, toward the light outside.

CHAPTER 10

...A time to seek.
Ecclesiastes 3:1-8

She needed air. Air, and escape from the dark and frightening memory pressing hard against her mind and threatening to take control of her sanity. A memory of some horror, some terrible tragedy she had no desire to remember. Something to do with her father, something she should remember, yet fought to escape. She had to get away from the suffocating pressure of it.

Outside the library, the thick and oppressive atmosphere did nothing to relieve her misery.

Gasping, Caroline plunged headlong up the busy sidewalk like a madwoman, toward the only place in this city she knew to go—home.

She ignored the stares and rude remarks of passers-bys whom she bumped and pushed unladylike in her rush. She tried not to be confused the strange lights and signals for cars, but found herself swept along with the tide of humanity all the same. She let the wave of people carry her, her only thought to find the brownstone where she'd lived with her father during their time spent in the city, where they'd spent so many happy winter evenings by the fire while Aunt Jess's lilting voice read aloud to them from novelists like Hardy and Dickens and classics such as Jane Austen. What precious memories, these were.

This day had been too much—too much newness and confusion, too many probing questions by Jake and his psychoanalyst friend. Too much forgotten...

She wanted nothing more than to shut her eyes and have it all be the way it had been so long ago, to close out the truth Jake had revealed and the questions he continued to ask. Having Francis dead suddenly seemed better than having this stranger who resembled him so, yet doubted her every word. She couldn't have been responsible for her father's death. He was alive when she last saw him...

The blackness threatened to surround her again, so Caroline let the thought go and turned to her surroundings. This had to be the block. She felt certain of it. Abruptly she stopped and scanned the area. This must be it. Surely, the house had been here. She looked around in dismay. No town homes here now. A building stretched for miles into the sky, steel and glass snaking their way into an eternity she could only imagine. People in modern day clothing came and went through revolving doors, oblivious to a girl standing on the sidewalk staring up.

"No-o-o!" She sank to the pavement.

Several people did indeed throw curious stares in her direction as they passed, but no one stopped to help. No one asked if something was wrong. No one seemed to care about the agony of one lonely woman sitting on the sidewalk in the middle of New York City, out of time and out of place.

Except one person.

Jake knelt beside Caroline and scooped her trembling body into his arms like a rag doll. She clung there to him for several minutes as he rocked back and forth, heedless of everything beyond her immediate pain. Caroline let him hold her as she wept for all the things she had lost—her home, her family, her friends, her world. Her time. Her life. She wept until she felt as waterless as an abandoned well deep in the depths of the Sahara desert. She wept until there were no more tears to weep.

When she finished at last, Jake eased her to her feet.

"Come on," he crooned like a parent, and she followed him like a child.

They walked side by side in silence for some time, down a street, around a corner, across a lawn, till finally she knew where he was taking her. Her face lit up when she at last she saw where he'd brought her, and Jake's heart skipped a beat at the return of her smile. He'd been afraid he'd really blown it this time. She'd seemed so sure of her ancestor's innocence. Jake had come firmly to the conclusion that his Caroline Lyndfield was a descendent of the original. Why else would anyone be so wrapped up in the Lyndfield family history? Obviously, it was important to Caroline to clear her family name.

Even if she didn't know it, there had to be a missing link somewhere. He smiled to himself at the irony of it all. Looked like May had been right. Maybe Caroline Lyndfield would give up her own secrets.

"So you remember the park, do you?"

"Who could forget Central Park? Outdoor concerts, boats on the lake, vendors selling hot dogs and popcorn?" She gazed around. "Doesn't seem to have changed much."

An amused smile touched the corners of his mouth. "Guess you're right about that."

They found a semi-secluded spot not far from the lake and chose side-by-side spots on the ground. "Father used to bring me here to sail wooden ships." She pointed to the water's littered edge with distaste. "It was crystal clear then. I'd pretend I was aboard those ships, being born to some far-off land, where my prince was waiting for my arrival."

"Looks like you made it, huh?"

A sad smile darkened her countenance. "I am here, but my prince is not, I'm afraid."

Jake met her gaze with a question that remained both unasked and unanswered. Of course she wouldn't reply. She loved a dead man. And not only was he dead, she believed she'd left him dead over one hundred years ago. Jake wanted to be angry with her but found his only thought to be that life tended to be incredibly bizarre sometimes.

He noticed her color seemed a little gray, and worried she might still be weak from her injury. "Are you feeling better? You don't look well? We can leave now if you're ready…"

"I'm fine, but it seems more difficult to breathe here than in the country. The air is heavy. Why is that?" She had deftly changed the subject, he thought, or had he?

"Pollution. Stuff in the air. And the water." He indicated the lake. "From cars, and planes, and factories. You'd think we'd have done better in the past hundred years. For all we've accomplished we haven't learned much, I'm afraid."

Her eyes met his in seemingly unspoken gratitude. "So much seems the same. Only the surface—clothes, vehicles, buildings—are different."

"Guess we seem a pretty strange lot."

"In some respects, I suppose. But people…I think at heart people remain the same. Don't you?" Without waiting for an answer, she continued, "Your May…she reminds me very much of my Aunt Jess, in manner as well as appearance. And Mitchell, he is a little like Evan, which I'm not certain is a good thing."

"And I, of course, am like Francis."

"Yes," she said softly, running her fingers through the green shoots on the ground. "Perhaps we see in others what we especially wish to find."

Jake touched her hand. "What did you hope to find then?"

Misty-eyed, she stared across the lake. "My lost love, I suppose."

Jake considered this for a moment and wondered what he'd hoped to find in Caroline Lyndfield. Certainly not someone he could love, he knew that much.

"Surely there are differences though?" he asked her. "Between people now and then?"

He couldn't resist continuing this baffling and outrageous conversation. He loved the way her eyes took in everything he said, rested on the horizon as her mind considered, then returned to meet his gaze with frankness and understanding. Whoever she was, wherever she was from, this woman was someone special.

"I think there is more talk of feelings, and more… more…"

"Openness?"

"Yes. I guess that would be a good way of expressing it. That openness has hurt you though. It hurt you today."

Caroline touched his hand lightly as a feather and Jake was moved by the simple gesture. "I know you did not intend to distress me." She shrugged. "I think part of the difficulty for me is the sense of having missed so much. Not just vital, important events in my own life, such as the one you spoke of today, but of the simple things as well—growth, changes, new things that might truly have happened in my lifetime. Believe it or not, Mr. Stanton, I was once very involved in the process of living."

Jake thought of the portrait above the mantle, and his sure feeling that Caroline Lyndfield was no ordinary Victorian woman. "I suspected Caroline Lyndfield wasn't much of a Victorian miss."

She raised an eyebrow. "What does that mean?"

"Women from the 19th century had a reputation for being prudish."

This brought forth the most exquisite feminine laughter Jake had ever heard.

"I assure you, Mr. Stanton, I was never a prude."

He leaned over and tickled her neck with a blade of grass in an effort to accomplish his objective. "Never?"

She shooed the grass away, smiling. "Never. I'm certain women of my time had vices the same as women of yours."

A slight irritation rose within him. What exactly were they, he wondered? "So do you want to talk about it?" he asked, hoping she'd reveal a few secrets.

Caroline brushed the dead grass and leaves off her slacks and stood. "What can I say? I loved Francis, with a very womanly love. I felt passion; I hoped to marry and love him the way a woman is meant to love a man. If that hadn't been possible—our marriage I mean, I would have loved him anyway." She paused for a long moment. "I loved my father, too. But it seems in the end I may have betrayed them both."

He watched as her eyes followed a tiny wooden boat bouncing to and fro on the water beyond. "I'm sorry, Caroline. I wish I could help. I really do."

"You could." She turned back to him, her eyes pleading for his understanding. "You could help me clear my name." She knelt beside him again and grasped his arm. "Won't you believe me? If not me, then her. Caroline Lyndfield is innocent."

"What you're asking me is impossible."

"Why? I can help you. Who better to help than the accused

herself?" She rose and leaned against the tree next to him. "But I do not blame you if you say no. This is insane."

Jake pulled himself from the ground and touched the tip of her nose. "It is insane," he told her. "But I'm always up for a good story. And you do tell some good ones, Miss Lyndfield."

Later, as they faced each other over burgers and beer—at Jake's insistence—"Live dangerously!" he'd advised—she told him the story of her life.

"My days were mostly my own. Until Francis came and we had lessons then. He was my tutor, you see. But in my free time, I walked or rode, in the summers. That's when we came to Lyndfield. After Evan came there to live all the time—I must have been about fifteen— he and Father were always off working on some new experiment. They fancied themselves inventors. They closeted themselves away in their laboratory for hours at a time."

"But you'd met him before, right? The diary?" Jake couldn't resist testing her a bit more. It was truly amazing how much she knew about the family.

"He'd been coming to see father off and on for years. Since I was very young. I believe he'd known my mother before she died. But I never particularly cared for him."

"Why?"

Caroline shrugged, and politely dabbed at her greasy mouth with a napkin. "I'm not certain. He was cold. And there was something about him...something..." She laughed a bit shakily. "Aunt Jess did not care for him either. She always did her best to keep him away from me."

Aunt Jess had been like a mother, Caroline explained. "After my mother died giving birth to me, Aunt Jess pampered and spoiled me as any doting aunt might do, but I loved her dearly and I believe she managed to instill in me some discipline as well as love."

"You say she was very protective of you?"

"Oh, yes. I think she feared some harm might come to me. Though I have no idea that she suspected any particular quarter. She'd been very close to my mother."

Then her aunt, too, had died when Caroline was ten, and the child had been left much to her own devices until her father hired Francis Monroe as her tutor.

"I loved him from the moment I laid eyes on him. I thought he was so beautiful, with his golden hair and slender hands. But it was only about a year ago that he discovered he loved me as well." She sighed wistfully as she sipped her beer—sipped beer, of all things—then continued. "We were so happy.... Then he died."

"And he just went out to the river one night and never came

back?" Jake was amazed that she could speak so calmly and with such assurance of events that had taken place over a hundred years ago.

"We had quarreled."

"About what?"

She hesitated. "My father wished for me to marry his colleague Evan, as I told you. Father had a dream that Evan and I would build an even greater empire together. I wanted to marry Francis, but I wanted to tell my father in my own time. Francis disagreed."

"So he was going to talk to your father that night?"

"Yes."

An idea was beginning to take form in Jake's mind. "Did it ever occur to you that maybe he...could he have..." Jake broke off, not wanting to upset her again. His eyes avoided hers and seeking another place to rest, locked on a large and faded painting on the wall over the bar. A slender slice of the moon hung low in the sky, casting only a thin shred of light on the dark river beneath its gaze. As Jake stared at the murky browns and greens of the water, the air seemed to mist around him. The noise and laughter of the bar's patrons, the smoky room itself, faded into the distance. Nighttime sounds—wind, the flutter of trees above, an occasional hoot of an owl—echoed around and bounced off the sides of his mind.

But suddenly, another sound drowned out all the others—a thundering roar. Close by. Powerful. The river plowed through the evening like an angry avenging god.

Bitter cold engulfed him. It seemed he'd been waiting in the rain for hours. He struggled to see through the dark. Where was she? He'd gotten her note. But why did she insist on meeting him here? In a downpour, no less?

Without warning, pain tore through the night and blinded him. Pain, followed by a push. A forceful violent push. A push toward something black and evil. Something that was not meant to be. Not yet. It wasn't his time.

Suddenly, back in the room, Caroline spoke to him. "Are you all right, Jake?" Then, with more concern. "Jake?"

He gave his head a hard shake, trying to clear the visions, the terror, he'd felt.

"Jake!"

Her tone said she was getting really anxious now, and he held up a hand. "I'm...okay."

"What on earth happened? It appeared you...you were not here."

He tried to shrug it off but knew his feeble attempt for what it was. "Just a chill, nothing important."

"You saw something. What did you see?" She reached across the table and grabbed his hand impatiently. "Please, tell me."

"It was nothing, Caroline." He removed his hand from her hold, lest it draw him back to a place he didn't want to go. "Nothing. I just got caught up in your story."

She drew a long breath. "Maybe you are a part of my story? You feel something here" she motioned to her breast, "don't you?"

More than anxious to get off this eerie subject, Jake shook his head adamantly and turned his head from her pleading eyes. Heedless of her feelings, he said, "Francis didn't kill himself, did he?"

Jake knew the answer. He didn't know how he knew, but his knowledge was accurate all the same.

Francis Monroe had been murdered.

They both had one drink too many. Jake had never shaken off the fear that accompanied his strange vision, and Caroline had probably been trying to shut out his words about Francis' death.

"Of course he did not kill himself!" But Jake thought he saw a flicker of doubt cross her face.

"What if your father said he couldn't marry you? Or her? That would be reason enough, wouldn't it?"

Caroline had been especially silent after that, perhaps wondering if it was possible that her father had betrayed her. But Jake hadn't let himself care about her discomfort. He was having enough of his own. He was getting too caught up in this thing. Now he was seeing things himself. Getting entangled in a dead man's life. It had to stop.

* * * *

His head quit spinning about four blocks after they left the bar. With the throbbing gone, his anger too had faded. He grabbed Caroline about the waist and waltzed her up the street toward Grand Central station.

At first she seemed shocked, and her eyes grew wide with amazement at his gaiety.

"Let's liven this party up a little, shall we, my dear?"

With a graceful tilt of head, she smiled in return, while he spun her round and round 'til he thought he'd drop to the ground with a dizziness that was more than the spinning.

"Thanks for this dance, my fair lady," he said breathlessly a few minutes later, sweeping her a low formal

"You are most welcome, kind sir." Caroline returned the bow then tilted her head up, wide-eyed with amazement at the twinkling lights far overhead. Their golden glitter was reflected in her eyes. She looked like a child in a fairyland of Christmas wishes come true.

"You okay?"

She let out a long sigh. "It is so very lovely. I can think of no adequate way to describe it."

"You're not afraid?"

"Of what?"

His arms swept wide about him. "All this."

"After the subway? Nothing could frighten me again."

Her delicate laughter surrounded him once more, and Jake wanted to take her in his arms and kiss her madly right in the middle of the street.

"I am not afraid," she continued, apparently oblivious to Jake's interest. "My father never allowed me to be afraid."

"And you never were?"

"Only once."

"When was that?"

"When I woke up here. Alone."

Sadness pasted over her features again and he wished he could strike it away. "Are you afraid of loneliness?" he asked softly.

"Not of loneliness." She sought his eyes, and finding them, locked his gaze to hers. "I am only afraid of a life without love."

Jake put his hands on her shoulders gently, suddenly clear-headed and sure of himself. He knew what it was like to live without love. He'd lived that way for too long now. But there had to be something inside before you could give to anyone else. May's lessons hadn't been a total waste. He'd never much thought about giving before: he'd always been more interested in taking. But he found himself wanting to give this woman more than just a physical relationship.

"I think you can learn to love yourself, Caro. May says that if you start there, the rest will be icing."

She giggled. "Icing? Like on a cake?" Caroline leaned against him just a little and Jake's body temperature shot up about five degrees.

"I'm not certain what that is supposed to mean, Mr. Stanton," she continued giddily. "But it sounds like a desirable place to start." She giggled again. "With the icing, I mean."

Jake laughed and steadied her. "We'd better get you home, Miss Lyndfield, "before you figure out you're drunk and have broken another rule of Victorian etiquette."

CHAPTER 11

...A time to throw stones.
Ecclesiastes 3:1-8

Jake expected trouble upon their arrival back at Lyndfield. Unfortunately, he wasn't disappointed.

Every light in the gatehouse glared like spotlights in waiting, and Henry McWilliams's car parked in front indicated those inside expected the worst. Amazing they hadn't called in the police as well... What did they think—that he might have abducted her—or that she'd driven him to the point of violence? He may have escaped with the princess for the day, but now the time had come to pay the piper.

With a gentle shake he roused a dozing Caroline, her head against his shoulder in the drivers' seat. "Wake up, sleepy-head, we're home!"

She stirred with a yawn. "So soon?"

Jake laughed. "Not so soon. It's late. You slept all the way from the train depot." His smile turned into a scowl as he pulled up the drive. "I'm afraid we're in for a bit of a row, as our British cousins would say."

She peered out the front window in confusion. "Whatever for?"

"Well, I'm pretty certain I'm suspected of kidnapping. You'll be safe enough if you play your part. The injured party, got it?"

"But I have not been injured! I shall defend your good intentions, sir!"

He gave her a light peck on the cheek. "Thanks, love, but I think you'd best look out for yourself here."

Jake put the car into park and got out, crossing around to help Caroline with the door. Before he moved toward the house, he paused for a moment, put both hands on her shoulders, and stared intently into her eyes.

"I hope I haven't totally blown our friendship today."

The smile he received in return beamed with warmth and acceptance. "No, I do not believe you have entirely 'blown' it, if I understand the meaning of that word."

He pushed an errant strand of hair off her forehead. "Good. Because I wouldn't want to think we weren't friends."

"There is one thing, kind sir."

Jake grinned at her continuance of their game. "Of course, my fair, fair lady. A dragon to slay, some treasure you seek? Ask and it shall be granted."

Now her bright eyes met his with complete seriousness. "Please don't give up the search...for my truth? You won't, will you? No matter what?"

He drew a long breath, wanting desperately to believe in her, but even more to find some way to help her, whatever that meant. "I'll do some digging around, okay? Maybe there *is* something I've missed."

Caroline's face lit with radiance and she stood on tiptoe to throw her arms about his neck. "Thank you. Thank you so very much."

Jake felt a deep blush creep up his neck, and hung his head so she wouldn't notice his embarrassment. "You're quite welcome, my lady."

Turning, he swept an arm in the direction of the house. "Shall we?" and a moment later they marched hand in hand toward the front door.

"Where have you been?" Mitchell demanded the instant they stepped into the front room.

Henry reclined on the sofa, a source of calm in the midst of the approaching storm. He sipped his coffee without a care in the world while May, just behind Mitchell warned, "Now, now, Mitchell. We said we'd let Jake explain."

"I'm letting him explain." The older man jerked back to Jake. "Where did you take this young woman? What have you been doing all day? You know she hasn't been well, and yet you drag her off to God knows where!"

Jake struggled to get his irritation under control. He was about to explain when Caroline laid a firm hand on his arm. "I asked Mr. Stanton to take me into the city," she said. "I hoped it might aid me in remembering something about my past." She gave a long, very convincing sigh. "Alas, I'm afraid it did not."

Mitchell's anger reversed to instant amazement. After a second or two of silence as the others waited with curiosity, he said, "But why didn't you tell us, my dear? I would have been glad to make your arrangements into the city. And to escort you."

Caroline glided to the sofa like a princess indeed, taking a seat beside Henry, who patted her arm and asked how she was feeling. "Oh much better," she responded then turned fluttering eyes at Mitchell in such a way that Jake felt sure she could only gotten the idea straight from a romance novel—until he remembered she was like someone from a romance novel.

"I know you would have done so, Mr. Johnston... Mitchell...," She continued with a coy smile, playing her game for all it was worth. "But I had a rather disturbing nightmare last night, and when I woke quite early and could not sleep again, I asked Mr. Stanton—who was already awake, you see, having had to give up his room for a very uncomfortable night's sleep on this very couch—if he might be able to assist me without disturbing either you or May. Was I wrong to do so?"

Mitchell suspected her of lying, but he couldn't resist her placating voice and flirtatious manner. He wanted to believe what he'd seen the previous evening was nothing more than a bad dream of his own. But this morning, when May had told him both she and Stanton had disappeared, he'd instantly feared that they'd run away together. Before he'd had a chance to claim her.

Yet here she was, sweetness and light, eyes pleading for his understanding and compassion. Perhaps he'd only imagined the two of them together in his desperation. Or perhaps, as he'd suspected, Jake had forced her into that embrace. At any rate, she'd come back now, and if he played his hand carefully, he'd have the chance he craved.

"Of course that makes perfect sense, my dear," he told her with newfound assurance. "We were only worried, you see."

"You could have left us a note, Jake," May reprimanded.

Jake shrugged. "You're right. I should have done that, and truthfully, I meant to. I just got sidetracked somehow. But, here we are, safe and sound, and no harm done."

"Exactly," Mitchell agreed, then to Caroline. "And tomorrow, I will help you move your things to the apartment I've prepared for you in the guesthouse, then you can tell me all about your trip."

As the girl smiled her loveliest smile in his direction, Mitchell experienced such a heat flood his body that he felt certain it could only be a foreshadowing of the magnificent things to come. For with each day that passed, he felt more and more certain that his destiny lay in making this girl his own. To seize the future Evan Ludington had left to him, and him alone. But then, out nowhere, came the bombshell he hadn't been expecting.

"I am sorry, Mr. Johnston," Caroline said with calm authority, "but I cannot accept your kind invitation. I've decided to stay here."

Mitchell reigned in his fury with a tight smile. "I'm afraid that won't do, my dear. As you yourself mentioned, Mr. Stanton has been put out of his space, and he certainly should be back to his work—without distractions. And May needs to get back to the estate." Mitchell saw Caroline's confidence waver, so he pressed on. "Besides, I've have a housekeeper who can check in on you from time. Right now I'm sure rest is the best thing, right Henry?"

"That's true," Henry replied, "although some fresh air isn't such a bad thing either."

"Then my lovely garden should be the perfect place for that as well," Mitchell beamed at Caroline.

"I'm sure neither of us minds if Caroline stays, do we, Jake?" May injected.

Jake knew better than to sound too eager. "Whatever works best for Caroline," he answered, meeting her eyes. "I can work up at the manor, if necessary."

Caroline spoke with hesitation, her hands nervous in her lap. Mitchell could tell the confidence she'd come into the room with had faltered. "It sounds like perhaps it would be simpler on everyone if I went."

"Nonsense, child," May chided. "You're not a bit of trouble."

"The girl can't stay here indefinitely, May," Mitchell reminded her. "Since we have no idea when she may recover her memory, or even if...I think giving her some space of her own to try and do that might be just what the doctor ordered. Isn't that right, doctor?"

"Well, I certainly can't argue with the suggestion." Henry turned to Caroline. "I'd be happy to check in on you regularly, my dear, wherever you are."

"All right. I suppose it's for the best." Caroline rose from the sofa. "I'm feeling rather tired now, so if you don't mind, I believe I'll go to my room."

Mitchell followed her with his eyes as she left the room, and didn't fail to notice his weren't the only eyes that watched her go.

* * * *

As Caroline lay in bed that night, she thought over the events of this most incredible day. Despite, and partly because of, the oppression and frustration and sadness she had experienced, this had been a day she would not soon forget. Still, she felt frustrated that she hadn't made as much progress as she wished. Definitely, she'd made a first step in taking a stand for herself. The look on Mitchell's face when she said she wouldn't be coming to stay with him! Caroline knew she'd made him angry, but Jake was right. Mitchell wasn't her guardian, or her father, or her husband. She was living in the year 2006 now—and she could make her own decisions about her life. She wanted to stay here, to be near Jake. Yet in the end she'd given in, something about pushing the issue hadn't felt right, and Jake certainly hadn't done much to stand up for her. Didn't he want her here? Would he be happy to have her go, even on the heels of his promise to help her?

Lying here alone, she still felt the pulsating warmth of his arms about her as they'd danced through the brightly lit fairyland streets of New York—such a different city, yet in many ways so much the same. The dark side remained, but the brilliance still shone through. New York had always been a place of great hope as well as great despair. Caroline wasn't really surprised that she should feel such passion within its realm. Earlier, she had thought this day somehow deepened her companionship with Jake. Was she wrong about that? Being closer to him felt like being closer to Francis, unreasonable as that might seem. She knew Jake still did not believe her story. Perhaps he would never believe that she had traveled here from another century. She could not fault him for that. But at least he was beginning to see her as a real person, instead of some feeble female prone only to vapors and fits.

Obviously, he had sophisticated taste in women. That had become clearly evident in the doctor she met this morning, with her classic gracefulness and chic apparel—once she had actually donned that apparel. Caroline blushed to herself as she thought of the long shapely legs and full bosom openly displayed when the woman had opened the door still dressed for sleep. Jake hadn't appeared the least shocked, which led her to believe that the relationship between Jake and the other woman had been anything but platonic.

Caroline bit her lip remembering the instant and unwarranted jealously that arose when he and the woman had closeted themselves in the next room. Of course they had talked about her. But what had Jake said? And what had the woman told him? If she hadn't been so upset about the information she had learned about her father's death, she would have asked Jake for details.

Would he really try to help her solve that mystery? Did he believe her enough? Why was his belief so important to her? Time after time throughout the day Caroline had tried to remind herself that this man wasn't Francis. It was Francis she'd loved with all her heart and soul, and she would not forsake his memory for some arrogant 21st century male who happened to resemble him. If Jake wasn't going to help her, she'd go to Mitchell's and try to find some way to figure out the answers for herself.

But even as she thought about leaving, she ran her fingers across her lips where Jake had kissed them last. *But you want to stay with him,* one part of her mind reasoned: while the other asked, *why?*

* * * *

Mitchell gently stroked the soft nightgown lying on the bed. All of Evan's hopes and dreams now rested in Mitchell's breast. Once he'd seen the girl for whom Evan had felt such desire, he'd understood why. She was everything any man could want. Soft. Sweet. Innocent. Made for taking. More than he had imagined she could ever be…He knew why Evan had wanted her so badly.

He turned and surveyed the before room. Everything was perfect. His housekeeper, Ruby Henderson, had washed and cleaned all day to get it ready. Pale lace curtains danced at the windows, fresh flowers graced the dressing table, a white satin comforter lay across the wide oak poster bed. This room had been where Evan had planned to bring his young bride.

Mitchell stared long into the mirror at his lined face and graying hair. He wasn't a young man any more. It wasn't hard to understand why Caroline had been drawn to Jake Stanton. He had the physical prowess Mitchell did not. Youth was on his side.

Sliding a hand into his pocket, Mitchell pulled out an hourglass he'd found with the diaries. Identical to the one May had discovered in Caroline's robe.

But we'll see who you come to love, my dear, Mitchell thought, feeling a sudden ache at his groin.

* * * *

May watched Jake with careful eyes as he poured his morning coffee. He'd slipped away to bed last night before she'd had a chance to question him about his outing with Caroline, but she wasn't going to let that happen now. Something was going on, and May intended to find out what.

Jake sat down next to her, and held up a hand as she was about to open her mouth. "I took her to see a psychiatrist friend of mine. I thought it might help."

May sputtered. "Not that...that...floozy?"

He grinned. "C'mon, May. Melanie's a good doctor and you know it."

"But how could you take that girl to see your...your..."

"My lover?"

May flung a cup towel at him. "Whatever she is!"

"She hasn't been anything to me for some time now, and I took Caroline to see her because she is a good doctor."

"And?"

"And... Caroline really believes she came from the past, and Mel said we should just leave her alone for now. She'll come back when she's ready."

May shook her head and turned by to the kitchen counter. "And if she doesn't? What if she can't come back because she was never here before?"

"Jesus Christ, May!" Jake knocked over the chair in his haste to stand. He picked it up and began pacing.

"What's wrong with you, Jake? Something's bothering you and don't you dare tell me it's not." May wanted to go to him, but she knew better. Since his parents' death, Jake hadn't liked to let anyone too close, emotionally or physically.

He took several deep breaths and appeared to calm down a little. "Would you believe I don't really know, May?"

"No," she said softly. "I wouldn't believe that."

Now he smiled at her. "Fair enough. How 'bout I'm not ready to talk about it?"

"I might be able to help."

"You might distract me, my dearest May." Jake crossed to her now and planted a quick kiss on her forehead. "Look, I told the girl I'd do some research for her. She, much like yourself, believes Caroline Lyndfield is innocent of her father's death."

May's expression perked up with interest. "You took her to the archives?"

"Yep." Jake sat back down and resumed drinking his coffee. "The weirdest thing happened, May. She found this old letter in a diary. It was hidden in the cover."

The older woman let out a gasp and clamped a hand over her mouth. "You see! You see!" she exclaimed, "That proves—"

"It proves what, May? That she really came from the year 1890? Give me a break, will you? It was a lucky find."

With irritation, she ignored his skepticism and asked, "What did it say? The letter?"

"Said that 'Evan did it.' And she hated him."

"Did what?"

He shrugged and took another long sip of his coffee. "That's the question, I reckon."

"Caroline didn't know?"

"Nope."

"That's curious. She knew about the letter but she doesn't remember what happened. What would cause that, I wonder?"

Jake laughed with evident sarcasm. "She didn't know because she wasn't there."

Sharply, May asked, "Why help her then? What's your interest in a 'crazy' woman?"

His laughter dissolved, Jake faced away from her, toward the window. The sun danced on the horizon, promising a fair day ahead. He still didn't know exactly what his 'interest' was. Caroline wasn't his type at all. She had none of the qualities he liked in women. She had a soft feminine romantic aura that frightened him and demanded much more than he wanted to give. Yet he felt drawn to her with a force he didn't understand. And right now he had no particular desire to try to understand.

"Jake?" May's voice softened now and he knew she'd gotten over her irritation. She only wanted to help, but he didn't like to let her.

He reached across the table and patted her arm. "I promise I'll tell you when I know. Okay? Right now I just can't explain it."

She nodded. "Don't be afraid of it, Jake."

He looked at her with curiosity. "Of what?"

"Of feeling," she replied. "Just feeling."

* * * *

Caroline put the last item of clothing into the small bag May had loaned her and zipped it shut, marveling once more at the wonder of the zipper. She scanned the room where she'd spent the last few days and tried not to be afraid of the days to come. After the initial shock, she'd felt safe here, knowing Jake and May were nearby and that she could see the manor from her window. Mitchell's house and apartment were farther back on the estate, down near the river, and while she didn't feel particularly uncomfortable with him, something bothered her about going there. But, it seemed she had no choice. For the time being, living off his generosity was necessary.

"All ready now?" May called from the doorway.

Caroline nodded and took up the bag.

"You know you really don't have to go, my dear. You're no problem here." May came over and took her arm.

"I think for now, it's for the best. Perhaps I'll learn something at Mitchell's that I wouldn't if I stayed here." Arm in arm, she and May walked down the stairs. She looked around, expecting to see Jake.

"He's over at the big house." May answered the unspoken question in Caroline's eyes. "Said he had some work to get started on early."

"Ah." Caroline felt the tears close to her eyes. He could have come to see her off.

"I want you to promise me if you're uncomfortable at all, or if it doesn't feel right there, you'll come back. Will you do that?"

Caroline shook her head and May gave her a tight squeeze.

"Well, then, you know we're here, dear, and you can visit any time. Jake'll be over to see you. Don't worry."

Caroline nodded once more and they both turned as the front door opened and Mitchell walked in.

"Are you ready, my dear?"

Putting on her bravest front, Caroline said simply, "yes."

* * * *

From the window of Lyndfield Manor, Jake watched as Mitchell helped Caroline into the car. She wore a dress today, a simply flowery affair that showed off her waistline—and her legs—even from this distance. Her hair drawn back with a bright ribbon, he thought she looked sad, and he felt guilty for not being there to send her off. Still, she could have said 'no'—no one was forcing her to leave. She could have told Mitchell she was perfectly happy where she was. Okay, she had tried, but she could have tried harder. Instead she let herself be coerced into doing something that maybe she didn't really want to do.

Anyway, Jake hadn't trusted himself to be there. He knew she wasn't going far, but he couldn't bear to think of her leaving, not to mention going to be in Mitchell's company and influence day after day, which Jake knew did not bode well for him—or her for that matter.

As the car rounded the turn past the house, Jake saw her look up to the window where he stood. For an instant it seemed their eyes made contact and held, acknowledging a world of unspoken thoughts and feelings. Then the car slipped beyond the circle of the drive and Jake went back to his work, certain she hadn't really seen him at all.

CHAPTER 12

...A time to keep silence.
Ecclesiastes 3:1-8

Though Lyndfield Estate boasted one hundred acres of farm and woodland in 1890, Caroline had no idea how much of her father's property might have been sold or given away since that time. It seemed she and Mitchell had been driving for a long time, but a quick glance at the little clock in the car told her in actuality less than five minutes had passed. The acreage they had traversed thus far had a vaguely familiar appearance, though perhaps more lush and wooded than those long gone days when she had had free rein of her father's estate.

As they rounded a sharp bend in the road, Caroline let out a little gasp. Once recovered from her initial surprise, she chided herself for not suspecting sooner. But it had been so long ago that she'd been there; she had completely forgotten the place. Evan's house was not a welcoming sight with its stark gray stone blocks, straight lines, and almost windowless facade. No flowering beds decorated its narrow walk, and even the trees seemed to frown with menace at their approach. Caroline's father had brought her here only once—when she was still a toddler—and the story Aunt Jess had told of the hysterics she'd thrown caused her to shiver even now.

Why hadn't she thought to ask Mitchell if *this* was where he lived? If she'd known that, she never would have come. Now, she was expected to stay here with him, to live in this place she'd hated each and every time she came, the home of the man whose twisted love for her had taken away the very man she had loved.

"Here we are, my dear," Mitchell broke into her pensive silence. "It's modest, I'm afraid, but it's home to me."

He stopped the car and came around to help Caroline out. His hand, hot and sticky, clasped hers possessively and she stifled a shudder. She took several long breaths in an attempt to calm herself as he led her to the front door.

"Ah, Ruby, there you are," Mitchell exclaimed as the heavy wood swung open and a graying middle-aged woman stepped from the interior of the dwelling.

The tall and coolly attractive woman in her forties acknowledged him silently, and standing with arms folded across her breast, watched the two of them closely as they approached. Her slight grimace and prying eyes reminded Caroline all-too-much of some villainous character straight from the dark side of Dickens' London.

"Ruby," Mitchell continued, apparently oblivious to the woman's formidable attitude, "I'd like you to meet Caroline. Caroline, Ruby Henderson, my housekeeper. She'll be here for you during the day."

Mrs. Henderson gave Caroline a curt nod and ignored the outstretched hand.

"I am pleased to make your acquaintance, Mrs. Henderson," Caroline said softly.

The housekeeper made a grunting noise and turning on her heel, marched back into the house. Mitchell shook his head and laughed lightly. "Never mind, Ruby. Her bark is worse than her bite," he informed Caroline. "She'll loosen up as she gets to know you better."

Mitchell ushered her inside, then waited quietly as Caroline's gaze took in the space. She had no specific recollection of having visited this room before—she'd been much too young to remember—but she felt almost certain the interior was identical to those days gone by. Clutter and collections filled every nook and cranny as was the fashion of Caroline's day, almost suffocatingly so, with chairs crowded together, books and framed pictures everywhere, ferns and other plants spilling like flowing green blood from their pots. Several oil lamps glowed with a low flame, and in the grate a fire burned brightly, adding to the already warm and heavy feeling in the air. She tried to draw deep breaths, but there seemed to be little air available.

Mitchell, noticing her discomfort, assisted Caroline in removing the sweater from her shoulders. "What do you think, my dear? Do you like my home?"

"It's quite nice," she managed, hoping the words concealed her slowly rising anxiety.

"I knew you'd like it. The old world atmosphere is wonderful, isn't it? I knew you'd feel more comfortable here than at the gatehouse."

Suddenly the heat and heaviness of the air seemed too much, and a wave of dizziness swept over her. She clutched the back of a nearby sofa.

Mitchell's expression changed to instant concern. "Of course, you're tired, aren't you? Yesterday was probably too much for you. Let me show you your room."

With an eerily distinct feeling that Mrs. Henderson had hidden herself in the shadows, watching and listening, Caroline allowed Mitchell to lead her up a side door to a connecting section of the house.

The dark narrow hallway he led her down filled Caroline with growing apprehension. How was she ever going to stay in this place? Then Mitchell stopped before a door and opened it slowly. Caroline clasped a hand to her mouth, astonished. It was her room—exactly as it had been back at the manor. How he had managed this she had no idea. She entered, moving from item to item, tenderly touching the flowers on the vanity, relishing the soft satin of the comforter and the smooth veneer of the mahogany bed. Her heart gave a little lurch when she saw the nightgown laid out on the bed. The same one she'd worn the night she set out into the storm. The night fate had thrust her forward in time.

She forced a smile up against the pounding of her heart. "This is wonderful. Thank you."

"I want you to feel at home, my dear. Anything you need, anything, just ask and it's yours."

Drawn toward the window with its open curtains, Caroline crossed the room to stare down into the sadly neglected garden. Shrubs and trees had been allowed to grow untended, and the fountain was a lifeless pool of dark murky water. *This is his lovely garden*, she wondered?

Mitchell had moved to stand next to her. "I'm afraid I've never cared much for gardening, but I suspected you might want to take it over yourself. I know you have a special love for that kind of thing." He paused. "Apparently the owner didn't have a knack for gardening either." He watched her face intently as he continued. "You may have known him. Evan Ludington?"

Caroline had not failed to notice how carefully he worded his question. 'You may have known him' not to mention his comment about her love of gardening. Whereas everyone else doubted her, Mitchell seemed to be taking special care to make sure she knew he believed she was whom she said. She didn't know whether to be grateful or skeptical. Something about this situation didn't feel right, and she remembered May's words about always knowing she had a place to come back to. "Yes," she answered Mitchell with equal care. "I knew him."

He sighed, as if he had some sense of her doubt. "Well, as you can see, we've both let the garden go. But it might be a hobby you'd enjoy."

Yes, the garden would at least be a pastime. Perhaps she would be able to tolerate her stay here after all.

"You've been so kind to me," she told him, meeting his still intense gaze with what she hoped at least appeared to be acceptance. "Thank you."

He raised her hand tenderly to his lips. His palm felt clammy and hot, his lips dry and cracked; Caroline stifled her immediate impulse to pull away. She couldn't believe she was in this place, with this person so much like the other she'd hated.

But she was.

* * * *

The old library in Tarleton left much to be desired in an era of computers and on-line databases, but it did have a good store of printed town history. Jake had used it several times for his preliminary research, but most of the family documents were in the archives in the city. Today however, he wanted to know about someone who wasn't a family member, someone who had lived and died right here in Tarleton—Francis Monroe.

Jake had only a skeletal outline of Monroe's life: Caroline Lyndfield's tutor, died young, buried—for some strange reason—under the sprawling beech tree behind the house. Before meeting Caroline, he'd never felt the need for more information than that. It had hardly been important to his research but now, suddenly, Francis' life had become a critical part of the story. He tapped his fingers impatiently against the table as he waited for the boxes of microfilm.

After a few minutes, an extremely attractive young woman in a brightly printed dress placed several boxes in front of him and proceeded to instruct him in the use of the machine. Maybe the Tarleton library had loosened up on some of its more conservative patterns—such as hiring the plainest—both in looks and attire— women possible to fill its openings. Normally, he'd have been more than happy to return the woman's pointedly interested stares in his direction, but these days, Jake had someone else on his mind. After the librarian—with a final disappointed look—went back to her desk, Jake gave his full attention to the machine, skimming rapidly through the pages of the paper for the year Francis' had died.

He scanned the paper carefully and after a moment or two found the headline he was looking for. "Lyndfield Tutor Found Dead." The story told a bit about Monroe's years as a tutor with the Lyndfield family, then described his disappearance and death by drowning. Jake ignored the shiver that crossed his spine as he continued to study the film. Apparently no foul play had been suspected—and no mention about Caroline in the article. Obviously, if there had been a relationship between the two of them, it hadn't been public knowledge.

Jake inserted a quarter into the machines and quickly made a copy of the page, then rewound the film and headed for the front desk. "Do you keep records of everyone who uses this material?" he asked the librarian, at once attentive to his needs.

"Why, yes, we do," she beamed, apparently more than glad to be of service.

"Do you suppose I could take a peek?" Jake asked, not wanting to offend, but merely to stay on track.

"Well," she hesitated, "it's not normally done." She reached out and touched his hand in an overtly and overly friendly manner then looking carefully around, she leaned close to Jake's face. "But I could make an exception, I suppose."

Jake smiled again, trying not to appear too eager. "Thank you," he whispered, "I'd appreciate that.

Breathing heavily, the woman sat back and unlocked a drawer beneath the counter. She pulled out a large black book and placed before him, opening it to a page that listed microfilm checkouts. Seeing he wasn't going to flirt with her any more, she went back to her work, leaving him with the ledger.

Quickly, Jake ran a finger down the list. *Look who's been here*, he thought as he noted the last entry in the book. Mitchell Johnston - January 16, 1994. So no one had looked at this microfilm since Mitchell, and that had been over ten years ago. Jake closed the book and waved the now-irritated librarian a quick farewell, then whistling, turned toward the exit.

* * * *

Caroline managed to pass away the day. She rested in the bedroom all morning, pleading a headache but finding she actually felt rather exhausted after the previous day's outing. When Mrs. Henderson knocked and announced lunch, Caroline drew a quick brush through her hair and came reluctantly downstairs.

Mitchell sat at one end of a long mahogany dining table and had a place for Caroline set at the other. She had to admit he had taken every opportunity to show her compassion and concern. Perhaps she had overreacted to him earlier. Now he seemed harmless and kind.

"How are you feeling after your rest?" he asked, rising from his chair to come and assist her with hers.

"Much better, thank you."

"Excellent." Sitting down again, he unfolded his napkin and spread it in his lap. A moment later, a somewhat irritated Mrs. Henderson arrived with a tray overflowing with bread, cheeses, and a various assortment of meats. "I hope you don't mind a rather light fare for luncheon."

Caroline shook her head, wondering what dinner would be like if he considered this a light fare. She helped herself to some bread and cheese, then hesitantly began to eat. After a few minutes, once she was sure Mrs. Henderson was back in the kitchen, she pushed her food aside and took up the topic that had been bothering her all morning.

"I'm afraid I'm not very hungry actually. Mr. Johnston...Mitchell...I must ask you... Why are you doing all this for me? You do not even know me."

The man smiled benevolently. "Ah, but I do, my dear."

Again, his gaze was intense, and Caroline found herself unwillingly drawn into it. There was something hypnotic about his eyes, hypnotic, and somehow familiar. She struggled against its pull, but found the more she resisted, the weaker she felt.

Then abruptly, Mitchell turned his attention back to his food and the spell was broken. "You see, Caroline," he said without looking up, "I believe you are who you say you are." Mitchell carefully dabbed at his mouth with a napkin, watching her carefully. "I am an expert on the Lyndfield family, my dear. You're too much like Caroline Lyndfield—both in looks and manner—to be merely coincidence. I believe something bizarre has occurred, and I intend to help you prove you are who you say."

Skepticism fought with joy in Caroline. It would be wonderful to have someone actually believe in her, to help her figure out what had happened to, but still something about Mitchell's interest in her felt wrong. "You will?"

"Yes, I will. But we must proceed carefully."

"Why?"

"Because there are those who would exploit you. Consider it, Caroline? You have traveled through time. People will want to know more about that. They'll want to question you, and study you, and analyze your history. It won't make for a very quiet and ordinary life. If the government gets its hands on you, it won't be a painless life, either."

"I hadn't thought of that."

"Of course you hadn't. There is much that is new to you right now, and all the implications of what has happened haven't fully hit yet. That's why I want to help. That's why I wanted you to have this place for yourself." He laid down his napkin and came to stand next to her. "I'm afraid Jake Stanton is one of those people, Caroline. You must be very wary of him."

"I don't believe Jake means me any harm," she said slowly. "He wants to help as well."

Mitchell laid a gentle hand against her cheek. "Jake Stanton has exploited young women in the past, both in his private, and his professional, life. What he says and what he does are often two different things. Please take care with him, Caroline."

Though she wanted to draw away from his touch, she held her place. After all, she had realized from the start that aside from looks, he was nothing like her Francis. She must take care not to be drawn in by the physical similarities of the two men. And thus resolved, Caroline held herself still as he stroked her cheek and even stiller as Mitchell Johnston leaned down and pressed a light dry kiss to her forehead.

* * * *

The handle of the door leading into Caroline's room turned slowly.

He told himself it was only to check on her. A moment earlier, when she hadn't answered his knock, Mitchell had assumed she might be sleeping and turned to go, but something stayed his hand and he found he couldn't leave without taking a peek.

With footsteps silent on the floor he crossed to where she lay sleeping on the bed. She'd removed the pale blue ribbon from her tousled hair, which spilled around her face like a shadowy halo in the late afternoon sunlight. Still dressed, a flowery bed of fabric caressed her body. Below, her feet were bare, and it was all Mitchell could do to restrain himself from reaching down to caress her unsuspecting foot and long slim leg. The light delicate smell of her pulled at him, and as he leaned closer, the low-cut dress gave him an excellent view of the rise and fall of her full breasts. The need in Mitchell's groin grew almost beyond endurance. His fingers itched toward her, and he ran just one across the smooth silky skin just above her neckline.

Groaning, he yanked his hand back and clasped it to the pain beneath his waist. *Not yet,* he told himself. Time enough to make Caroline fall in love with him. He must go slow and easy. But he'd never manage it this way. Wanting her. Needing her with such agony. Thank God for Ruby Henderson. What he needed was near at hand. Abruptly, Mitchell fled from the room.

The kitchen, where he'd expected to find her, was deserted. Turning toward his study, a sudden thought came to him. "Oh, yes..." he breathed softly. "That's the thing. Practice makes perfect."

Mitchell paused only long enough to retrieve the hourglass from his top desk drawer. He held it to the light for an instant, letting the white sand slide back and forth. He'd wondered how he could be sure it would work though he'd had a hint at lunch that his practice would pay off. Now, he had the perfect solution for a test.

He found Ruby upstairs, mending some clothes. He slid quietly into the room and closed the door behind him, turning the key with a quick click. Only then did she look up, a brief flash of annoyance evident on her face. "It's you then," she said. "What'd you do with the princess?"

Mitchell shook his finger back and forth at her in mock annoyance. Ruby could be more than a little difficult at times, but ever since the day ten years ago when Mitchell had saved her son from jail over a petty theft, she'd shown her gratitude. She wasn't attractive to him, but Mitchell never cared about that. His "Caroline fantasy" served all of his aesthetic purposes and Ruby offered him simple physical release. She could be cool and standoffish more often than not, but she liked her "roll in the hay" from time to time, and she never made demands for anything more. Unfortunately, she'd never been too eager for some of

Mitchell's more unusual and daring appetites, but now he might be able to change all that.

"Ruby," Mitchell said, toying with her in a deep and commanding voice, "What do you make of this?" He held the slender cylinder up in front of her, not near enough to touch, but where the light and her eyes would catch the sand as it slid from one side to the other.

She gave it a brief inspective. "Don't make anything it." Ruby went back to her stitching.

Mitchell remained patient. "Look carefully. Watch the way the light catches the colors of the sand and reflects off the glass."

Now she turned her eyes upward, and he saw their gaze being drawn into the motion. He continued speaking in his low monotone, relaxing her muscle by muscle, until finally her eyelids slowly closed and the fabric she held slipped to the floor.

Mitchell moved close to her and touched her chin. She remained still and motionless. "Ruby," he said, running his fingers across her face, "I want you to suck my forefinger. With pleasure."

The housekeeper drew his finger into her mouth, then ran her tongue playfully back and forth across it. Mitchell smiled to himself as he felt his already-rising passion. He reached out and cupped the woman's breast.

It worked, his mind sang joyously. *Perfectly.*

For a moment, he considered waiting, knowing when his time came with Caroline it would be all the more precious. But his body, fully stretched against Ruby's now, was still demanding release. Moving close to Ruby's ear, whispered his request.

* * * *

Lyndfield Estate, 1890

Evan sloshed some water into the bowl on the bureau then plunged his hands into the cold liquid. He hadn't suspected it of his friend at first. Lila had been so taken with William and seemingly he with her that Evan thought it was simply true love on both their parts. Now he knew better. Highly doubtful William Lyndfield ever loved the girl at all—his main intent had been to steal the virginity of a fourteen-year-old.

He'd stolen her life as well.

Evan stared down at the long cylinder lying next to the bowl and pitcher. For a moment he wanted to fling it far out the window, so far he need never look upon it again. The hourglass had just taken his future from him, and at the moment he had no idea how to get it back! He hadn't intended to kill William Lyndfield —they'd argued, the gun had gone off, and William, and suddenly the man he'd hated for so long was gone in an instant. Neither had he meant for Caroline to be blamed for her father's death—his marriage to her was part of a grander plan to not only make William's daughter his own, but the wealthy man's fortune as well. But something had happened, some emotion had gripped and thrust his love away from him, and now Caroline's disappearance had led to a sequence of events beyond his control. The girl and his future—all gone in an instant. He'd had to make it look like she'd stolen at least some of her father's money, lest he himself be accused of her father's death. Oh, he'd need that money to do more tests on his experiment, to figure out where she went and how to get her back...the rest of it, what was left, would be tied up in this estate forever.

And now, he was alone.... How long had it been since he had a woman? Much too long, that was for certain. Now, it occurred to him that he'd been alone since Jess's death—another lunatic Lyndfield, though her lunacy harmed no one but herself in the end.

He let out a long sigh and slumped against the windowsill. Jess had obviously thought she was protecting Caroline. Little did she know it wasn't himself that the girl needed protection from. It was someone other than him. 'The sins of the father....' Or maybe Jess suspected even that, and just wanted to keep her niece safe from both of them.

Still, he couldn't help but believe her desires had been partly for herself. Night after night she'd come to his room, baring her body to him, exploring his as if it were some uncharted course begging for navigation. He had lain there beside her, inside her, and taken his release, letting her think as she would. Never admitting he had any knowledge or part in the accusations she flung his way. Never promising to keep away from the girl.

Then came the night when Jess got too close to the truth—too close for her own good. But there'd been no need for him to act. William himself realized what the ramifications would be if the truth came out, and it was he who administered the fatal dose of poison. Evan had felt no guilt when he'd looked down at Jess lying still and silent in her satiny coffin—and he felt no guilt now. Only this incredible urge....

Switching his thoughts abruptly to Caroline, Evan stared out into the night, and dreamt of his future.

CHAPTER 13

...A time to pluck up what is planted.
Ecclesiastes 3:1-8

May stared at the ceiling and tried to think about getting out of bed. She'd felt so tired lately, so heavy, as if the weight of the world threatened to crush her. Since that odd experience in the garden with Caroline, with its memories from the past of another life, it seemed the vitality and energetic life force sapped from her body a little more every day. She ate less and slept more—and worse still, every fiber of her being shouted that something was wrong—very wrong.

Tossing the sheet aside with determination, she slid her feet to the floor and headed for the bathroom. As water from the old-fashioned shower nozzle drizzled down her aging body, May attempted to relax a little, letting the warm spray renew her. A fierce pain shot through May's right arm and she gripped the side of the stall to keep from falling. Unable to turn the faucet off, water gushed into her eyes and blurred her vision as she groped outside the door for a towel. She gasped as the pain continued to throb. Finally slipping out of the stall and onto the tiled bathroom floor, she lay motionless for what seemed like an eternity, biting her lip against each new tremor of agony. Then suddenly, as quickly as it had hit her, the pain disappeared.

May closed her eyes and took several long deep breaths, filling her lungs with fresh spasm-free air. The vision crept upon her before she could bid it to stay away—and she wasn't sure she would have if she could. Somehow, May knew she must face this horror, if all was to come out right in the end. So took another gulp of air, and steeled herself to face the images from the past.

She knew the man, and she didn't—of course she saw his portrait every day. But this was different—this was a living, breathing version of the formidable William Lyndfield himself, and something seemed personally familiar about his presence. Broader than she would have guessed, and handsomer; May could understand why women would be drawn to his charm as well as his fortune. But he was also a terrifying figure. She knew she shouldn't be here, about to witness this dark secret side of his life. May pushed herself far back into the black shadows of the corner, praying he would not detect her there.

She hadn't noticed the bed at first, her eyes had been so full of him. But now, as he moved closer to his intent, she caught sight of the tiny motionless figure lying there. So small...too small...for him to be about to... *Oh my God*, her mind raged. He slid over the little form, a menacing shape of madness and lust. His breathing grew heavier and labored and suddenly—

Her own sharp indrawn breath filled the room to astounding proportions. She emerged from the shadows and struck out angrily, hitting, kicking, biting at whatever came into her path.

But she was too late. The deed had already been done. She hadn't been able to prevent the horror. Not that time. Not in that place. And as the world faded to black before her, May wondered if she would have the strength to prevent it this time either.

Some time later, up at the manor, May watched carefully as a small group of tourists lined up along the plastic runner in William Lyndfield's dark study. Since her experience in the shower, she felt extremely uncomfortable in this room. William's ominous presence permeated the very depths of this room, and the cold and calculating eyes in the gilt-framed photograph on his desk seemed to follow her every movement.

"This is Mr. William Lyndfield's study," she began, "where he conducted many of his elaborate business deals, and began preliminary work on his inventions. Through that archway," she gestured toward the heavy mahogany paneled wood to her left, "is the extensive family library which he used for his research in both areas."

"What was he most known for?" a particularly obnoxious young man in spectacles asked as he peered curiously around the room.

May tried to give her light laugh a natural sound, but its tone rang false in her own ears. *For abusing young women*, thought irrationally, then even more hauntingly, *perhaps his own daughter*. The word sent chills racing down her spine.

Curtly, May answered his question as best she could. "Making money."

Moving to stand between the two rooms, she allowed her gaze to rest on the portrait of Caroline over the mantel in the library. Truly amazing how much the young girl looked like their own Caroline. Not only in features, but manner as well. Soft and almost timid-looking on the surface, but with something confident and certain about the eyes. But though the pose held self-assurance, the girl clutched a thick shawl about her almost protectively, despite the seemingly sunny and spring-like background of the portrait. May wondered why.

"Excuse me, miss," a dreamy-eyed young woman, who'd been carefully eyeing the photo of William on the desk, broke into May's thoughts. "Why didn't he ever re-marry? He was certainly an attractive man. You'd think he would have wanted to find a good mother for his daughter."

"I don't know," May replied with a stilted and angry tone, causing the woman to stare in open-mouthed astonishment. She followed her statement with a stern, "Now if we could move on."

But as May reached up to switch off the light, something in the painting distracted her attention. Only for a moment, but in an instant so illuminating that she could only wonder that she hadn't thought of it before. The birthmark! That was the proof! The birthmark. The real Caroline Lyndfield had a tiny crescent-shaped birthmark on the upper inside of her right ankle. It was barely visible in the portrait because the younger girl was barefoot. May had never even considered looking for it on this Caroline, for until she'd had her terrible vision, she wasn't sure she really believed the girl's story. Not really... But this...this evidence could confirm the truth of it. Wouldn't it—in spite of the fact that it seemed impossible.

Suddenly May knew why Caroline was here. For escape...she was trying to escape the evil of her past. And somehow she'd wound up here. Here—with Jake...whom Caroline had seen as so very much like another young man. There was something else, too...something May had read once but couldn't quite recall. Poised right on the edge of her memory, she knew it wouldn't come back to her until the time was right. She'd just have to wait it out. *Wouldn't it be something,* she thought, the ramifications of this discovery were mind-boggling. Too much so to further consider now, but soon, very, very soon. Quickly, she turned from the room and hurried to catch up to the chattering group down the hall.

* * * *

"You look like hell!" Jake said as he strolled into the office at the manor house later that day. "What happened?"

May ignored him while she finished taking a long sip from the cup of tea on her desk. A neat little ceramic pot sat next to its saucer, evidence of her morning ritual. "I slipped in the shower this morning. Nearly knocked myself silly and I haven't quite recovered."

Watching carefully as she set down her cup and began to tally up a long column of numbers on her adding machine, Jake determined what she'd just told him was more than likely not true—and it wasn't like May to lie. He sat down on her desk and began to play with her Rolodex. "What's up?" he asked, trying to be casual. "Wanna talk?"

"No."

"Okay." He continued to flip through the cards.

"Would you please stop that?" She turned to him with irritation. "I'm trying to work."

He stopped but he didn't leave. "What do you want?" she asked at last, stopping what she was doing to give him her full attention.

112

Jake got off the desk and paced the office. "I'm looking for Johnston. I came in yesterday, but he wasn't here."

"I assume he took some time off to get Caroline settled. Why didn't you go there?"

Jake let out a snort. "Yeah, right. Just walk up to the door and ring the bell. I'm sure I'll be met with open arms."

"If you're not willing to do what's necessary to find him, then why did you ask?" May pulled a pile of unopened mail toward her and began to slit open the envelopes. "What did you want him for then?"

Jake drew up a chair next to her. "May...what do you know about Caroline Lyndfield's tutor? Monroe?"

The woman proceeded with her absentminded opening of the stack of mail. "Not much. He drowned, didn't he?"

"Do you think Caroline was in love with him?"

"I suppose it's possible. They were both young. He'd been with her a long time. It could have developed into something."

Jake placed a hand over hers, halting her haphazard task. "I'm asking you to help me here, May. You said you'd help, and now I'm asking."

Her gaze suddenly locked on his, full of fear. "Maybe we should just let it go, Jake. Take Caroline at her word, but help her start a new life here. Maybe it's not wise to press so deeply to understand the past."

Jake drew nearer to her. "This isn't like you, May. What the hell is the matter? Tell me what's happened."

Tears began to form at the corner of her eyes and she opened her drawer and reached for a hanky then dabbed at them. "Something terrible, something I saw."

"What? Tell me."

Slowly and in a whisper, she told him about the vision she'd experienced earlier that morning. "I don't know what I'm supposed to do," she concluded finally.

Winding his way behind the desk, Jake drew her into a close embrace. "It's okay, probably just a bad dream because of your fall. But maybe you should ask Henry about that knock on the head—it could be serious."

Angry, May jerked out of his hold. "It was *not* a bad dream. I was not in bed and I wasn't dreaming. And I don't need Henry to tell me I'm perfectly all right." She lowered her voice. "I'm afraid for you and Caroline."

Surprise registered on his face. "Why? This has nothing to do with us."

"Don't you understand, Jake? That man is...was...as the case may be, Caroline's father. He may have done something terrible to her.

There is a secret there, a dark secret. That may be why she's blocked out her past. But there's something more—I can't explain it, but I really feel there's a threat, right here in the present. Something evil…"

"Oh for Pete's sake." Jake went back around the desk and plopped back down in the chair. "First of all, May, you're implying that our Caroline *is the* Caroline, and you know how I feel about that. It just isn't possible. But I think there may be a connection between the two, so I'm willing to pursue this theory that something sinister could have been going on in that family. Which maybe triggered some childhood trauma in our Caroline."

May stared in open-mouthed frustration, but seemed to lack the energy to argue further. "So what now?" she asked. "What do you plan on doing?"

Jake looked relieved that she hadn't pressed. "Later today I'm going back into the city to see if I can find out anything else about our Mr. Monroe. While I'm there, I plan to do a bit of investigation into Ludington…and your William. Fair enough?"

Satisfied for the moment, she gave him a warm hug. "Thank you. In the meantime, I'm going to start work on finding a way to get Caroline away from Mitchell. I have a bad feeling about her being there."

"May," Jake went on, "why do you think Mitchell would have been interested in Monroe? The library records show he's been doing a good bit of research him."

She shrugged. "You know he thought he would be the one to write the history. I expect he was just getting his ducks all lined up."

"I suppose you're right," Jake agreed with reluctance as he turned to head out. "That must have been the reason."

At the door, he stopped. "Here's a thought…why don't you ask Caroline to come to work here? God knows she familiar enough with the family history."

May practically jumped over the desk in her haste to give him a hug. "That's a perfect solution," she said, squeezing him like a rag doll. "Will you ask her, if you're going out that way?"

"Who said I was going out that way?"

"Well, aren't you?" She grinned slyly.

"I am now." Jake kissed her forehead and headed for the door, not particularly sorry to have his errand to the city delayed.

"Jake," May called to him, "before you go, there's one more thing. I really think you should see this."

Curious, he followed her down the hall to William Lyndfield's study. Two minutes later, balanced on a stepladder with a small magnifying glass, he inspected Caroline Lyndfield's painted ankle.

"You see it?" May asked impatiently.

Jake inspected the tiny red crescent with care then began to back down the ladder. "Yep," he said, "I see it." Then after dusting his hands, "so?"

"For Pete's sake, Jake, don't you see what that means? If our Caroline has that same mark, then somehow, bizarre as it may seem, she is who she says…"

Jake laughed outright. "You are nuts."

May began treading back and forth across the carpet. "Why? Why am I nuts? It would be too coincidental for two people to ever have the same birthmark in exactly the same place."

"But it really is possible, isn't it?"

"Well," May hesitated, "I suppose it could be possible. But not likely."

"And you're suggesting it's more likely that she traveled through time? God, May. Get real."

"But it's all too much, Jake. Too much." May had begun to pale and he moved to take her to the sofa.

"May," he said tenderly, "don't get so worked up about this. It's not important."

"But it is important. Don't you see? It terribly important."

"Why?" he asked calmly. "Why is it so important?"

"When are you going to start believing?" The look in her eyes compelled, as always.

Lightly shaking himself from her gaze and grasp, Jake replied, "I will never believe she traveled through time, if that's what you're asking. When did *you* start believing?"

May heaved a breath of frustration. "Almost at once," she said simply. "There's something about her that's not of this time, and my gut tells me she's telling the truth. You know I always listen to my instincts, and this feeling is strong. I've got to help her. Something is going on here. And you're involved." Her eyes penetrated his. "Don't you feel it?"

Ignoring her question, Jake pushed the stepstool back in its place and turned to leave. "The only thing I feel is pissed off at Mitchell Johnston for trying to control her life like some sort of father or something. And the only thing that's going to help her," he said, "I mean really, help her, is for Caroline to get her memory back."

Rising slowly, May followed him from the room. "Then why are you so interested, Jake? If you don't feel anything, if you don't sense anything, then what are you trying to prove?"

"I think her amnesia is somehow tied to the Lyndfield history, plain and simple. Something happened to her that has something to do

115

with them. And she's gotten it confused in her mind."

"She doesn't have amnesia, Jake," May said with a calm he couldn't fathom. "She is who she says"

Of course she doesn't, Jake thought *with a shiver as he headed out the back door. But what exactly is wrong with her then?*

* * * *

Caroline did little more than sleep the next day. After her evening with Mitchell, she'd felt under the weather, and decided to use that as an excuse to remain in bed. If the truth were told, Caroline felt more than a little afraid to be alone in Mitchell's company again. Something about his intensity last night frightened her, and she didn't like the way she'd been unable to control her actions in his presence—as if he had some kind of magical spell on her.

Of course, feigned illness had done her little good in the end because Mitchell insisted on remaining at home with her, and coming to bring her meals and to read and sit at her bedside. He'd been nice enough during those visits—friendly and nothing more—and again she'd begun to feel she must have been imagining the other scene. But the image refused to leave her mind all the same.

A light tap at the door reminded her she could not continue this charade indefinitely. Today she must face the world again. Besides, perhaps if she got out of bed, Mitchell would go back to work and leave her to her own devices.

From outside the door, Mrs. Henderson asked, "Will you be coming downstairs this morning, Miss Caroline?"

"Yes," she called back. "In about fifteen minutes."

As the footsteps faded into the distance, Caroline rose from the bed and dressed quickly. Sitting before the mirror at her dressing table, she studied the woman before her. Her appearance seemed much the same...a trifle pale and thinner perhaps, but then she had not been eating too well over the past few days. The last time she remembered enjoying her food was...she sighed. Of course, the night she'd been in New York with Jake. Beer, and strange greasy meat and bread he called a hamburger. She'd certainly had nothing like that here. She smiled a little and then broke off into a frown. What would he be doing today, she wondered? And why hadn't he been to see her? She'd thought surely he'd have something to report to her by now. After all, he'd promised.

Suddenly aware of the passing minutes, Caroline jumped up and ran downstairs, completely unladylike. What did she care? Wasn't this the 21st century, after all? Who would care if she ran unladylike through the house?

Mitchell waited for her in the garden. As he'd promised, a gardener had appeared the first afternoon she'd been here and begun reconstructing the park. It still seemed dark and tangled to her, with obvious improvements, such as the freshly trimmed lawn and beds laid out with shrubs. He'd had Mrs. Henderson set up breakfast on a table there, and laid aside the paper he read as she approached.

"My dear," he exclaimed, rising. "I'm so glad you felt like joining me this morning. Does this mean you're feeling recovered?"

Caroline nodded as she approached the table. "I think I've taken enough of your time for one week."

He eased out her chair then pushed it in after she'd taken her seat. "Nonsense. I couldn't go away and leave you in unfamiliar hands, now could I?" Resuming his seat, he continued, "But now that you're well, I think I'd better get to our search, hadn't I?"

Caroline still found it difficult to believe that Mitchell wanted to help her find out the truth about her family, that—on some level—he believed her story. Sipping juice from the crystal at her place setting, she watched him carefully. What does he really want from me, she wondered? He'd been much kinder and considerate to her than Jake had ever been, a thought that made her sad.

"You're look unhappy," Mitchell observed.

She sighed a little. "I'm missing someone from my past, I suppose."

"Your fiancé."

Caroline clenched her fist, somehow certain he wasn't speaking of Francis. "Evan Ludington was not my fiancé."

Mitchell leaned over and patted her hand, as if she were a child, or perhaps a favored pet. "I don't want to push you, my dear, but if you do feel a need to speak of it, I hope you will turn to me." His eyes penetrated, burned with a passion she didn't want to see. Caroline found herself being drawn...again...toward something she didn't want to be drawn to.

Mrs. Henderson's sudden appearance broke the spell. "Mrs. Whatley's on the phone, sir," Ruby announced with stern disapproval after a glance at Mitchell's hand on Caroline's. "She'd like to speak to you about some papers she needs signed."

With a curt nod in her direction, Mitchell stood from his chair and Caroline felt her body go limp. "Will you be all right if I leave you today?" he asked.

She shook her head in affirmation. "I think I'll work in the garden," she replied, wondering with a look toward the window how she might go about adding some color to its dreary elements as Mitchell once again seemed to read her mind.

"That's a wonderful idea, my dear. If you need anything, ask Ruby to take care of it for you."

* * * *

After Mitchell hung up the kitchen phone, he turned to find Ruby staring at him in deep contemplation. "Is something wrong?" he asked.

The woman shook her head and gave him a thin smile that spread little by little and finally touched her eyes. "I was just thinking about the other night," she said glibly. "And wondering why you haven't mentioned it?"

He raised an eyebrow in mock curiosity. "What about?"

She shrugged. "What you did. You know. I rather liked it, I think."

Shock coursed through him that she remembered any of what had happened. Had she simply been playing a game with him, or had he forgotten some critical element of the hypnosis? Mitchell crossed the room in two seconds flat and pinned her next to the counter. "What are you talking about?" he demanded.

A shrill laugh emitted from the woman. "Oooo," she trilled like a schoolgirl, "Don't pretend you don't know. You thought I was out of it, didn't you? Gone under...hypnotized? But little ol' me was right there, enjoying every minute of it."

His heart pounded unreasonably. "I read up on hypnosis," she continued, oblivious to his grip on her arm. "A person can't go under unless they want to. So I guess I wanted what you did to me then." She pressed her body close to him suggestively. "But you knew that already, didn't you?"

"What exactly do you remember?"

"All of it—before, during, and after—especially after. You didn't tell me to forget any of it, now did you?

Mitchell heaved a sigh of relief and allowed Ruby to nuzzle his ear for another moment or two. Of course he hadn't told her to forget it, a stupid mistake he wouldn't make again. Right now, it wouldn't do to make her angry. He needed her to keep an eye on Caroline. At least he knew he needed make certain to remind her next time to recall nothing. Not to mention there was always the drug, which he hated the thought of using, but now felt certain he would if he decided to take Caroline before she was ready. Any liaison with her must not be remembered. She would be upset—more than upset. But with Evan's potion and the hypnotic trance, he could have her body at night and woo her to his love in the daytime.

Mitchell sighed, causing Ruby to slide her hand below his belt and rest against the hardness there. After a moment more, he carefully pushed her aside. "Later," he said with a firm voice. "Duty calls." And with that he left her frowning and headed toward the front door, whistling as he went.

Glass Hours

* * * *

The day fell into a dull routine as Caroline surveyed the garden and began to lay out a plan for its renewal. Normally she loved working in a garden, figuring out what could be salvaged and what needed to be added, finding unexpected surprises in the rare flower or herb. But this particular garden had no life to it, and even Caroline, with her green thumb and passion for plants had no desire to make this garden grow. Still, she plunged in to the work, for lack of anything better to do with her time. Weeds and scraggly shrubs had taken over most of the beds, so she spent the mornings pulling and hoeing in an attempt to discover if any of the original bulbs remained. Ruby Henderson brought her iced-tea around midday, but other than that, the woman kept to herself.

As the afternoon grew warmer, Caroline sought the inner sanctity of Mitchell's library and discovered in its dark cluttered room books that once belonged to Evan. His library had been extensive, consisting not only of books on science and Victorian technology—his passion— but also with novels and a large collection on both the paranormal and the occult. Not for the first time, she wondered just exactly what Evan and her father had hoped to prove or discover with their scientific experiments. And did Mitchell find all this so fascinating that he'd failed to incorporate books of his own into the library? From the frontispieces of the books, it appeared he'd added little of his own reading material during his tenure here.

Caroline found herself fascinated by the transcendental literature. She'd always been drawn to the spiritual aspects of life, but had little knowledge of the subject. Her father had not been a church-going man, and while Aunt Jess had introduced her to some of the more didactical aspects of religion, she'd never considered faith beyond the simple belief that each person might have the capacity to maintain a spiritual existence of their own. One book particularly intrigued her with its mention of something called "astral travel," whereby the spirit was able to leave the body for certain periods of time. Except for the fact that she was actually still in her body, she couldn't help but wonder if something similar had happened to her. Certainly she had traveled somehow from that time to this. For the first time, the thought crossed her mind that perhaps Evan or her father might have been behind whatever had happened to her but she tossed it quickly aside, for why on Earth would either of them have wanted to send her away from them? Certainly not Evan—that would have been the very last thing he'd have wanted. Still, she read on, her mind now alert for clues that might help her understand the past, whether that meant her own, or her father's and Evan's.

Right in the midst of a particularly impressive passage, the doorbell clanged, breaking the still and eerie quiet that permeated the house for most of the time. Ignoring decorum and Mrs. Henderson's scorn, Caroline jumped up, tossed aside her book, ran to the front door, and threw it open with enthusiasm.

A sheepish-looking Jake lazed before her, a wilting spray of wildflowers in hand. "Well," he said with barely a trace of his usual sarcasm. "The lady of the manor herself. I'd have thought you had people to help you with things like answering doors."

In her surprised joy, Caroline chose to ignore his remark and tried hard not to seem too glad to see him. "Won't you come in?" she said with as much primness as she could muster.

Ruby Henderson appeared in the foyer, arms folded across her chest like a German field marshal. "Mr. Johnston said you weren't well enough to have visitors," she ordered.

"Nonsense, I'm perfectly all right. Haven't I been working in the garden most of the day? That's strenuous work, and I'm fine."

Frowning, Jake acknowledged Caroline's introduction of Ruby, wondering where exactly she'd come from. Mitchell had never mentioned having a housekeeper until Caroline arrived, and this one didn't appear to be typical. More like a guard dog, if first impressions said anything. "So you've been gardening, have you?" he asked, returning his attention to Caroline.

"Well, in a manner of speaking," she replied. "It needs a lot of work. Would you like to see?"

He followed her past the displeased housekeeper and through the back door.

Caroline had indeed been at work. Jake had only seen Mitchell's garden once before, at a cocktail party he'd given for the staff, but he well remembered its state of neglect. Caroline had definitely cleared some of the beds, but the ground looked like it had a way to go before it came to life again—if it ever did.

"If anyone can make things bloom here I'm sure it will be you." Jake told her and received a pleased smile in return for the simple compliment. "What else have you been up to?"

"I've done some reading, but that's about it. Yesterday I slept, mostly. Maybe I did need the rest."

Keeping to the spot where she stood, Caroline twiddled a branch with her fingers. "I missed you."

For what seemed like the thousandth time, Jake studied the way the light played with the colors in her hair, and cast a soft shadow across the side of her face. She was dressed in a flowing print skirt and blouse, and her feet were bare. Right now, she reminded him very much of the portrait at Lyndfield.

"Come here," he said with quiet authority to which she immediately responded. He reached up and pulled her down onto his lap and into his arms and cradled her there for several moments, savoring the wild sweet smell of her thick hair as it lay like heather against his face. She allowed the embrace for a time, then drew back and studied him. "What have *you* been doing?"

"You want to know if I've learned anything, right?" She nodded then rested her head back on his shoulder. "Bits and pieces, but I'm not sure how anything fits together." He patted the ground beside him and she moved there and curled her legs up beneath the full skirt. He decided to keep May's premonition to himself—for now—even though his eyes automatically drifted toward her bare ankles as she wrapped them beneath her skirt. *Did she have the telltale birthmark?* Jake wasn't even sure he wanted to know.

"Tell me, Caroline, are you sure you don't know of any family secrets? What about William? He was a wealthy man...and money will buy a lot of silence." He noticed her shiver slightly, but she only shook her head in response. "How come he never remarried?" Jake probed.

"I don't know. I think he loved my mother very much."

Frustrated, he asked bluntly, "Who was Nan Callahan?"

Caroline's face froze and he knew he'd struck a nerve. Still, he was amazed she'd even heard of Nan. The digging he'd had to do to come up with that little mystery...

"Well, are you going to tell me or not?"

"I...she..." Caroline's breath started to come in short spurts and Jake instantly wished he hadn't sprung the name on her so suddenly. He'd reached the point of honestly not want to send her into paroxysms of shock every time he told her something.

"Easy," he said, filling his voice with as much calm as he could manage, "Take your time with it."

Finally Caroline's breathing slowed and she was able to continue. "She...was a maid...at Lyndfield."

"And?"

"And what?"

"What happened to her?"

"I didn't know anything happened to her. The last time I saw her was the night I disappeared...she brought me a cup of tea."

"That's it? You didn't see her later?"

Again Caroline hesitated and Jake knew instinctively there was something she did not want to remember. Which meant the memory would only come to her in its own time.

"Look," he said, "Let's drop it for now, okay?"

She shook her head, obviously relieved to leave the past for now.

"How are you doing here?" he asked with real concern, remembering May's earlier worries. "Is Mitchell treating you all right?"

"Yes. He's been considerate."

"But..."

She seemed reluctant to go on, but eventually said, "Something about him that troubles me. I don't feel comfortable with him, if you must know the truth."

He laughed. "There's something about him that troubles me, too." He pushed a strand of hair back from her forehead. "Seriously, I think he's harmless. But he can be pretty intense at times. Do you want to leave?"

"Where would I go?"

"You could go wherever you wanted to go. Mitchell's not your father, or your guardian, or even you husband. You can just get up and walk out if you want to. That's what modern women do, Caro. Come back and stay at the gatehouse, if you want."

"Do you mean that? All of it?"

"Of course I do. Don't let people push you around. Just because you can't remember your past doesn't mean you can't start to work on your future. You're probably better off not remembering anyway. The past often holds a lot of pain."

"Does it for you?"

Jake drew his eyes away from her and focused on the birdbath, where a cardinal had just landed and was cheerily bathing. "Yeah, it does," he said at last.

"If you ever want to tell me..."

"Yeah..."

He rose abruptly and made a show of brushing off his pants. "Listen, May had an idea...why don't you come to work up at the Manor? She could use some help with the tours, and you know plenty about the house and the family. What do you think?"

Caroline's eyes grew wide. "I could actually work for her. She would give me that chance?"

"Have confidence, Caro. Of course she would. And honestly, you should think about coming back to live with us if you're feeling weird about being here. I mean it, and May would agree. And don't let Mitchell give you grief about it either."

"All right," she answered. "I'll talk to him. I'll do it. I'd rather be there with you...and May."

"Good girl. Why don't I tell May to come and pick you up later this evening? Just in case Mitchell gets his goat up about you leaving. I'd do it myself, but I'm going to the city and I'm not sure when I'll be back."

"That would be perfect," she beamed. "Thank you so much, and thank May for me too."

"You can thank her yourself." Jake grinned then looked toward the house. "Guess I better get going. I'm sure the Gestapo has phoned the Fuehrer by now."

Her puzzled expression brought a laugh from Jake. "You need to start reading some modern history books," he suggested, teasing her. "You have a lot of catching up to do."

"Oh," she said, rising herself. "That reminds me of something I wanted to tell you. Evan was heavily interested in the occult. I'm starting to wonder if perhaps it played some part in his experiments?"

Jake bit back another sarcastic remark and shrugged. "I don't know, Caro. I think I'd better stick to family history, you know? That's my specialty." He held out a hand and led her toward the door. "Talk to May about it. She's got..." he paused to consider his words before speaking again. "She's got a gift in that area."

"You mean she sees things before they happen?"

"Sometimes...but it's more of a knowing." Jake stopped and watched her face again—so trusting, so innocent.

"Caroline," he said on impulse, touching her chin. "Don't be afraid to know the truth. Whatever it may be, not knowing is worse."

She smiled and he leaned down and touched her mouth with his. Her lips were warm and ready and tasted a little like honey-sweet nectar. Suddenly Jake found himself wishing he'd kissed her earlier, and that he didn't have to leave now. That he could stay here and kiss her all afternoon. Kiss her, and hold her, and... She was vulnerable, this one, and he wanted to somehow protect her. But she was tough too. Tough, and determined to remain true to the truth she professed: that she was who she said she was. Too bad that truth was an utter impossibility.

But as he walked her back to the house, his eyes couldn't help but stray down, and as the breeze blew her dress just slightly, he saw the tiny crescent-shaped mark on her ankle.

CHAPTER 14

...A time to speak.
Ecclesiastes 3:1-8

The drive back to his house seemed endless to Mitchell, and the voice in his head clamored for attention he didn't wish to give. He tried to keep his thoughts focused on Stanton. The nerve of the man, thinking he could simply show up without waiting for an invitation. Thank God Ruby had called him at once. Mitchell had known he could trust her. Still, he must be careful. Unfortunately he couldn't be quite sure how understanding Ruby would be once she knew his plans about Caroline. He feared the woman might be becoming more attached to him than he'd planned, the problem being that after he and Caroline were married, there would be no place for Ruby at all.

He'd deal with that later, when he had to.

He turned into the drive and quickly hurried up the front walk. Just before he reached the door, however, he stopped and drew a few deep breaths, knowing he must calm himself. Caroline mustn't suspect how angry he was. Still, this relationship with Stanton could not be allowed to continue.

The foyer's mahogany walls hid the late afternoon shadows as Mitchell quietly closed the door behind him. He took a quick peek in the library only to find it empty.

"She's resting now," Ruby said softly, coming up behind him and looping lean arms about his waist. *The woman is insatiable*, he thought, feeling he'd unleashed a monster.

Deftly, Mitchell freed himself from her embrace. "How long did he stay? Did anything go on between them?" he asked, trying to keep the irritation from his voice.

"Not much...and not long," she replied. "Why does it matter so much?"

Suddenly she eyed him with suspicion. "You've never told me much about why she's here."

"She's a distant relation of the Lyndfield family." Mitchell knew what would appeal to Ruby's interest in the family fortune. "She may be worth millions some day. But first I have to establish the connection. And... I want to be the one to do that, Ruby—not see it fall into the lap of the likes of Jake Stanton."

With a smug smile, she ran a finger down his cheek. "Of course you do. You should be, after all. And you know I want that for you, don't you, sugar?"

With only a slight wince at her throaty endearment, Mitchell let her kiss him on the mouth. "I might even re-consider my rule about marriage," she told him after a moment. "If you had millions."

Realizing the time had come to be firm, he pushed her from him. "Ruby," he said, commanding his most authoritative tone, "you know our agreement. I need your help, and appreciate your help. You'll be well compensated for it. But the Lyndfields...my work...this work, is my first priority. I want...and need...to keep it that way. I hope you understand."

Peeved, Ruby drew herself up like a queen. "Of course I understand. But don't think for a moment you can pay me off like some common whore. You and I are more than that to each other." Then instantly returning to her cool demeanor, she headed back to the kitchen without another word.

Satisfied for the moment with his results, Mitchell headed up stairs to change for dinner. Ruby certainly had her uses, but he didn't intend to let anything—and that included Jake Stanton—stand in the way of his ultimate goal—having Caroline.

* * * *

The evening meal unfolded over an uncomfortable silence. Caroline knew Mitchell must be aware of Jake's visit. It had been obvious to her from the instant she'd arrived her that Ruby's loyalty laid with Mitchell and with him alone. Evidently he intended to wait until after they'd finished eating to bring up the subject. What exactly *was* Ruby's relationship to him that she would carry such tales, Caroline wondered with annoyance? Jake's words about her 'choices' came back hauntingly.

I can make my own choices, regardless of what Mitchell says, she thought with growing courage. And no matter what happened right now, May would be here soon to take her home. Funny, if anyone had told her a week ago that she'd soon be calling the gatehouse 'home,' she would have laughed in their face.

Abruptly though, she wondered if Mitchell could have her put off the estate? He seemed to have so much power over both Jake and May. Was the reason neither of them had fought to have her stay before, because they were afraid? She wanted to believe Jake's developing affection meant he would fight for her, and hadn't he said as much today, encouraging her to come back and stay with them. Still, at the expense of his employment, he might feel differently. If that happened, and she had to leave, where would she go? What would she do? *No matter what happens, I can take care of myself*, she reasoned, knowing she must be strong. Something like the 'modern' women Jake had spoken of in New York. Those women...the women of this day and age...would not let the likes of Mitchell Johnston, or any other man, push them around.

The sound of the older man clearing his throat broke into her timidly courageous reflections. She gazed up from her plate to find his eyes trained on her with an intensity that caused her to shiver, despite the room's heat.

"Yes?"

"My dear," Mitchell began, "I don't mean to chastise you..." he paused slightly, as if giving his words careful attention. "I understand Jake Stanton was here today."

"Oh, yes," she said, determined to keep a light tone, "he was. He wanted to make sure I was feeling better."

Mitchell gave her an irritated glance, then tossed his napkin on the plate and came to help her from her chair. Something about his motion brought other nights back to her, nights at her father's table, with Evan often finding irritation at some comment Francis had made, then tossing aside his napkin and heading toward the drawing room for his brandy.

"I see," he was saying. "Let's go in the drawing room, shall we?"

Reluctantly she followed, as she'd so often followed her father and Evan for after dinner conversations. A few minutes later Caroline found herself sitting before the fireplace trying, as Mitchell bent to light the logs, to muster as much calm as she could for what was to come. Though she felt it much too hot today for a fire, he apparently did not. Suddenly Caroline a chill crept over her, as she remembered the way Evan had always insisted on having a fire, sometimes even in the middle of summer. Being here—in this house—with another man who made her very uneasy was not comforting. More and more she wanted the evening to be over and to be away from here—if only she could find the courage to make it so.

"Now there," Mitchell said as he rose and dusted his sooty hands, "we can talk."

He crossed to the bar and poured two glasses of sherry, then he took a seat next to her on the sofa. "So, do you want to tell me about Stanton's visit?"

Caroline sipped the sherry with care, letting its warm sensation slide easily down her throat, hoping it would help build her resolve. She finally met his gaze with as much directness as she could. "He came to offer me a job, actually, one that I've accepted."

Mitchell's mouth formed itself into a hard line and she had the distinct impression he struggled with intense anger. "What do you mean he offered you a job?"

Caroline held tight to her courage like a lifeline. "I'm going to work at the manor house, to help with the tour groups."

"Jake Stanton is in no position to be offering you a job with the estate." Mitchell laughed, but the sound of it was tight and forced. "The nerve of the man."

"Actually, May offered me the job, and Jake just came by to say hello and pass along the message." She paused and took a deep breath. "If the estate can't pay me, it's fine, but at least I'll be doing something to take care of myself, and making a contribution for everything you all have done for me."

Now Mitchell appeared truly at a loss. "But why should you need to take care of yourself, Caroline, or contribute anything to anyone? You have everything you need right here, my dear."

She knew she was treading on extremely thin ice, but she had to forge ahead. If May arrived before she told him that she was leaving, Mitchell would either be furious that she'd kept it from him, or terribly hurt—and Caroline didn't want either of those things.

"I can't stay here, Mitchell. I'm sorry because I know you're only trying to help me and I do so appreciate that. But being here doesn't feel right, whereas staying at the gatehouse, with May and Jake, it feels like the place I need to be right now. Please try to understand." Here she added a little white lie. "I've spoken with May, and she'll be coming for me in a bit."

He set his drink down and moved closer to the fire. Silently, he fiddled with the hourglass on the mantle, turning it one way and another until the white sand began to slip down its glass sides, silt running away the minutes of time. Mesmerized by it, Caroline loosened two buttons at the neckline of the only thing she'd been able to find in her closet this morning—a long lacy-sleeved Victorian dress. Just the type of outfit she'd been forced to wear in the past—and shunned when she could for artists' robes and riding slacks. Though she'd only had the few items May had bought to bring with her, she couldn't imagine why Mrs. Henderson had taken them all away at once. She longed for the light summery dresses May had helped her select in town. She dabbed a handkerchief at the base of her throat, as the heat turned to damp moisture against her skin and still Mitchell didn't speak. His posture seemed stiff and unbendable, and she feared the worst—his anger.

Surprisingly, when he finally turned and came to her, he was calmer than she would have expected. He knelt on the floor in front next to where she sat, and placed his lined hands over her own. "Caroline, I don't wish to see you hurt. Jake Stanton may have all the qualities to draw in a young woman such as yourself, but in the end, he will hurt you. I must forbid you to go back to that house."

His dark eyes bore into her own, once again attempting to draw her into some deep and spidery web. As she fought against his hold, the heavy air seemed to press against her; heat crept over her body until she could actually feel the drops of sweat beading up between her breasts. Behind him, the sand in the hourglass continued its silky flow toward the future.

"No!" She ripped her hands from his and struggling to rise from the sofa.

Mitchell's gaze pierced her skin as she moved to the outer edge of the room and tried to restore her breathing. "Are you all right, my dear?"

"You will not tell me whom I may or may not see." She forced the words that threatened to remain locked in her throat. "You are not my father." Caroline paused for a moment, calling up her strength. "I thank you for all you have done for me, but you do not own me."

With great patience, he waited until she had finished her tirade to approach her. Caroline could feel the energy within him, strong and commanding. She fought against a sudden rising nausea.

Mitchell's hand came up and touched her cheek then he ran his finger down her neck until it rested at her collarbone. She kept her place, determined not to move one muscle or show one iota of fear. "You're quite worked up, my dear," he said, "and I think you've misunderstood. It was not my intention to order you. Of course you do whatever you please. It's just that I'd hoped you would stay here."

Caroline felt herself begin relax. *I've done it,* she thought with pride. She had made her stand and had been taken at her word. "I know that," she whispered and even as she spoke an idea began to formulate in her mind. This hadn't been so very difficult. Jake was right. She could choose. She had made a decision on her own.

"I too want us to be friends," she replied with the first stirrings of confidence, "and I promise we'll continue to get to know each other better, regardless of where I am. I'll even come here to visit, perhaps to help you with your garden, if you wish."

His penetrating eyes now seemed nothing more than murky brown. "You'll keep that promise?"

She found herself smiling with more ease than she would have expected. "Of course, I will." She patted his hand. "Thank you for understanding, Mitchell."

Caroline couldn't be sure, but she thought she felt just the slightly flinch in his touch.

* * * *

Jake's visit back to the New York Public Library didn't produce any results beyond another look at Caroline Lyndfield's childhood diary. Something about the innocence of her words brought to his mind the woman he knew, and he thought again of the birthmark he'd seen earlier today on her ankle. Could it be a mere coincidence, a family trait handed down through the ages—because really, there was no other plausible explanation beyond that? People didn't travel through time.

The same dour librarian who'd brought the containers before appeared before him with a small cardboard box. "I found this tucked far back in the corner of the shelf, Mr. Stanton," she informed him as she set the box on the table. "I'd be surprised if anyone's looked at it since it was put there, and I knew you'd want to see it right away."

Wow, he thought, maybe this will provide some of the missing clues he'd been searching for. If nothing else, it was a new piece of information for the family history. He removed the lid with care and stared into the container. The only thing inside was a pile of letters, all tied up with a faded green ribbon. More letters from William to his wife, he wondered, doubting those would be much help to anyone.

But when he pulled the first one from its delicate yellowed envelope, he found the very thing Caroline had been telling him all along—these were love letters, and they were from Francis. He read the one on top, but the words were so intimate, and rang so *true* to him, he couldn't bear to continue with the others. But she would want them, he knew, so he rearranged some items from the other box, slipping some of those into this one, and slid the letters into his jacket pocket. He was as bad as Caroline had been, peeling the cover back from the diary, but irrationally, he knew it was important that he give her these. He slipped the little diary in his pocket as well, thinking perhaps it might later reveal more than seemed apparent at the moment.

He motioned to the librarian to let her know he was finished with the material. "Did you find anything useful in that box?" She seemed much friendlier now that Caroline wasn't here, but he wasn't in the mood to flirt today.

"Not really," he lied, thankful she hadn't explored it too carefully when she brought it.

Jake thanked her and headed toward the front of the building. Just as he was rounding a corner, he ran into the last person he wanted to see while in the City—Melanie.

"Jake!" She beamed with pleasure. "I was just thinking about you earlier today. How funny to run into you. I would say small world but it's not really, in a city of seven million people, it's amazing."

She could say that again but she didn't. "Hey, Mel," was really all he could think of to say.

"I was just leaving. Why don't we grab a bite to eat?" she asked.

Jake knew he could say 'no' and he wanted to; he was in a hurry to get back to the gatehouse and see how Caro had ventured with leaving Mitchell's. Still, Mel had been a friend for a long time, and if nothing else, he owed her dinner for seeing Caroline that day.

"Sure," he said, and a short while later found them sitting across from each other at a bistro they both liked.

Mel fingered the stem of her wineglass and studied him with intense eyes. "You're different," she mused, her full lips pouting just a tad. "Let me guess, you still have a thing for that girl."

Jake hadn't really expected her to be so perceptive, but then she was a psychologist—not to mention a woman—after all. "I guess you could say that," he told her, feeling some relief that she wasn't surprised and didn't seem particularly upset either.

"How's she doing? Any return of her memory?"

"Oh, her memory's intact, it's just not realistic," he responded, taking a long swig of beer.

"So she still claims to be from another century?"

"You got it."

She laughed. "Well, maybe she really it. Happens all the time in romance novels."

"Get real, Mel. We both know that's not possible."

She reached across the table and squeezed his hand, and for the first time he realized that even though they were basically breaking off their relationship, she really was a friend. "Would it matter, if she never figured out who she really is?"

Jake shook his head, amazed he could admit that he felt this way. "No," he told her. "I don't think it would."

* * * *

Mitchell felt incredulous that he'd been able to restrain his temper as Caroline gathered the few belongings she'd brought with her and drove off into the night with May. The voice in his head blared at him to kill May on the spot, then take Caroline upstairs and ravish her. How he would have loved to do just that. To feel her silky skin, bare beneath his hands, to flick his tongue across her nipples, to have her cry out for him, to love only him and no other. He wanted that now, wanted it bad enough to kill for it. He pressed his head between his hands, wishing he could silence the voice inside forever, not wanting to share his thoughts of Caroline even with it.

"Are you all right, darling?" Ruby's husky voice slid from the shadows. She moved toward him, placing a hand on his shoulder.

"I'm fine," he answered, more forcefully than he meant, shaking off her hand.

Ruby wouldn't be shaken off however, and stayed him with

130

another touch. He remembered he might need more of her help at any time, and allowed her to hold him in place. "Now that she'd gone, we can be alone again," she said, reaching up to touch his cheek. "I'll do whatever you want, my darling."

He grabbed her wrist and twisted, wanting more than anything simply to hurt someone, anyone, and Ruby happened to be the person at hand. But she didn't seem to care, and simply pressed herself into him and ignored any pain she might be feeling.

Evan's voice, the voice he'd come to know so well, taunted him to use this opportunity to perfect his skills, to make sure he had full use of them when the time came. He'd do that then, he thought, he'd use this woman who so desperately wanted to be used.

"Why don't we just have some wine, first?" He filled his voice with as much passion as he could muster. "I'd like to wind down a little, if you don't mind."

Ruby laid her hand on his chest. "I'll just open a bottle. Shall I bring it up to you?"

"Why, yes," he smiled, "that would be wonderful." He watched as she headed toward the kitchen, thinking at least the evening wasn't to be a complete waste.

CHAPTER 15

Time, you thief...
Lord Byron

Caroline woke before dawn the next morning, determined to begin her first day helping at the estate office with a cheerful disposition. How strange would it feel to be back in the house she would always think of as home? She couldn't say she really missed it all that much—mostly she missed her garden and Francis. Now her conservatory was little more than an empty shell, her wonderful flowers and herbs gone with the sands of time. But at least she had something purposeful to do, and for that she had Jake and May to thank.

As she fussed with her hair in the mirror, she thought again of the absurdity—and the irony—of it. Her father had always groomed her for unique employment: running the estate after his death. Now, she would be indeed be working in her own home—but it would be as an employee. If only people knew and believed who she really was, they would be amazed. Her life had certainly become an unpredictable bundle of tricks.

Once dressed, she turned to tidy the room she'd come to think of as hers, much more so than the one Mitchell had replicated. It might be Jake's in reality, but here, she felt connected, even more than she ever had at the Manor house—all more than likely due to the fact that she was with people she trusted—Jake and May. They were here and now, but they so reminded of those she'd trusted in the past. Why, she wondered, had she never completely felt that trust with her father?

Brushing away the unbidden memories, she turned her thoughts to the previous evening. Thank goodness there hadn't a scene when she'd left Mitchell's. Mitchell had taken her leaving much better than she'd expected him to, and she'd promised she'd come and visit him often, perhaps dinner in a couple of days, and certainly continue they would continue to develop the friendship they had started. But she knew she didn't mean it, and she hoped never to set foot in that house again. The thought of it—of him—terrified her! And what was even more terrifying was that she had no idea why she was so frightened of him!

As she pulled up the sheets and comforter on the big poster bed, a vision of Nan came to her mind. Nan, she recalled sadly, who used to make the bed for her every morning, who did so much, each and every day. Why had Jake asked about her yesterday, and why did she have the feeling something terrible had happened to her friend? Although the girl had now been dead for over a century, Caroline had left Nan safe and sound back in her own century. Hadn't she? What exactly had happened the night she disappeared, only to wake and find herself in this century? Icy fingers of fear told her it was something terrible, something she didn't want to remember.

Shaking negative thoughts aside, she noticed a loose scrap of notepaper on the bedside table and reached for it, wanting to leave the room tidy and neat before going downstairs. There was no need for May or Jake to have to pick up after her; she didn't want either of them to regret her decision to return here. She would show them she could take care of herself. As she turned the paper over, she discovered it had words written on it. Absentmindedly, Caroline began to read, and then gasped as the impact of the phrases knocked the very breath from her. Of course she recognized them instantly—from the poem Francis had given her the day he first proposed—filled with his hopes and his fears, he'd told her, and his one most fervent desire—for her to be his wife. How had it gotten here? This paper wasn't yellowed with age. Had someone copied it? Surely there must be the explanation.

Feelings rushed over Caroline once more as she recalled the morning Francis had first shared this poem with her. They'd spoken of the fear their union might not be accepted by her father in the same breath they'd spoken of their dreams for a future together. She shivered with something between excitement and sadness, remembering the way Francis had brought her fingers to his lips and run his tongue across them lightly. He'd asked her to have courage; and she had promised she would, but in the end she'd had no courage at all.

She rubbed her temples, wishing she could so easily rub out the painful memories, then tucked the paper in her pocket and headed downstairs. May was fixing breakfast, humming a little tune, the image of domesticity, when Caroline walked into the kitchen.

"Morning, dear," the older woman chimed out. "Did you sleep well? You must have been exhausted after all the excitement yesterday."

"I guess I was tired," she admitted, taking a seat at the table and setting the piece of paper to one side. "I don't believe I've had taken a stand like that with anyone before. Today, it feels good, but yesterday, well, it was terrifying." She looked around the kitchen. "Has Jake left already?"

She'd barely gotten to see him last night. She was already settled into bed in 'her' room when he'd finally gotten home from his trip to the city. He'd popped his head in to say goodnight.

"Welcome back," he grinned, "and good for you for standing up to the ogre."

"You're sure you don't mind giving up your room?" She eyed him doubtfully, wondering if sleeping on the sofa was terribly uncomfortable for him.

"Not to a pretty lady like you." He blew her a kiss goodnight. "See you in the morning."

She'd hoped she would indeed, but maybe it wasn't to be. "He went out with the dog for an early morning run," May informed her now. "Do you want some eggs and bacon? You've got a full day ahead."

Caroline beamed at the thought of it. "Yes. I'm quite excited. My first employment."

With a cheery laugh, May placed a plate of steaming scrambled eggs and bacon in front of her. "Well, you seem to be more than qualified for it. Even if we aren't sure exactly how you came by those qualifications."

"I'm a bit nervous, all the same." Caroline fidgeted with the eggs on her plate. "I don't want you to regret this decision."

"You'll do fine," May told her. "People are just people. Work is just work. Life's very simply when you remember that."

Caroline nodded and began to eat, realizing suddenly she was famished. After a bite or two, she remembered the piece of paper.

"May," she asked, picking it up and handing it to the woman. "I found this on the table beside my bed. Do you know where it came from?"

"Looks like Jake's handwriting. It's a poem." May's face lit with sudden recognition. "It's from the diary. I was reading it last night and I saw this."

Caroline put down her fork. "My diary?"

Wrinkles creased May's forehead as she shook her head. "I know, I know. He shouldn't have taken it. But he thought there might be something there that would help us figure all this out. He's promised me he'll return it." She studied the paper again. "Anyway, this poem was copied there, near the end." She looked around the kitchen, not finding what she sought. "I had it in here last night, but maybe Jake reclaimed it this morning. We'll ask when he gets back."

Caroline frowned. "I did copy it in there...I wanted to make sure it was a part of my life forever. Do you think Jake copied it from there? But why would he?"

"He must have." She gave Caroline a girlish smile. "Maybe he was plagiarizing, hoping to make an impression on you?"

"I hope you're not talking about me. A writer could get a bad rep over gossip like that." Jake entered the room with Sam close on his heels. The dog headed immediately for Caroline and began to lick the hand she extended.

Then she turned toward the man, feasting on the way his skin glistened with perspiration from his early morning run. She watched as he took a carton of orange juice from the refrigerator and poured himself a glass. The short pants he wore clung damply to his strong lean legs; she licked her lips without thinking as she remembered the morning she'd seen another's long and familiar legs glistening in the morning light. She did not think she could go on like this. She ached with desire—for both of them, whether they were one or not.

"This poem," May replied, handing it to him.

"Oh that," he said with a slight blush. "It's nothing. I was just playing around. Can't believe I actually wrote the damn thing. Sounds like some kind of Victorian posy, doesn't it?" He glanced at Caroline. "No offense intended," he told her with a little laugh. "I thought you'd like it so I left it by your bed this morning."

A hot sensation rose in Caroline's breast. Sam, who had stretched out on the floor beside her, sensed her anger and let out a low whine.

"This only offense I take," she said sharply, "is that you would claim to have written this poem yourself, or to trifle with the affections I held so dear!"

"Well I did write it!" He slammed his glass on the table, sloshing the juice at the bottom. "Who else? It's my handwriting, after all. Isn't that right, May?"

"But didn't you copy it?" May asked him.

"Where the hell from? William Butler Yeats?"

"From my diary, of course," Caroline answered for both of them.

"From your diary? Are you referring to the diary we found in the archives?"

Caroline's blood was boiling now. "You know I am. The one you stole!"

Her theories about his connection with Francis were far from her mind. Now he was Jake Stanton, 21st century male, and he was being impossible.

"Well, I'm telling you I wrote this poem last night. It popped into my head while I was reading, and I wrote it down, plain and simple—and the only reason I 'stole' it was to try and help you!"

May held up a hand in protest. "Enough arguing, I think. Where is the diary now, Jake?"

Abruptly, he left the room and came back a moment later with a puzzled look on his face. "I left it on the coffee table. It's not there."

May eyes searched the kitchen. "So you didn't come and get it from the kitchen this morning?"

"No. I've been out. What was it doing in here?"

"I couldn't sleep last night," May told him, "so I got up and came downstairs. I saw it lying in there and brought it in here to read a bit. That's when I read the poem."

"Why didn't I see it then? I went through the entire book, looking for something that might give us information about Caroline's father."

May got up and began to clear the table. "Some of the pages were stuck together. Remember, you mentioned it to me yesterday. I steamed them open."

Jake stared at her with disbelief. "And you're trying to tell me that the poem I wrote was in the diary?"

"Of course it was," Caroline shot out. "Francis wrote it for me and I copied it into my diary." Then sudden realization dawned in her mind. She brought her hand to her mouth and stared at him in astonishment. "Don't you see, Jake? This proves it. There is some connection between you and Francis! You wrote this poem...and you hadn't even read it yet."

"Oh for Christ's sake. It's a conspiracy." He downed the last gulp of his juice then stalked out of the kitchen.

Caroline looked helplessly at May. "Why won't you believe it? I believe you. Why can't you believe me?" Her eyes brimmed with tears and May placed a comforting arm around her shoulder.

"It's not so easy for Jake, honey." May engulfed her in a motherly embrace.

After a moment she pulled free. "And does he think it's easy for me? I did not plan to come here, to leave my father. To have him murdered and myself convicted without evidence or trial. To find a man who is so much like the one I lost, but who hasn't an ounce of his courage. I hate it! I hate it all!" She burst into harsh sobs and stormed out the back door.

Pain tore through Jake as he listened from beyond the door. It was impossible. It just could not be. And yet with each passing day, it seemed more and more it was. That he was who she said he was.

* * * *

After giving her a few minutes alone, May wandered out to find Caroline puttering in the garden beside a bed of daffodils, strangely subdued after her outburst. "Are you all right?" she asked the girl.

Mutely, Caroline nodded, staring into some distant past.

"Rather childish, wasn't I?" she said, frowning as she cleared a few weeds from around the bulbs.

"Not really," May said, taking a seat beside her. "You were upset. Do you want to talk about it?"

The girl stopped fiddling with the dirt for a moment and faced her with sad eyes. "What's to say? I think he is Francis. Somehow, I have no idea how, he is Francis. It seems impossible, but that is what I believe."

May, not to be idle nor make too much of their conversation, pulled on a pair of worn gloves and busily began helping her weed around the fragile golden bulbs.

"Working with the earth always helps clear my mind of troubles," she told the girl as she tugged at a clump of crabgrass. "Doesn't it you?"

"It was my whole life once..." Caroline replied, wistfulness evident in her eyes. "I knew so much. Aunt Jess and I made medicines, perfumes, cleaners..." She laughed a light and airy laugh. "We were always quite pleased with ourselves when we came up with a new concoction. After she died, I always swore I would continue the work she and mother loved so well. I would give back to the world what they had given to me. Now that seems impossible."

"There's still a need for that kind of work, work with nature. Maybe it isn't so impossible," May told her in a positive vein. "Just like your being reunited with your Francis isn't impossible."

Caroline's eyes lit and she turned quickly. "You've said something like that before. Do you really believe it?"

"I've always believed in reincarnation." May smiled, then brushed away a speck of dirt her gloved hand had deposited on her cheek. "Souls move from one path to another, until they've completed their tasks on this earth. Then perhaps, they move to some greater realm."

"My father used to read a lot on the subject," Caroline told her, again staring into the distance. "He and Evan talked about it often. Evan wrote quite a lot about metaphysics, I believe, and was interested in the occult. I think they hoped to find some kind of scientific explanation for it all." She smiled a little. "I used to think they were both a little mad over it."

"But you don't anymore?"

"No. I don't." She gave May her full attention. "I don't know what I think exactly. I don't know what to believe. It seems so very unbelievable. I only know how very much I loved Francis. And how much I want it to be possible."

"I believe sometimes a love between two people is so strong it transcends even death to bring them together again. It's rare when it happens, and it's certainly a miracle, but miracles happen, don't they?"

"And you think this really could have happened with Francis and me?"

May leveled a steady gaze at Caroline. "It doesn't matter what I think. What do *you* think?"

She shrugged and gazed away. "I think I'm afraid, May. Sometimes I'm so afraid I can almost imagine my fear severing me from him forever. I'm afraid of doing the wrong thing. Of making the wrong decision." She angrily pulled an errant blade of crabgrass from the damp earth. "Jake tells me my father was murdered. And I was blamed for his death—because of my disappearance. I'm torn between a need to go back and find out what happened, and to stay with the man I love. And I don't have the means to do either."

Compassion spilled from May's smile. "You have the means, my dear. And only you can decide which is more important. Listen to your heart."

"I wouldn't know where to begin to try and go back. But something feels wrong about the playhouse, so perhaps there is a clue in the diary. But first and foremost, I think I must not abandon Francis. I did that once before. His death was the result."

May's tone turned firm. "You mustn't let fear make your decision for you, Caroline. You must act. You must take the risk. Taking the safe road is never the right choice. Sooner or later your destiny—your real destiny—is going to catch up with you. Be strong enough to let it be your guide, instead of forcibly having its way with you."

Caroline remained silent, considering. The woman hoped she had given the girl the kind of guidance she needed, the right words. Unfortunately, it always came down to this: only she could ultimately decide what to do with her life.

"If it comforts you at all, my dear, I also believe that love always wins in the end. If you follow your heart it will never lead you to the wrong place. Be it 1890 or 2006." May reached over and put both arms around Caroline's still form. "Why not just wait for a few days then? And see how you feel?"

She sighed and leaned into May's embrace. "You are so wonderful," she said. "And you remind me very much of my Aunt Jess. She was always there with good counsel for me. But this...this is almost asking too much. For you to believe me is...it is very special."

She placed a soft kiss on Caroline's forehead. "I've never had very conventional beliefs, honey. Now what do you say we put this aside for now, freshen up a bit, and set off to our work? The work they're paying us for."

* * * *

Jake watched them walk arm-in-arm toward the Manor, still shaking with his uncontrollable combination of anger and fear. He *had* written that poem. Not some man who'd been dead for over a century. Sam watched him closely. "What are you looking at?" He threw a wad of paper at the dog. Sam, who normally would have grabbed it for a game of fetch, got up and left the room. "Great. Now my dog doesn't even want to be around me. So much for man's best friend."

His gaze roamed the empty kitchen, and it dawned on him suddenly they'd never found out what happened to the diary. It must be around here somewhere. He wanted to read the poem Francis Monroe had supposedly written for himself. After a quick search revealed no sign of it, he returned to the living room.

"Damn!" he said aloud after a minute or two. "Books just don't get up and walk away."

He tried to turn his attention back to his own book, much too neglected these day, and spent the morning working on his manuscript. Still, he couldn't seem to shake the loss of the diary. The more he thought about it, the more he had a sneaking suspicion about what might have happened to it, and the thought made him more than a little angry. Only one person had as much interest in Caroline as he did, and that was Mitchell Stanton. But how dare he come sneaking into the gatehouse in the middle of the night? Just because he ran the estate didn't give him the right to come and go in their private quarters.

Finally, Jake decided he'd had enough 'thinking' about the situation and decided it was time to take action. He'd confront the man head-on; at least he could possible gauge from his reaction whether he was involved or not. He headed toward the Manor, resolute, and once more accompanied by Sam.

"So you've forgiven me, have you?" he asked the dog, and Sam licked his hand in reply. The day, sunny and clear, gave him a bit of a lift, even if he wasn't looking forward to the task at hand. He didn't like confrontations, even if it was for a good cause.

A short time later he faced Mitchell across from the older man's desk, fairly sure by his immediate defensiveness that he had indeed taken the diary.

"I have no idea what you're talking about." Mitchell's tone oozed sarcasm and dislike. "But I can tell you this, Mr. Stanton, if you took property from the archives and lost that same property, you are in grave trouble."

"Oh get off it, Johnston. That's exactly where you'd like me to be, isn't it? In grave trouble. No pun intended, I'm sure. I know May told you about the book, and I'm sure you couldn't wait to get your grimy hands on it. So cough it up."

Jake watched as Mitchell twirled a pen around in his hands. "If I did have the book, I certainly would not 'cough it up' for you, as you request. That book belongs to the estate, and in light of that, in the archives."

"And I'm the historian who's writing a book about that estate," Jake reminded him. "I need to have access to all its records."

"I've already given you access to all the records I have." Mitchell bent his head and began to study the open ledger on his desk. "Is there anything else I can do for you?" he asked without looking up.

Jake had already risen and started for the door. "Not today." He made a point of slamming the door on his way out. Nothing to do now but head back to the library in town, try searching the newspapers again. Hopefully he'd find some clue somewhere, to tell him what exactly had happened to the mysterious Caroline Lyndfield. What he'd do with that information, he had no idea.

* * * *

Once Jake had gone, Mitchell rose and locked his office door. He opened a drawer and took out the little book he'd gotten last night. Thank God, he'd gone to the gatehouse after he'd finished with Ruby, just to check on things. When he's seen Jake with the diary, he'd known he better get it and find out what the girl knew about Ludington and her father. Thank God again, there'd been nothing in it about either man. The young Caroline had suspected nothing of her father's insatiable lusts or Evan's part in providing for them. Those secrets were still his alone.

There was, however, one problem he hadn't reckoned on. Francis Monroe. According to Evan's journals, he had merely been waiting for the right moment to make the girl his. They'd been engaged, for heaven's sake. But it suddenly seemed to Mitchell Caroline's claim of the love between her and Francis might actually be true. Had Evan had some hand in that man's death, he wondered? More and more, Mitchell realized Caroline had lived amidst men with uncontrollable lust. Whatever had catapulted her out of that scenario, now she was under his protection. Jake Stanton was not going to interfere with that. It was about time he started planning to deal with him. And May too, in necessary.

Snapping the diary shut, he opened the hidden drawer in his desk and shoved the book inside. Her love for Francis Monroe was certainly an obstacle to be overcome, but overcome it he would. Mitchell would use all he'd learned to make Caroline his and his alone. He might not understand how or why she had come to be here, but however it had happened, she was here. And he intended to see that from now on, she was safe from all harm.

* * * *

May noticed at once that Mitchell was furious. Although Caroline was present, he asked her to step into the hall with him and launched into his tirade at once.

"This time your nephew has gone too far," he told her sharply. "Absconding estate property and then 'misplacing' it. The board will be informed at once. He had no right to take that book from the archives.

None whatsoever. I wouldn't be surprised if he weren't removed from the project entirely."

May drew a long breath and began rearranging papers on her desk. "He meant well, Mitchell. It was my fault as well. I should have made him hand it over to you immediately."

"That you should have. Still, the board must be informed. I wanted you to know my plans." He stared beyond her into the room where Caroline was studying the wall paintings, considering. "I have reason to believe your Jake may have removed some other items of the estate's as well. From my office."

Now May was stunned. What on earth was he talking about? "Jake would never take anything from your office. You know that."

"I know no such thing. In fact, it sounds like just the kind of thing he would do, and I intend to see that it's investigated thoroughly."

Leaving her to stare after him in silence, he turned on his heel and headed back to where Caroline waited. She followed, uncertain what else to do or say.

"Now," he said as the civility returned to his voice. "How's my new tour guide doing her first day on the job?"

Caroline faced Mitchell with a frown. Evidently she had heard a portion of their exchange and wasn't pleased.

"She's doing beautifully," May replied, determined not to let Mitchell's announcement get the better or her. More than likely the man was simply bluffing. "She's gone through two tours with me this morning, and I think she'll be ready to give her first when we re-open tomorrow. She does know a lot. It's really quite remarkable."

"Excellent," the man said, with a rapt smile on Caroline. "And you haven't forgotten my dinner invitation tomorrow night? You did say you'd spend time with me, you know, and I'm missing our chats together already."

May watched uneasily as the girl blushed a little. Why did she have the feeling that Caroline was incredibly uncomfortable in Mitchell's presence? And why did the girl seem to be avoiding his eyes?

"No," Caroline replied with a nervous frown. "I haven't forgotten. What time would you like me to be there?"

"Well," he said, puffing up, "I thought you could leave here a little early to freshen up, then I'll drive over and pick you up about 7:00. How does that sound? You don't think you'll be too tired after your first full day of work."

Caroline smiled and May thought perhaps she imagined the earlier discomfort. "It sounds wonderful. And I'm sure I'll be fine. I'm really feeling completely like myself now. Whoever that may be."

"Excellent," he smiled. "I'll see you now."

After Mitchell headed back toward his office, Caroline sat down and drew a long breath. "Don't you want to go?" May asked.

Caroline looked up. "I don't mind really. He has been so kind to me. But I always feel a little...strange...with him."

"In what way?" May asked, taking a seat next to her.

"It's difficult to explain. Oppressed somehow...afraid."

May reflected on their conversation that morning. If it was possible for Francis to be here in the form of Jake, what about the others? May did not believe an evil person could be reincarnated, but what about the evil itself? Could Mitchell have something to do with the terror Caroline sensed?

May realized how very little they knew about William Lyndfield or his eccentric friend Evan Ludington. Could some tragic event from the past be drawing them all together again? She shook her head to clear it. Time travel. Reincarnation. Lives and deaths intertwined. She believed it all, but she'd had enough for one day. Mitchell could close up shop; that's why he made the big bucks. The last tour had come and gone and she needed some fresh air and mindless activity.

Rising, she took Caroline's hand and pulled the girl up from the couch. "C'mon," she told her. "We've done enough and talked enough about all this for today. Let's go shopping."

Smiling at the pastime that apparently could cross all lines of time, Caroline followed her friend from the room.

CHAPTER 16

They know not I knew thee,
Who knew thee too well...
Lord Byron

Jake shoved his chair back from the microfiche machine and rubbed his eyes. He must've looked at thousands of pages of microfilm today alone and his head warned him to stop now before he lost his eyesight completely. When he'd gotten here just after lunch, he hadn't even known what he was looking for. But there had to be something. Some evidence, some clue, something to unlock the Lyndfield family's mysterious past. Something historical to help him understand the bizarre present.

He remembered a book he'd read once about a woman who claimed to be the lost princess Anastasia, youngest daughter of Czar Nicholas II. Supposedly, she escaped the massacre at Yekaterinburg only to have her identity rejected time and again by both friends and family—yet since that time science had proven that Anna Anderson couldn't have been the Grand Duchess Anastasia. People wanted hard facts and hard evidence before they allowed history to be re-written. Specific answers to questions which sometimes had none. They also wanted fairy tales to come true, not end unhappily like Anastasia's life did. In the end, things had ended badly.

So what *facts* did Jake have to unravel this mystery? Caroline Lyndfield had disappeared in 1890, never to be seen or heard from again. The papers all carried detailed accounts of her father's murder and her disappearance. Her father had been stabbed to death in the playhouse. Granted, that in itself proved interesting—that the Caroline he knew was terrified of going inside the playhouse, almost as if she knew something terrible had happened there. Was it recorded history she knew, or actual experience?

Jake rubbed his chin thoughtfully and stared out the open library window. It was a sunny cloudless March day, filled with breeze and birdsong, and he wished he were out with Sam taking a long walk instead of sitting here in a dark and dusty old building trying to piece together a hundred-year-old mystery. He picked up his notepad and studied the scrawls he'd made there. What could he have missed? It all seemed so straightforward. Beyond the murder of William Lyndfield, it was pretty much the usual parade of births and deaths, with an occasional crime or disappearance here and there. Life, pretty much.

"Are you finding what you need?" a feminine voice asked. Jake looked up to find the incredibly attractive librarian he'd seen before bending suggestively over his shoulder. He grinned.

The young woman wore a short, low-cut dress and thick blonde hair fell across her shoulder and rested seductively against the bare skin of her chest. Her cherry-red mouth, full and sensual, enticed and her movement sent a waft of heavy musky smelling perfume every now and then. Opium, he'd bet. Jake knew by the way she leaned toward him and brushed his arm slightly she was definitely available—and interested.

He was just about to begin the now familiar game, when suddenly another face came to mind as it seemed to frequently these days. A face with a slow smile that more often than not was pursed into a pout, with wide innocent eyes that glistened like emeralds nestled in a treasure chest. A face surrounded by wild and swirling tresses of burnished golden brown. Caroline. He wanted her, not this woman.

"No," he told the librarian with a slight frown. Then abruptly, he realized maybe she could help him, though not in the way she might like.

"Actually," he said just as she was about to turn away, "You could do me a favor." He held out the notepad on which he'd been writing. "I'm doing some research for a book. I've been sitting here all day looking for a common thread. Some kind of link to solve an old mystery."

She held out her hand. "I'm Wendy Jordan," she said.

Jake shook her hand. "Jake Stanton."

"So you're writing about the Lyndfields?" she asked after a cursory glance at his notes.

"Yeah. I've been commissioned to write their family chronicles."

Wendy gave him a full smile, broadcasting an either near-perfect or very expensive set of white teeth. "I'd think Mr. Johnston would be able to help you with this. According to our director, he used to be the library's most ardent patron." The young woman pointed toward an overweight aging woman in a dull gray dress sitting at the reference desk. "Of course, Mrs. Rudley could be biased since I'm positive she's had a crush on him for years."

Jake laughed. "I wish her luck. He's one cold fish." He turned back to her. "You say he used to spend a lot of time in here? Researching the family?"

She nodded as she pulled up a chair at his table. "That was a few years ago though. Before I came. But Mrs. Rudley talks about him a lot. I think she misses his visits."

Looking over his shoulder, Wendy examined his notes. Jake could smell her perfume, sweet and flowery, too heady. He thought of the fresh meadowy smell of Caroline and an ache began to develop somewhere deep in the core of him.

After several minutes the young woman next to him looked up. "It's quite a mystery, huh?"

Jake let out a frustrated sigh. "Yep, it's that, all right. Do you see anything? Maybe something that didn't directly have anything to do with the Lyndfields at all?"

"Not really, but I have an idea. Come with me." She motioned to her lips with one finger. "Quietly."

Jake followed her behind the stacks and round toward the back of the library. She slipped through a partially open door into a room that obviously housed reference materials.

Wendy opened a file cabinet that looked like something straight out of a forties' detective novel and removed two large manila envelopes. "I think you might find this interesting," she whispered conspiratorially. "But you'll have to be quick. If Mrs. Rudley discovers I've let you in here, she'll be furious."

Opening the first folder, Jake let out a whistle. "Wow!" was all he could say.

"Yeah," Wendy acknowledged. "They're Mr. Johnston's records. Evidently he was very secretive about it all and even swore Mrs. Rudley to secrecy, but she couldn't bear to throw away anything he touched. She even Xeroxed some of the information she found for him and kept copies. No telling what you'll find in there." She eyed the door a little nervously. "She'd die if she knew I let you see this."

"My lips are sealed. This is great, Wendy."

"Well, good luck. I hope you find something helpful. I'll go out and keep watch. If anyone's coming, I'll whistle."

Jake, already deep into the notes, gave her a silent nod. "Thanks a million," he said without looking up.

After she'd gone, Jake quickly perused the files, which consisted mostly of Xeroxed news clippings. He was amazed!

Here, laid out side-by-side, he the pattern presented itself at once. Three deaths and three disappearances in a five-year period. All young girls fifteen or younger—most a lot younger, only the last was fifteen. Of course all had occurred with seemingly normal explanations. One drowned, one committed suicide, one had a heart attack; one ran away from a bad home, one eloped with some unknown beau, one went back to live with her family in another state—after the disappearance of her mistress. That last intrigued him the most—Nan Callahan. Jake remembered he'd seen a story about her before; she too had disappeared mysteriously, and she'd been Caroline Lyndfield's maid.

Because of all the confusion and uproar over William's death and his daughter's disappearance, Nan hadn't actually been reported missing until a week later. But then it was quickly assumed she'd gone home to her family. Jake wondered if anyone had known that for certain.

Obviously, Mitchell had felt these deaths were somehow connected. Why else would he have gathered them together like this? But what did they—aside from Nan—have to do with the Lyndfields? Jake jotted down the names of the girls on his notepad. At least it was something to start with. He remembered the odd reaction he'd gotten from Caroline when he asked about Nan. Could she have known about these other young girls? He'd have to ask her. She seemed to be a fount of information about everything else. He might as well take advantage of it, suspect though it might be.

The second folder proved something more of a mystery. It contained photocopies with several marked passages from a journal entitled "Paranormal Phenomena of the 19th Century." Where had he heard that title before? He'd seen it somewhere recently, he felt sure of it.

Before he could read any further however, he heard Wendy's sharp whistle. *Damn*, he thought as he'd shoved the folders back into the file cabinet. Still, he'd gotten a lot more than he'd expected.

Wendy waited like an expectant sentry as he slipped from the room. The hefty Mrs. Rudley was just rounding the corner. "Are you helping this gentleman, Wendy?" she asked suspiciously.

"Of course, Mrs. Rudley." The young woman gave her a dutiful smile then winked at Jake once she'd moved away.

"Thanks, Wendy," he said as soon as the other woman had gone, "you have been very helpful."

She gave him a wide smile and placed a hand on his forearm. "It was my pleasure, Jake," she said in a husky voice. "If there's anything else I can do..."

He tried not to focus on her lips. "There is, actually." He handed her the piece of paper on which he'd written the name of the journal. "Could you copy the pages for me from this book? I think they may be quite important to my research."

Skeptical, she asked again, "Why don't you just ask Mr. Johnston about all this? Surely that would be simpler than all this sneaking around?"

"I can't ask Mr. Johnston for the same reason you can't let Mrs. Rudley know I've seen those files."

She gave a soft acknowledging laugh. "Understood. Okay, I'll do it. Why don't you come back later and pick them up?"

She followed him toward the large open doors of the building, obviously reluctant to part with his company. "If you need anything else," she said leaning close and gazing meaningfully into his eyes as Jake stepped out onto the pavement, "please don't hesitate to call."

Jake gave her a wide smile. *Probably not a good idea*, he thought, and turning, ran directly into Caroline and May.

Caroline bit her lip at the sight of Jake and the beautiful young woman who was obviously flirting with him. Flirting much more boldly than women of Caroline's 19th century would have dared. And he, it appeared, was eagerly flirting back.

"Oops," he said, a guilty blush creeping across his face as he stumbled into step next to the two them. "Fancy meeting you ladies here. What's up?"

"We decided to take a break and do a bit of shopping," May explained with an impatient turn of the head. "Caroline has a dinner engagement tomorrow evening and wanted to look her best." She evidently was not pleased with Jake's behavior either, Caroline inferred.

Jake's gaze shot instantly in her direction. "Dinner? And what dinner engagement might that be, Miss Lyndfield?"

Caroline's ire rose at the emphasis he placed on Miss Lyndfield. He just couldn't let go of the insinuation that she was lying. And how dare he question her plans. After he'd just been carrying on shamelessly himself.

"If it's any of your business," she replied, cool and creamy as a bowl of sherbet, "Mr. Johnston—Mitchell—has invited me to dine at his home. And I have accepted."

Tight-lipped, Jake fell silently into step beside them. "Well," he said after eying the shopping bags, "Isn't that nice? And you've been away from him for so long now. Looks like you've bought a lovely new outfit to wear. Aren't you spending your earnings a little quickly?"

Inwardly, Caroline flinched. She did hate the idea of May buying her things, but for the moment there did not seem to be any way around it. Of course she intended to reimburse her new friend fully once she received her first wages. But Jake had definitely struck a nerve here.

"Never mind," May said, casting an angry look at Jake.

He lowered his head, sufficiently chastised. "Okay, truce then. If you two ladies are free for lunch, it would be my pleasure to have your company."

May turned to Caroline with a silent question, leaving it to the girl to decide.

"Oh, come on," Jake said, linking arms between them. "At least let me buy you lunch. You can't stay angry with me forever, you know."

Sighing, Caroline nodded her assent and within ten minutes they were seated around a table outside a small cafe. "So what have you been up to all morning?" May asked Jake after they'd ordered lunch. "Besides the flirtation?"

"Research," he said, his eyes never straying from Caroline's face.

"It certainly *looked* interesting," the young woman replied with a hint of sarcasm.

Jake smiled and leaned toward her. "I think I detect a note of jealously in your voice, Miss Lyndfield. I didn't realize I'd made such an impression."

"You've certainly done that." She took a long sip from the glass of lemonade she'd ordered.

"So did you find out anything interesting?" May interrupted, obviously tired of their bickering. "About the Lyndfields?"

"As a matter of fact, I did."

May let out an exasperated breath. "Well are you or are you not going to share it?"

He held up a hand, laughing. "Okay, okay. I don't know what it means exactly, but I found some interesting facts. Wendy did, that is."

"Wendy?" Caroline asked, feigning innocence.

"Yeah, Wendy. She's the librarian."

"And they were?" May prodded.

"They were great," Jake answered with a tease.

May slapped at him. "The facts?"

"Oh, those." Jake drew a breath and took his time. "Well, actually the facts were all in two folders of information about the estate. Information complied by Mitchell Johnston."

May gasped. "Mitchell!"

"Yep, that's right. It shouldn't surprise you, May. You know he always thought he'd write the family history."

"So what did you find out? What did he find out?" May asked.

"Well, I never would have caught it myself, because it all seemed so normal. But collected in those folders, it does seem to form some kind of pattern."

Caroline leaned forward with interest as he continued.

"It appears there were several deaths and disappearances on or around Lyndfield Estate—within a five-year period. All relatively young girls."

A chill coursed down Caroline's spine. Some thought stirred deep within her that she did not wish to waken. But it was too late. Jake had already done this. For her. She had asked him to find out what he could, and she couldn't change her mind now about wanting to know the truth. Whatever that truth might be...

"So what was strange about the deaths?" May asked.

Jake kept his eyes trained on Caroline's face and somehow she knew he was trying to carefully formulate his words so as not to distress her. He'd come that far, at least.

"I'm not sure yet. Like I said, they all seemed to have natural enough causes. But why would Mitchell have collected them in the file if they weren't related to the Lyndfield history in some way?"

Caroline clung to the tablecloth. The arrival of their meal temporarily halted the further revelations and she thanked God for it. She didn't want to know. She couldn't bear to know. But she knew.

Several moments passed while May and Jake settled into their meal. Caroline picked at her own, finding her appetite suddenly gone.

"You aren't eating, dear," May noticed. "Is something wrong?"

Caroline placed her fork down on the table and directed her gaze toward Jake. Her voice trembled slightly as she spoke. "You asked me the other day about Nan. It *was* Nan, wasn't it? Nan Callahan? She was one of them, wasn't she?"

His face shot up from his own plate. *Bingo!*

She must have read his thoughts, for she shook her head and brought the corner of her napkin to her eyes. "I had a feeling something had happened to her," she said simply.

"Well what exactly do you think happened to her then?" Jake asked.

"I do not know. I only had a feeling."

"So what did happen, Jake?" May asked.

"She disappeared. Must'a been about the same time Caroline did, only no one noticed right away with the murder and Caroline's disappearance. Some assumed she went back to her family in another state. Or perhaps with her mistress?"

"She didn't," Caroline said.

Suddenly Jake believed her. It hit him like a ton of bricks but it was true. He didn't know how or why and he didn't really want to pursue his feelings about it at this point. He just knew she was telling the truth. Nan did not run away with Caroline. But maybe Caroline did indeed run away. He doubted that as well. Because his gut told him now that somehow, some way, Caroline Lyndfield—*the* Caroline Lyndfield—was sitting across the table from him now.

"Okay," he said, trying to maintain a calm his pounding heart didn't feel. "Then what we have are several young women who either died or disappeared. Now all we have to do is figure out how they were connected to the Lyndfield?"

Caroline's eyes met his with gratitude. She seemed to sense his acceptance—at least for the moment.

"Just supposing," May said, watching them carefully, "Just

supposing our Caroline is who she says she is, Jake. Maybe the other young women disappeared the same way she did. Maybe it was some kind of experiment."

"But what about the deaths?" Jake asked.

"Maybe they were too. Or maybe they saw something they shouldn't have," May suggested.

Remembering the contents of the other file, Jake faced Caroline with purpose. "What kind of experiments were Evan and your father conducting? Did they ever talk to you about time travel? About the paranormal?"

He couldn't believe he was actually going along with this. But somehow it felt right. Just like holding her in his arms had felt right. "Remember all that stuff on the occult in Evan's library at Mitchell's? Could that have been part of it?"

"They never spoke much about their work," Caroline told him. "They both had a great interest in the metaphysics, so I always assumed their experiments might have something to do with that." She drew a deep breath. "I think Nan was murdered. I feel certain she died a violent death."

Jake brushed her arm with a gentle touch. "Were you there?"

"I think I was. I know something terrible happened." Her eyes begged him for understanding.

"And you think it has something to do with the playhouse, don't you?" he asked with tenderness. She had suffered so much. Kind words were the least he could offer her now.

Jake saw tears forming in her eyes and once more he instinctively knew she'd had enough for one day. There was so much more he wanted to ask her. So many things he needed to know—to understand. But there would be time for questions later. And hopefully, more answers.

May evidently caught the drift of his thinking for she cheerfully suggested they talk about something else, and promptly proceeded into a lengthy description of the two new dresses Caroline had bought and which would be best for her dinner date the next evening.

Jake watched them in silence, trying not to give away his irritation. The thought of Caroline spending an entire evening alone with Johnston chapped him immensely. He'd seen the way the older man looked at her and he didn't like it one bit. Then abruptly, he had an idea that might make it worthwhile.

"Caroline," he said, excitement rising in his voice, "maybe it is a good idea for you to have dinner with Johnston."

He saw he'd struck a nerve with her again. For someone who claimed to be a Victorian, she certainly had a fierce independent streak.

She did not like to be told what to do.

"Look," he went on, "No one knows more about the Lyndfields than Mitchell." He shot May an apologetic look but she waved him ahead with acknowledgement. "Maybe he'll tell you something he wouldn't tell us."

"And how exactly am I supposed to find out what he knows?" Caroline asked.

"Ask him," and then with emphasis he added, "Tell him you are. See how he reacts. He's obviously infatuated with you. Talk to him about the experiments and see if he knows anything about them. About the deaths... He'll never tell me or May, but he just might open up to you."

"So you want me to play spy for you?" she asked slowly.

He let out an exasperated breath. "No, damn it...just ask questions. This is your ball game, isn't it?"

May joined her plea with Jake's. "You needn't feel you're spying on him, Caroline. After all, you are working on the estate now and you need to know as much as possible. I've always felt Mitchell knew more about the family than he said. He used to drop little hints about family secrets, but after he found out he wouldn't be writing their history, he never mentioned it again. Jake's right. He might tell you."

Caroline softened. "But he's been so kind to me. I feel it would be using him."

Jake tossed down his napkin and sat back in the chair, arms crossed. "Look do you want to know the truth about your father or not?"

She took her time answering his question, her eyes staring into the distance, perhaps to a past only she could truly see. "I want to know," she replied. "I think..."

CHAPTER 17

Long, long shall I rue thee,
Too deeply to tell.
Lord Byron

Caroline couldn't remember ever having such a case of nerves. As if having a secluded dinner with the eccentric Mitchell Johnston wasn't unsettling enough, now she was expected to play the parts of enchantress and spy as well. What next, she wondered? All day she'd played out various scenarios that evening. Luckily Mitchell hadn't come in to the Manor office today, pleading other business to attend to. He'd spoken with Caroline on the phone, briefly, to remind her he still planned to pick her up at seven this evening.

Now, only minutes away from that time, she slipped the flowery spring dress May had helped her choose over her head and studied her reflection in the long mirror behind the bathroom door. The dress boasted a color assortment of peaches and greens and, as May told her in the shop, did much to highlight her skin color, now warmed by time spent in the sun without a dreaded bonnet. The dress itself wasn't too short; she'd insisted on having something at least mid-calf. Her attitudes about clothing hadn't changed entirely, though she did love these loose and flowing 21st-century garments. They offered such incomparable comfort and convenience.

Typically, her hair was a mess of tangled curls, so she refrained from using the hairbrush and tied it back simply with a green ribbon. Next to her shoes lay the new pair of "pantyhose" May had insisted she buy to wear with the dress. Evidently these were stockings with which one need not wear underwear or garters. Caroline ripped open the package and took out the fine nylon material. She held them in front of her and laughed aloud—amazing the things this century had thought of! Standing next to the bed, she tried to roll them up but found she couldn't manage her foot, the panty, and standing all at the same time. Frustrated, she sat down and attempted to put her foot in again. The stretchy material twisted and clung to her leg. Completely frustrated, she threw them to the ground. *"In Christ's name,"* she said aloud, immediately regretting her profanity. Hardly Christ's fault she was in this predicament.

"Are you all right, my dear?" May queried from the doorway.

"No, I'm not," Caroline replied vehemently, holding up the twisted pair of leggings. "These....I do not like them at all!"

May laughed outright as she entered the room. "They're quite comfortable once you get the hang of it." Crossing to the bed, she took the hose from Caroline and showed her how to roll up the panty with her hands and then pull the legs on one at a time.

After another try, Caroline managed to get her new peach legs on straight. She grinned proudly. "Now I see. It's not so complicated after all, is it?"

May hugged her in typical motherly fashion. "Not so very. But I can see why you might have been frustrated. Especially when you're nervous and in a hurry." She surveyed Caroline up and down like an approving parent. "You're quite lovely. Too bad it's not Jake you're going to be spending the evening with."

Caroline blushed like a naughty schoolgirl. She'd been thinking the same thing but wasn't about to admit it. She moved toward the window and stared out at the rapidly falling twilight. She wouldn't give Jake Stanton the pleasure of knowing she actually enjoyed spending time with him. Even if her reincarnation theory proved to be correct, much had changed in the man since she'd known and loved him. Right now she wondered if love really could prevail over centuries of time.

"Give him time," May said, almost as if reading her mind. "He'll come round."

Caroline turned back to face her friend with a wistful smile. "Do you really think so? Do you really think there's a chance he'll believe?"

May came to stand beside her and together they gazed out on the evening like old comrades reminiscing about days gone by. "I believe if something's meant to be it will be, Caroline. Why cross centuries if not to reclaim something you lost before its time was due?"

"I feel more and more certain that must be what has happened," Caroline said. "I am being given another chance to prove my love. To be worthy of it."

May squeezed her waist and Caroline allowed the older woman's love to permeate her being. "You've always been worthy of it, my dear," May assured her. "You only need prove that to yourself. Maybe this is simply where you were meant to be. I think—oddly enough—you may have a lot to share with our world."

"Really?" Caroline looked amazed. "Me?"

"Of course—your knowledge of plants for one thing. People in this day and age have gotten so far away from nature and its remedies. Here you are—someone young and energetic, someone who knew their secrets in a time when those secrets were more accepted, when we hadn't allowed science free rein over our lives. You can share these things with today's young people. They don't need to know how you came by your information: they only need someone with enthusiasm to

153

share it with them."

"I certainly would love to do that. I miss my gardening. I miss healing."

"Which reminds me," May said abruptly, "some brochures came for you in the mail today. From the EPA and also, there's one from Ellon Bach."

Caroline smiled with anticipation. "Jake must have called about them. EPA must be the environmental group he mentioned, but this Ellon Bach isn't familiar."

Arm in arm, they moved as one toward the open door. "Ellon Bach," May told her, "is a manufacturer of flower remedies. *I* called about that one. When Jake mentioned your interest in plants and healing, I thought you might like to learn more about them."

Caroline spun about with excitement. "That must be the same Dr. Bach who was researching the medicinal flowers in England in the late 1800s. I only heard about him because he and Aunt Jess met once. She had my mother's love of plants and gardening and was intrigued by the notion flowers had healing powers for the emotions. I would love to see how far they've progressed in their research."

"Quite far," May replied assuredly as they entered the living room. "I've used them for years." She nodded her head in Jake's direction, who sat observing them somewhat sullenly as they approached. "But I'll tell you more about all that later," she whispered.

May paraded Caroline in front of Jake like a child dressed up for her first special outing. "Well, what do you think?"

He studied her up and down, frowning. "Maybe you overdid it just a little. After all, it's only Mitchell. He's an old man."

May gave Caroline a knowing look. "Humph," she snorted, jerking her head in his direction. "Men. I hope you get a more complimentary reaction from Mitchell, my dear."

Inwardly, Caroline shivered a little, her case of nerves suddenly returning. What if she said something tonight to give herself away? Could she play this little game of intrigue?

The doorbell's chimes interrupted her thoughts. Jake, up in a flash, put one finger to his lips and headed toward the kitchen, apparently not wanting Mitchell to know he had been in the room.

"Hello, Mitchell," May was saying as Caroline turned to face her dinner date. He had dressed for the occasion—an elegant black suit and silk tie—even though they only planned to dine at his home.

"Good evening, May," he returned graciously as he slipped into the room. "Ah, my dearest Caroline...you are breathtaking."

She smiled at his exaggeration. She knew she did not look 'breathtaking.' The compliment was nice all the same, but did nothing to salve the guilt of her forthcoming subterfuge.

"Well, my dear," Mitchell went on, oblivious to the silence on Caroline's part, "We really should be going. I've asked Mrs. Henderson to have our dinner on at 8:00, which gives us just enough time for cocktails. We could have walked, but I brought the car as I thought you might be tired."

A few moments later they slid down the long drive in Mitchell's sleek black vehicle. Caroline watched the scenery roll past with real interest. Though Lyndfield Estate boasted one hundred acres of farm and woodland in 1890, she had no idea how much of the property might have been sold or given away since that time.

Once again, Evan's Ludington's house was not a welcoming sight with its stark gray stone blocks, straight lines, and almost windowless facade. She dreaded going back in, but stuffed down her fear. The house's owner was long gone, and she'd convinced herself she had nothing to fear from the doting man at her side.

Mitchell stopped the car and came around to help Caroline out. His hand was hot and sticky as it clasped hers possessively, and she held back a shudder. Taking several deep breaths in an attempt to calm herself, she followed him to the front door.

The malevolent Mrs. Henderson was nowhere in sight, and Mitchell lead Caroline straight to the drawing room, stiflingly hot as before. She tried to draw some deep breaths, but there seemed to be little air available.

Mitchell, noticing her discomfort, assisted Caroline in removing the sweater draped across her shoulders.

Did she imagine it, or did his fingertips linger on her bare skin just a bit longer than necessary? Suddenly the heat and heaviness of the air and the intensity of Mitchell's gaze overcame her with a wave of dizziness. She clutched the back of a nearby sofa.

Mitchell was next to her instantly. "You're not well. I knew the work at the estate would be too much for you."

Caroline put up a protesting hand. "I'm fine. Truly. Just a bit warm, that's all."

"Of course," Mitchell said, "I shouldn't have asked Ruby to lay the fire." He motioned toward the open door. "I'm sure it's much cooler in the garden. Why don't you wait out there while I prepare us a before-dinner drink?"

With scarcely less apprehension, Caroline stepped out into the night.

* * * *

"Well," May said to Jake after Caroline and Mitchell were gone, "I guess now we wait."

"What do you mean, 'we wait'?" Jake had already started pacing. "You don't think I'm going to let her spend the evening alone in that lecherous fool's company, do you? We have work to do."

The older woman stared at him, aghast. "You don't mean you're going to spy on them?"

"That's exactly what I'm going to do. And you're going to search his office."

"What?"

Jake placed both hands on his aunt's shoulders and stared pointedly into her eyes. "We have to make the most of this chance, May. I need your help."

"Since when have you suddenly become the lady's knight in shining armor?" she teased.

He dropped his hands and shrugged. "Isn't that what you wanted me to be? Lancelot du Lac. So...here he is. Now are you going to help me slay dragons or not?"

"So while I'm playing Watson to your Sherlock, what is it exactly that I'm supposed to be looking for?"

Jake embraced her with a big bear hug. "That's the spirit." He handed May the Xeroxed pages he'd picked up from Wendy just before the library closed. "Anything to do with this."

May cocked an eyebrow in surprise. "'Paranormal Phenomena in the 19th Century?' What's this all about?"

"I don't know. That's why I want you to look around his office. See if you can find anything. Notes we don't know about, books on the subject. Anything." Jake rubbed his forehead. "Something's very odd here, May. Something weird was going on at Lyndfield, and I'd bet money Mitchell Johnston knows what it was."

"So you do believe her, don't you?"

"You might say I'm coming round."

May wrapped motherly arms around Jake and kissed his cheek. "I love you," she told him. "I'm proud of you."

He held up a hand in protest, not wanting her to go all woo-woo on him. "Don't go too far, May. I believe something. But I haven't sorted out what it is yet."

"Don't play tough with me, young man. That might work on Caroline, but I'm on to you." She pointed to her chest. "You're feeling something, aren't you?"

He laughed. "Right-oh. I'm feeling something, all right. I'm feeling like Johnston's been gone five minutes too long with Caroline. And my knightly blood is telling me to get to work. Okay?"

Like a pair of mischievous children on their own secret mission, they headed for the front door.

* * * *

Mitchell watched with longing as Caroline stepped into the evening. She was here. His for now, and soon his forever. Turning back to the bar, he poured himself a whiskey neat, then set about preparing Caroline's drink. He knew from Evan's diaries that she liked sweet drinks, so he mixed a white Russian with Kailua and the cream he'd asked Ruby to bring in earlier. Ruby had become quite a treasure to him. She would do as he requested and ask no questions of her own. Thank God he'd been around to help the woman's son out of a jam with the law years ago. Too bad he wouldn't need her services much longer. Once Caroline was his, he could put such lust aside. He would finally have everything he'd ever wanted.

He opened the top drawer of the buffet, took out a small brown vial, and poured the thick liquid into Caroline's drink. He couldn't afford to take any chances tonight—he'd have to use the drug to accomplish his goals.

Stirring his concoction, he then turned toward the open door leading out into the garden.

"Here you are, my dear. This should revive you a bit." Mitchell handed Caroline the milky white drink and watched as she took a slow sip. "Do you like it?" he asked eagerly.

"It's quite good," she said, smiling as she took a sip. His being so nice to her made things harder. She took another drink from the glass, puckering slightly at the bitter under-taste.

"Are you feeling better now?" Mitchell asked.

"Oh, yes. I think I just needed some cool air. I'm fine now." Caroline's eyes scanned the garden, dimly lit with several gas lanterns. Too bad the garden would again go neglected. Again, she felt the intensity of his stare as he continued to watch her silently. *What does he want from me*, she asked herself?

"Does it bother you that Evan lived here, Caroline?" Something in his husky voice wrapped itself around her heart and demanded reply.

"Yes," she said dully. "A little."

"You knew all about him, didn't you? All his secrets?"

Caroline searched his eyes for some sign of warmth. Dark fathomless eyes, and in that instant they reminded her very much of Evan's. They pulled and sucked at her like dark leeches sucking life's blood from their helpless victims.

Mitchell leaned close and whispered in her ear with alcohol-tainted breath. "I need you to tell me about Evan, Caroline. About you and Evan." He touched her hand briefly. His hands, which had been hot and clammy earlier, were now ice-cold. She shivered and for the moment, he dropped the subject. "Now you're getting cold. We should go inside."

With reluctance, she rose and followed him back into the drawing room, her glass still in hand. Somehow, she'd felt safe in the darkness. There in the drawing room, she feared some nameless horror lay in wait for her.

* * * *

"Damn," Jake said aloud after Caroline and Mitchell had gone back inside. Out here, he'd been able to hear their entire conversation and could keep an eye on them as well. Now, however, all he could do was wait.

He watched their shadows silhouetted against the curtained window. At least he could tell if the lecher laid a hand on her. And if he did, Jake wasn't about to wait to be invited inside.

Their plan seemed to be working better than he'd expected. Caroline hadn't even had to bring the subject of Evan up. Mitchell had done it for her. But what had he meant by 'you know all his secrets?' Did Mitchell really believe in this time-travel theory? If only he were inside; Jake could hear the rest of it. He looked toward the window. Caroline sat motionless; Mitchell paced back and forth in front of her. When would they go in to dinner, Jake wondered? Or had that merely been a ploy to get her here?

Absentmindedly, he stripped a leaf from a nearby shrub. As he ran a finger across the glossy fiber of the plant, the scene before him shifted and changed. Jake fought the change, but seemed powerless to prevent the swelling tide of memory that swept over him like a violent sea.

They had been in the greenhouse—the glass intact, the steel moldings shiny and new. She stood like a gypsy, surrounded by a forest of deep green, barefoot, with the last rays of the sun catching the red highlights in her hair and casting a rosy glow on her ivory cheeks. She didn't know he was there. She worked, and for a time he merely watched in silence as her slender hands cut and pruned the plants before her. He needed no words. Love burst like a song from his heart.

At last, he moved slightly and she saw him. She smiled with her eyes as they met his and held out a dirty but beautiful hand.

"I've just been grafting these two varieties of roses. The flowers should produce some interesting treatments." She spoke to him as he came close enough to take her hand. "What do you think?"

"I think you're beautiful," he said, bringing her palm, dirt and all, to his mouth. "I think I love you."

Laughter light as fairy chimes spilled from her lips, and she came eagerly into his arms. The warmth of her permeated the fabric of his shirt. Her full breasts caressed his chest; he longed to yank away her clothes and lay her down—a flower among the flowers. He lowered his head to hers and claimed the kiss he'd been aching for moments earlier.

"Do you love me?" he asked.

"More than anything," she murmured between mouthfuls of his kiss.

"You'd do anything for me? Anything?"

"Of course." She smiled once more and with her smile lit even the most remote core of his being.

"Caroline..." he said, knowing he meant to ask something of her. Something important.

Then as suddenly as she had come, she was gone. Her warmth. Her love, and light magical laughter. Everything. He remained there, alone. Under the shattered glass and rusted steel of the dead greenhouse. How he'd gotten here he had no idea. Shivering in the cool night air, Jake glanced down at his watch. Nine-thirty. Two hours since he'd been at Mitchell's, and he had no idea where the time had gone. He only knew one thing. He was here—and Caroline was alone with Mitchell Johnston.

He had to get back there. Fast.

CHAPTER 18

And the eyes of the sleepers waxed deadly and chill...
Lord Byron

Mitchell slammed the book in his hands with frustration and tossed it aside. He'd followed its instructions to the letter—the exact dosage of the herbal potion, the precise verbal phrasing, the sands of the hourglass on the table in front of them—but to no avail. Caroline appeared to have no affection for Evan Ludington or knowledge of his experiments. Question after question only produced confused responses from her. But surely Evan would have confided what he was doing to the woman he was about to marry? Even if she had been in love with another, he hadn't known that secret. He knew it now though, and the voice pounded furiously at his head, desperate to get out.

"If you want her back so badly, why don't you just tell me how to send her?" he demanded of it. That silenced the voice, and for the first time he wondered if perhaps Evan himself wasn't sure how to get Caroline back. Perhaps that's why he was seeking answers from her as to how she got her.

The combination of the drug and hypnosis had helped proved certainly proved helpful in confirming Caroline's identity, if nothing else. She knew intimate details about the Lyndfield family that could only have come from first-hand, personal experience. But she apparently had no knowledge about her father's lecherous appetites. Understandably, that secret had been well protected. He studied the girl closely, still sitting upright as royalty in the chair across from him. Reaching out a lined hand, he stroked her cheek. Skin soft as an infant's. Her blank eyes gazed out at nothing. Mitchell trailed a finger down her neck then across her breastbone to where the delicate fabric of her dress began. Stopping at a tiny green button, he toyed with it, remembering the way her mouth had tasted the day he'd kissed her. How he wanted her now...now. They both wanted her... But still, it was too soon.

A blast of frigid air struck him and Mitchell turned toward the fire, wondering why the evening had suddenly gone cold. The flames still hissed and crackled in the grate, but icy tendrils seemed to be creeping their way throughout his body. He shivered, intending to move closer to the heat.

Then, for an instant, he caught sight of himself and Caroline reflected in the mirror behind the chair where she sat. Auburn curls crowned her head and next to it he saw his own face, aged and frowning. Then he saw something else—the red crescent outlined against his temple, now blood-red and angry-looking like a devil's mark. He put a finger to it, then pulled back quickly at the sting of his touch. Where had it come from, he wondered? Why wasn't it going away? Perhaps he should have a doctor look at it.

He rubbed his hands together, trying to rid them of the frosty tingling in them. Caroline looked warm enough, like a breath of summer almost. Her skin glowed golden with just a slight flush of red. Mitchell put his hand toward her again and the ice in his fingertips thawed slightly. He drew his own chair closer to hers and rested his knee against her leg. Heat began to permeate him at the contact point and spread itself throughout his limb. Perhaps now he could free himself from this near-frozen stupor!

Drawing his breath in and out heavily, he once more put his finger to the button at her neckline. It slipped loose with a quick fluid motion, as did the next, revealing full cleavage pressing against her lacy brassiere. The cold receded and was replaced with heat—a heat more penetrating than any he'd ever known. White heat. He touched the pale skin of her breast and thought he felt a slight shiver beneath his hand. Could he arouse her this way? Would she respond?

His hand slipped further, and he groaned as his fingers made contact with the fragile tip of her nipple. Mitchell leaned forward and drew in a deep breath of her. She smelled of sex. He wanted her more than he'd ever wanted a woman in his life. Why not now, he asked himself? *Now, right now.*

* * * *

Quite pleased with herself, May slipped out of the big house and carefully locked the door. She'd found exactly what Jake was looking for. At least she hoped it was what he was looking for... She also hoped Mitchell didn't miss the file she'd taken out of his desk. From what little she'd been able to make out in the dark, she'd discovered handwritten notes concerning paranormal phenomena and some type of experiment. What kind of notes, she didn't know yet.

"May!"

Startled, she turned toward the conservatory to find Jake running in her direction. "What on earth are you doing here?" she asked. "I thought you were watching Caroline."

Her nephew appeared confused. "I was," he said. "Something weird happened. I'll tell you about it later."

Jake put a hand to his head then shook it as if to clear it. "Right now I need to get back there...Can I borrow your car keys?"

"Of course," she said, fishing around in her pocket. "Where's yours?"

"Still hidden near Mitchell's, I think."

"You think?"

Jake grabbed the keys and set off at a quick pace. "I'll explain later," he said over his shoulder.

"Well, what are you going to do with two cars there?" she called out as he left. "I'll figure something out," he called back as he disappeared into the darkness.

Puzzled and absorbed now with Jake's curious behavior, May resumed her trek toward the gatehouse, the near-forgotten file still under her arm.

* * * *

Jake threw the car into park and raced up the walk to the house. He knew exactly what he was going to say. He'd been out for a drive, noticed the time, and decided to save Mitchell a trip back to the gatehouse by picking Caroline up. It wasn't original, but he thought it would work. He'd worry about getting his car later. Mitchell wouldn't notice it tonight.

He started to ring the doorbell then on an impulse, tried the handle.

Unlocked. What luck.

For some reason he himself didn't quite understand, Jake did not want to make his presence known. Like a cautious cat-burglar, he let himself inside, then allowed his eyes a moment to adjust to the dimly lit hallway. Why was it so quiet? Shouldn't he be hearing voices, laughter?

He eased his way down the corridor. Candles at the center of the dining room table had burned low, outlining place settings for two, but dinner did not appear to have been served.

Anxiety began a slow descent over Jake's body. Where was Caroline? He approached the closed door at the end of the hall, estimating that to be the room where he'd last seen Caroline and Mitchell. Was she still in there? Why was it so quiet?

Heart thundering in his breast, he slowly and carefully turned the doorknob and peered through the crack not certain what to expect. The scene appeared normal enough at first glance. Caroline sat where she had previously, her back to his, and Mitchell was bent forward over her like a specter of Satan about to lay claim to his innocent prey.

But then Jake recalled the similar intimacy he'd experienced with her in his mind only moments before. How could she sit there, now, and let another man touch her? His temper exploded with a venom that momentarily surprised even him, "What the hell's going on?"

Mitchell jerked his head up and away from the girl, apparently

162

stunned by Jake's unannounced arrival. Caroline remained motionless in her chair, something eerily out of place about her still and silent behavior. The older man bent quickly to her ear, whispered something, and abruptly, she lifted her head and turned toward Jake with a dazed expression.

"Caroline?" Pain coursed its way through Jake's veins. How could she? How could she, after what was between them?

Grasping the arm of the chair for support, she rose on unsteady feet. She looked crumpled and dazed, several buttons of her dress were loose at the neck and her eyes glassy. *What's wrong with her,* he wondered? What had they been doing before he came in?

"Hello, Jake," she said in a dry voice that cracked as she spoke. "What are you doing here?"

Jealously pierced his reply. "I was just asking myself the same thing."

Mitchell, seemingly in control once again, faced Jake angrily. "How dare you come into my home without knocking?"

"No one answered my knock," Jake lied coolly. "The door was open. Obviously you were occupied. I came to offer Caroline a ride home." He faced her. "Maybe you don't want a ride home...Maybe you were planning to stay the night?"

With a pained look, she put a hand to her forehead as if she had a terrible headache. "No...no...I do want to go home. Please..."

Something in her words tore at him, but Jake wasn't about to let himself be swayed. He didn't intend to let himself be affected by this little 'poor me' routine.

"You don't have to go, my dear," Mitchell's honeyed voice cut in. "I can take you later if you're still not feeling well. There's no need to rush off."

"No," she said, and Jake wondered if he merely imagined her sudden firmness. "I really must go. I'm very tired."

"Let's go, then," he said more sharply than he intended. "Unless you and your *friend* need a private moment to say goodnight."

The older man glared at him while Caroline gathered up her fallen sweater from the back of the chair. Jake noticed that she paused for a moment to retrieve something from the floor. An instant later she turned back to them. "Thank you for dinner," she said with somewhat slurred speech, and held out a hand to Mitchell.

"Yeah, some dinner, I guess." Jake laughed bitterly as Mitchell bent his head over her hand, then headed out the door, leaving her to follow on her own.

"So what the hell was going on in there?" Jake demanded the minute they were in the car.

Caroline cradled her head. The throbbing was almost unbearable. And her mouth was so dry she could hardly speak. On top of all that, she had no idea why Jake was so angry.

"Well?" He slid the car into reverse and gunned it out of Mitchell's drive.

"Nothing was 'going on,' as you put it. We had dinner. We talked."

Jake revved up the engine and spun forward. "Dinner? You had dinner? What'd you have for dinner, Miss Lyndfield?"

They drove for a moment or two in a silence broken only by the insistent drumming of Jake's fingers against the steering wheel.

Finally, she faced him in confusion, tears forming in her eyes. "I don't know," she whispered. "Why are you so angry?"

He slammed on the brakes and threw the car into park. "Why am I so angry?" He grabbed her arm and yanked her to him. "I walk in and find some old letch looming over you, and you ask why I'm so angry?"

"Nothing happened between us. Nothing. How could you think such a thing?"

He pulled her into his arms and crushed his mouth down on hers. She struggled against his embrace.

She managed to break free of his hold and open the car door. The night welcomed her like a mother with outstretched arms. She flew into its shelter, wanting only to get away from him and away from the pain in her temples. She dashed through the trees, and shortly found herself standing before the old conservatory. She slipped to the ground, suddenly deflated, and began crying against the hard cold dead earth. Everything else was gone—the plants, the flowers, the love. This had been the place she loved most, the place where she had felt the greatest passion—for all things. Now, it was lifeless and cold as winter. As was her heart.

"Why?" she whispered tearfully to the solid ground beneath her cheek. "Why? What am I to do?"

She never saw him come in, but he knelt beside her as he'd done that day in New York, with such tenderness she knew at once he was filled with remorse at his own behavior. She wouldn't forgive him this time, she thought. She would not. Finally, she had had enough of his doubting.

But the next instant she was swept up into his arms, and he was pushing back the damp strands of tangled hair from her face and covering it with heart-wrenching kisses. Begging her to forgive him. Begging her to love him. His eyes were suddenly the eyes of another: he touched her with the hands of another. And somehow, she knew now, as she had known once before, it was right.

Everything changed the minute he swept her into his arms—as if

Jake had never left the greenhouse, never seen or talked with May, never gone to Mitchell's to pick-up Caroline. All that was the dream...this was the reality. The two of them were just as they'd been earlier...arm in arm in a sea of forest green, color-tinted here and there only by the fading of fall roses and the final foliage of summer. Errant ivy provided a carpet still-warm with the last vestiges of the sun's heat, but Jake drew off his coat—his dark linen waistcoat—and spread it as a quilt. He noted with brief curiosity the initials FM engraved in the center of his silver cuff-link, which shone against the pale white of his tailored shirt. He knew he owned no such shirt, but here, now, it was right. It was his shirt—Francis Monroe's shirt.

With no more thought for who or when, his mouth sought hers again, tracing the pink fullness of her sensual lips with his tongue. Like petals, they parted gently and he inhaled her love like the breath of life itself. How he adored this woman! He would never love like this again, he knew. This was the stuff dreams were made of...lying right here in his arms.

He raised his head and searched her eyes, questioning. He drew his fingers through the thick web of curls spread on the ground beneath her, then buried his face in them. She smelled of sun and roses. She smelled of dark earth. She smelled of love. Passion.

He pushed aside the apron she wore and fingered the tiny pearl buttons at her neck. Caroline lay beneath him, still and open. His sex strained at his tight pants, pushing against her leg. He wanted her. He supposed he'd always wanted her, but had only just discovered in the past year. Then, the power of it had hit him like a swirling tornado, sucking, twisting, threatening to consume him with its force. Love was something...

She seemed to realize he'd stopped kissing her and tugged tenderly at his neck. "Francis?" Her eyes were pools of sea-green curiosity. She wanted him to go on, he thought. But there was so much left to be resolved... And he wanted her first time to be special.

"Should we?" he asked as he twirled a tendril of long hair around his finger. "Is it right?"

Her smile, full as the moon on a midsummer's eve, beamed love. "What is right? What is wrong?" She brushed a butterfly kiss against his cheek. "Do you love me?"

"Forever," he replied, cradling her face. "Always."

"Then we will be man and wife someday, will we not?"

"If I have anything to do with it..." He ran his finger across her temple around her eye then down to the tip of her nose. She smiled again.

"Why, then," she asked softly, "should we not begin our love here, in this moment, at the peak of its passion? Will there ever be another moment so right? A place so right?"

He shook his head, then undid the first pearl button.

She'd been so angry at him, but the anger had evaporated like a summer shower, replaced now with the fullness of joy. She didn't mind that he wanted her here, on the cold dead earth that had once pulsated with the life of their love. Now, as she lay in his arms, the soil seemed to take on new life. Caroline realized it wasn't completely dead, for the ground on which they made their bed was laced with ivy gone wild with time. Somehow, this was appropriate. Together, in another moment, they had lain here in love. Why shouldn't they be re-united in this same place?

Caroline breathed his scent like a prayer as he reverently undid the tiny buttons at the neck of her dress. Encouraged, his hands moved faster, till he was able to slide aside the fabric and deftly unhook the opening to her bra. With slight amusement, she recalled how much simpler this was than in days gone by, with the many-layered garments they both had worn. Francis had lost a cuff-link that day, she recalled, and had never been able to find it. All those many years ago...re-born in this moment. Love was something...

As his tongue traced the tip of her now-bare breast, the days seemed to melt away, leaving only the two of them and their love— together once more. How it could be she did not know. She only knew that it was.

A warm glow ignited somewhere in the depths of her and made its way up, suffusing her with pulsating energy. Her heartbeat magnified and blended with his, until it almost seemed they were truly one soul, instead of two...joined. And somehow, knowing she had once lost him forever made her passion all the greater. Even in the heat of this moment though, she knew she must not fail him again.

Caroline moaned against his ear as his fingers and mouth kneaded her nipple with savage urgency. Before, he had been gentle. He had taken time. But now, too much time had been taken from them; she knew he needed her as desperately as she needed him.

He shoved up the crumpled fabric of her dress and struggled for a moment to strip the binding pantyhose from her body. She smiled at the unexpected imprisonment the future had made of her womanhood; his smile joined hers in mute warfare. Freed of captivity, his hand sought the warm and throbbing dampness between her legs even as his mouth claimed hers again. Caroline thrust against him, hot and wanton.

"Yes..." she murmured as his head bent to her breast once more. "I want you."

His eyes sought hers and finding them, acknowledged with a single look his own desire. His passion. His heat. His need. His love. With a deftness of hand that amazed even himself, one by one Jake slid open the buttons to his trousers. Though he was out of them in the blink of an eye, he did not fail to notice that one second seemed an eternity to both of them. It was here. Now. The moment he had waited so long for. An eternity.

She stroked his sex with a gentle caress, and he gasped at the pleasure her single touch evoked.

"Caroline..." he whispered. "God, Caroline..."

She drew him to her quickly, yanking open the front of his shirt and pressing her mouth to his chest, her tongue trailing warm and feathery kisses around the tips of his nipple. He wanted to take his time, to be tender, but she seemed to have some other unknown agenda, an urgency he could not fathom. Eagerly, welcoming, her legs spread beneath him.

Then, he was in her—so easily—shuddering, aching with the sudden velvety enjoyment. Their bodies moved in unison: he thrust deeper and deeper, touching her depths and merging with the very core of her being. He gasped as her voice arched into the night, begging for release.

Jake let go. Filled her. Lost himself. Was one. And suddenly it was crystal clear to him. It was then. But it was also now.

Caroline did not hold back. She ached with the joy of him inside her and felt no shame as her cry of passion forced its way into the night. Quivering waves of sensation swam over her, circles of hot energy that she prayed might never stop caressing her with their god-like embrace. She allowed her physical pleasure to run its course, then breathed him into her heart. His name, either of the names she had come to know him by, no longer mattered. Now, he was simply her love. Her one and only love.

When he raised his eyes to hers, it was evident for the first time that he understood. Believed completely. Drawing deeply of the night air, she traced a line down from his eyebrow to his cheek. He sighed a long light sigh. Tears sprang from her then like a river newly-flooded with the cool waters of spring.

"Oh!" she said and drew him as close as she dare. She shivered against his chest, filled with unspeakably joy.

Not understanding, he pulled back with instant concern in his gaze. "What is it, love? Are you cold?"

Caroline shook her head and pressed herself closer to him. So close she might actually be a part of him. So close they might never be separated.

His hand cupped her face. "What is it, then? Did I hurt you? I'm sorry I wasn't more tender. More gentle."

She wiped the moisture of her happiness from her cheek. "You did not hurt me," she whispered. "Not in the least."

"Then why, my dearest love, are you crying?"

With barely a breath of a kiss, her lips grazed his and she slid her hands, still-warmed with their lovemaking, across his back.

Jake sighed again and this time she smiled. "I'm weeping for your sigh," she said at last. She ran a slow finger across the line of his mouth. "For Francis' sigh. You've come back to me."

He buried his face in the depths of her lush tresses, and knew it was so. When he raised his eyes again, he asked her simply, "Do you think we could find my cuff link?"

CHAPTER 19

The heart must pause to breathe,
And love itself have rest.
Lord Byron

Fury tore a fiery tirade through Mitchell's breast. The time had definitely come to deal with Jake Stanton. Once and for all... It had been almost more than he could do to restrain his hatred when the young man strode in— unannounced—earlier that evening. How dare he? And to intrude at that particular moment... Mitchell slammed his fist onto the desk at which he sat. "Damn him to hell."

A light tap at his study door was followed by Ruby's voice. "Excuse me...are you all right?"

"Come in," he barked.

Not intimidated by his obvious displeasure, Ruby entered the room. "Can I get you anything?" Ruby asked him, and Mitchell sensed the unspoken request.

But he didn't want her now. The very sight of her, the thought of being with her—like that—sickened him. After the shimmering pale and silky skin of Caroline Lyndfield, he knew he could never be with another woman again. That heat he'd felt from her... He thought once more of the icy cold, and then of the white fire. Both were gone now, vanished completely at the departure of the girl. Where had they disappeared to, he wondered? Those extremes of temperature that made him feel as if he were poised on the brink of hell?

With an effort, he forced his attention back to the woman who stood before him. She would do whatever he asked. Not many men could boast of having such a faithful servant. But how could she help him with the task at hand: Jake Stanton?

Mitchell looked down at the letter opener in the hand, and briefly imagined it covered with Stanton's fresh blood. But how? When? Where? He had no idea how one went about plotting such a crime—his special was antiquities, not murder.

But abruptly, he knew someone who might. Suddenly, he thought he knew the way to get Jake Stanton out of the picture once and for all.

He looked up at Ruby, face brightening visibly at his sudden thought. "Ruby?" Mitchell smiled his warmest smile and motioned her forward to the chair next to his desk, then leaned toward her eagerly. "Ruby, what's you son up to these days?" He grappled to remember the name. "Gordon?"

* * * *

Jake suggested they leave his car and walk back to the gatehouse. He wanted to be alone with Caroline for a little longer, not in the car where they'd fought, but under the night stars, where the twinkling sky glittered with possibilities. Besides, May's inquisitive eyes would note the change between the two of them instantly, and Jake wasn't ready to provide explanations. Right now all he wanted to do was savor Caroline's company, enjoy the delicate feel of her hand in his, see the love in her eyes.

What he felt right now was indescribable—and incredible. How he could know what he knew and be who he was, he had no idea. Jake only knew that when they had made love in the greenhouse, his life had suddenly merged into a complete picture, and he not only remembered the times he had known her before, but he knew beyond a doubt that they had once—in another lifetime—made love in that very same place. They had shared a special love in that place which, like the flowers around them, had one day blossomed into full passion. Then it had been lost. Jake's thoughts and memories grew cloudy at that point, and for some reason he sensed he must not pursue them now.

Caroline turned eyes brimming with love to him as they cleared the little grove of trees near the playhouse. As usual, he sensed her tension upon approaching this spot.

"Caroline?" he filled his voice with the full measure of the tenderness he felt. He accepted her anxiety now, even if he didn't completely understand it. Something about this place held terror for her. Real terror, not imagined.

Her gaze still held her joy, but fear and uncertainty lay close at hand. He drew her palm to his mouth and bent to kiss it gently. "It doesn't matter now," he told her. "We're together again. I promise I'll take care of you."

"But it does matter," she replied. "I don't know how, or why...but it does. There is something I must do...or know...or something. A force threatens to pull me back here. Back...to before..." She threw herself into his arms. "Oh, Jake...I don't want to lose you again."

"You're not going to lose me, darling." He held her close and kissed the top of her head. He liked the way she'd called him Jake. Somehow, it made their love seem stronger, knowing she accepted him for the man he was now, as well as the one he'd been then. There were differences, he knew, just as there were things in this life he'd yet to resolve. But she accepted him. That mattered most.

"We'll figure it out, Caro... Piece by piece. Day by day. Let's just be together right now, okay?"

Feebly, and forcing a lightness he knew she did not feel, she smiled up at him, and they resumed their walk past the old building and toward the places they'd both known as home. Once again content, Jake let the night and her love wash over him like an ocean of calm. With every step he took, past and present merged more and more into eternity, and somehow he believed what he told her had been the truth. This time they would be together forever.

Caroline turned to him as if she read his mind. "And always," she whispered.

* * * *

May stared at the notes spread out on the coffee table. Everything suddenly made sense, in a bizarre sort of way—Jake's confused behavior, Mitchell's irrational interest in Caroline, her own eerie and foreboding intuition.

William Lyndfield and his friend Evan Ludington hadn't been ordinary scientists—theirs had evidently been a study of not just the paranormal, but the abnormal as well—malignancy, demonism, and ritualism. May still couldn't be sure exactly how it all fit together. She wished she had something to specifically prove the two of them had been up to no good, that William's daughter had nothing to do with his violent death, which—if what she suspected were true—he probably deserved. What was obvious from these notes of Mitchell's was that the *proof* she wanted wasn't here.

The front door opened, announcing the arrival of Jake and Caroline.

The second she saw the two of them, May knew they had resolved whatever age-old problems were between them. Their faces beamed with their love. May felt moisture instantly gathering in her eyes and dabbed at it with a Kleenex. She waved them in. Silently, they joined her on the sofa.

"Well, it's certainly been an interesting evening, hasn't it?" she said lightly.

They laughed together, and then shared one huge bear-hug. Jake had always been distant—unemotional—almost as if he'd been born with a broken heart, but tonight May thought she saw real happiness in him for the first time. His fractured heart seemed healed.

"So..." she said softly, "I suspect you two have found each other at last."

Jake kissed his aunt on the cheek. "Yes," he said simply. "We have at that."

"Well," the older woman continued tactfully, "then I won't ask what you two have been up to. I will, however, share a bit about my findings."

May wanted to be careful what she said around Caroline: it

171

wouldn't do to alarm the girl unnecessarily. She could discuss that with Jake later. Caroline had had enough hurts for the time being. Best to let her revel in her renewed love for now.

She picked up several sheets of paper from the table and pushed the remainder to one side. "I've been going over these."

"What are they?" Caroline asked.

Proudly, May smiled. "They're confiscated papers from Mitchell's office. Jake's idea, actually. These are personal notes Mitchell made about some experiments both Evan and your father conducted."

Confusion spread across the girl's countenance. "But how did he find out about them?"

Jake had begun rifling through the pages. "I think I'm getting your drift here, May," he said. "You think there are journals." He pointed out several notations in the margin to Caroline that read 'see journal entry dated...'

May beamed. "Precisely. Either Evan or your father, Caroline, must have kept records about the experiments. And since your father was mostly an apprentice in this arena, I'd guess it was Evan."

"But where are the journals?" Caroline asked. "Why have you never found them?"

May patted her arm. "That, my dear, is a very good question. But I have a feeling it's because Mitchell has never shared them with us. The nerve of him, to accuse Jake of stealing that little diary, when he's been hording Evan's journals for years."

She rose and went to the window, considering. When she faced them again, she found Jake kissing Caroline's hand and gazing at her with adoring eyes. She smiled. It was so good to see him happy, happier than she'd ever seen him. Somehow it seemed all the pieces of his life had snapped into place. It was right, for the first time ever.

"You know," she said, "whatever we may think or not think, or know or not know about their experiments, you, Caroline, are the proof that love can endure."

"That's for sure," Jake said smiling. "Damn sure."

"But what should we do now?" Caroline asked. "I'm here, but I don't know if I'll be able to stay. I don't want time to somehow sweep me away again. I want to stay...I feel I belong here, but what about my father? I need to know what happened to him? Did my leaving somehow cause his death?" Her eyes pleaded with Jake.

He clasped her to him, and May thought the girl actually drew strength from their embrace.

"We'll find your answers," Jake told her calmly. "But you're not going back. I won't lose you again either."

Distress registered in Caroline's face. "But it's my fault we were separated to begin with. I didn't act. I was afraid." She clutched his hand to her chest. "I know this is important, Jake. There is something I must do."

He kissed the tip of her nose. "Tomorrow, then," he said, and May nodded in agreement.

"Tomorrow will certainly be soon enough," she said as the two of them rose from the sofa. "We've all had a big day, and Nurse Whatley says it's off to bed with the two of you. You'll be able to think a lot clearer after you've gotten some rest." She winked at them as she gathered up the papers strewn about the coffee table. "And try to get a bit of sleep, won't you?"

May noticed Caroline's instant blush, but Jake merely returned the wink. "I'm sure we'll sleep quite well," he said as they headed up the stairs.

* * * *

Caroline woke to find herself nestled in the crook of Jake's arm. With his eyes still closed, he appeared boyish and vulnerable and she found herself wanting to protect him from any more cruelty life might have to offer. She brushed the sandy hair back from his forehead, and at her touch, he stretched and yawned sleepily.

"Morning, love," he told her a second after opening his eyes.

Caroline had wondered for a moment if he would remember their love in the light of day, or if somehow it would all turn out to have been a dream after all. But he did remember, it seemed: all was real.

She snuggled up close to him, relishing the earthy male scent of his body. Last night, they'd both been exhausted and had fallen into an instant sleep, but now she re-lived that magical moment in the greenhouse when past and present had suddenly become one. The hardness of his thigh against her own leg brought a quick blush to her cheeks as she recalled that other hardness she'd drawn into her own body the night before. Her gaze suddenly met his, openly inviting.

Jake laughed softly and kissed her cheek. "You are a little wanton, aren't you? I always suspected there was something very un-Victorian about you, Miss Lyndfield."

She giggled. "Do you mind terribly?"

Without answering, he thrust his hand between her legs and found her wet and more than ready. "Jake!" she gasped and pressed herself to him as his fingers began stroking her with an even rhythm.

"Do you want me, baby?" He breathed against her neck and his tongue traced its outline. "Are you hot for me?"

Her body thrilled even more at the new and sensual words. "I want you," she murmured, struggling with the bedclothes to find that part of him she craved.

At last she had it, the hard shaft of him, the glorious part that so easily merged with her. "Suck me, Caroline," he told her in a husky voice. "I want you to kiss me there."

At first her eyes widened with shock, then suddenly it all seemed so right, so natural. She rearranged herself so as to take him into her mouth, then her tongue flicked up and down, savoring the pulsating throb of blood through his steel veins, delighting in the taste of his most private place. His hands kneaded her breasts, his fingers expertly pulling at her nipples like a baby suckling its mother's milk. Finally, it was he who could take no more of the exquisite torture. He moaned and pulled her up, astride him, and with a quick motion plunged deep into her.

"Oh, Jake..." she cried, rocking back and forth in time with him like two dancers joined in perfect unison. His fingers found her open mouth, and she sucked them one at a time as he drew her closer and closer to ecstatic release.

A second or two only but what seemed an eternity between them, their passion exploded like a stormy summer afternoon, cleansing, refreshing, then bringing them back to a sultry lazy rest, sated and happy, and somehow ready to begin— again.

* * * *

May found Jake whistling in the kitchen when she came down to prepare breakfast. It looked as if he'd already made quite a dent of the task himself.

She smiled to herself. She had woke to the muffled sounds of lovemaking from Jake's room, and had spent a few moments happily remembering her own times of passion before getting up for bath. She really must call Henry soon. It had been much too long.

"Morning," Jake told her cheerfully. "Eggs, bacon, and biscuits okay with you?"

"My, my. Aren't we feeling energetic today?" She poured herself a cup of coffee and took a chair at the table.

"Well, I wanted to do something special for Caroline this morning. Her first real day of work and all."

May laughed. "I bet that isn't the only reason."

Jake cracked an egg in the skillet then wiped his hands on a cup towel. "Ah, dear May, you know me too well, don't you?"

His aunt joined his laughter then spoke seriously. "How do you feel, Jake? Is that what last night was all about?"

He flipped the egg and watched it silently for several seconds. "Yes," he told her at last as he slid the egg onto a plate brimming with bacon and biscuits and joined her at the table. "I don't really know how to explain it, May, but it feels complete."

He searched for a moment, as if carefully choosing the right words. "I feel like I found a part of myself that's always been missing. Always...even before Mom and Dad were killed."

She squeezed his hand. "I'm happy for you."

"I'm happy for me, too. But I'm still a little in shock, I think. I mean, what happens now?"

"What do you want to happen?"

He laughed. "I want us to live happily ever after. But somehow I don't think the odds are in our favor. C'mon, May, you're the expert on weirdness, what do you make of all this?"

"Thanks for your recommendation." May picked up a fork, thoughtfully took a bit of her egg, then put the fork down again. "I think you have to forget how and why and think about what you both want, Jake."

"But how are we ever going to be sure?" he asked her, sounding more doubtful that he had all morning. "How can we know she's not just going to disappear again someday? Back to her own time?"

"She's gone from that time forever, Jake. Historically, we know that. What we can't know is the future. You and Caroline have to make that happen. What I sense—and this is my 'sense' only, mind you— what I sense is that you two let each other down...maybe she more than you. Here's another chance for you to work together, to strengthen your love, to overcome..." She paused briefly and considered whether or not to tell him more about what she really felt.

"Overcome, what?" he prodded.

"Overcome the evil..." Caroline said from the doorway.

Her hair was still slightly damp, but already full with its lively curls. She came in, dressed for her first day as a tour guide. Suddenly it occurred to May that she looked very young and very frightened. Vulnerable. Did she realize more than they'd thought, she wondered?

"Isn't that what you were going to say, May?" Caroline asked.

May nodded. "Yes." She turned back to Jake. "I think you two have somehow, through the power of love, found each other again. But I also believe just as love can cross centuries, so can evil. Whatever force parted you once, may attempt to do so again. And, depending on the two of you, may or may not succeed."

Shivering slightly, Caroline joined them at the table and took Jake's hand in her own. "Well," he told her, "let's hope we've learned from past mistakes. I think we have."

May began eating once more, talking between careful mouthfuls. "I'm sure you have." She looked at Jake. "So, Sherlock, what's on the agenda today?"

Jake dived into his own breakfast thoughtfully.

Caroline fumbled around in her pocket, then after a moment, withdrew something from her pocket. "I think we should begin with this." She held out not one but two small hourglasses.

"Two?" Jake held out his hand for the objects, examining them carefully. "Where'd you find the other?"

"On the floor," she told him. "Last night at Mitchell Johnston's."

CHAPTER 20

Dashest him again to earth—there let him lay.
Lord Byron

Though Caroline hadn't expressed her feelings to May or Jake, she dreaded encountering Mitchell at the estate office this morning. When she finally managed to draw her thoughts away from her love for Jake long enough to think about what exactly had happened last night before he came to take her home, she remained at a complete loss, most of the evening remained little more than a blur. She remembered very little after she and Mitchell had gone to the garden. *Why*, she fretted? She had the nagging feeling the hourglass had something to do with it. But what, exactly?

Jake and May agreed with her that the hourglass might somehow be connected to the gap in her memory, but with the morning slipping away, they'd decided to postpone further discussion until later. She and May had to be at the office, and Jake, eager to spend more time deciphering the notes May had confiscated, planned to make another trip to the library to look at the forbidden files. Which, Caroline thought with a stab of jealously, might well require more flirting with Wendy. There would be the whole day to be gotten through before she saw him again, when fifteen minutes seemed an eternity.

Despite this, Caroline put on a happy face as she and May made their way to the house, and luckily, Mitchell was not in his office when they arrived. He'd left a message on the answering machine, however, to say he'd be in around midday.

As she went about her morning, Caroline couldn't manage to shake the odd feeling she'd forgotten something important about the previous evening. What had she and Mitchell done for the rest of their time together? Could it somehow tie in with Evan and her father? What kind of bizarre experiments had the two of them been conducting?

If only she could get back into Mitchell's house, Caroline thought, perhaps she might find some clue to unravel the mystery. Right now, she wanted answers more than anything. Instinctively, she believed that only solving the mystery of the past would allow her to stay in the present. And Caroline knew beyond a shadow of a doubt she wanted to stay where she was—in the year 2006. With Jake Stanton.

Caroline glanced over at the clock in her father's study. Eleven-thirty. The tours had been small today, and she'd had no difficulty adjusting to the routine. Or, amazed as she was with all the newfangled gadgets of the 21st century, had she had any further problems operating them. She and May had taken the first group through together, and Caroline had flipped switches like any modern woman might. Then May left her on her own, promising to relieve her for lunch at noon. The thought occurred to her that perhaps, if Mitchell had arrived by then, she could slip over to his house and tell the housekeeper she'd left something in the study...or better yet, that Mitchell had sent her to retrieve something. *About time I followed my instincts*, she mused as she ushered the last of the tourists downstairs to the gift shop. Tonight, she too, would have a contribution to add to May and Jake's.

"How is your day going, my dear?" Mitchell asked just as she was about to go up to the office to let May know when she'd return. Caroline forced back the shiver that threatened to overcome her. She'd hoped she would miss him, but apparently no such luck. Why, she wondered, did she always feel so cold when he was near?

"Good, morning, Mitchell." She made herself stand firm and stifle any quivers of fear. "It's going quite well, actually."

Mitchell peered at her intently. What exactly was he looking for? Did he suspect something had happened between her and Jake? May had noticed at once, but she knew Jake well and both he and Caroline had been together then. What changes could Mitchell detect in her as she faced him now?

The fathomless pitch of his eyes attempted to draw her into their sticky depths, but Caroline held herself in check and physically took a step or two away from him.

"Are you feeling all right?" he asked, concern in his voice. "You didn't seem well last night."

"Oh...no, I'm quite all right," she said, briefly wondering if the faint spell she'd had in the parlor had anything to do with her lapse of memory.

"Well," he continued, "I just wanted you to know how very much I enjoyed out evening, my dear. I hope we can do it again soon. When you're feeling better—without the interruption." He reached for her hand and brushed his dry and cracked lips across it. She struggled to maintain a calm she did not feel and again to refrain from shivering at his icy touch.

"Don't overtire yourself today," he instructed as he headed up the stairs toward his office. "If you begin to feel ill, call me."

"No, I won't..." She breathed a sigh of relief at his departure. "Would you mind telling May I've gone to the gatehouse for lunch?"

The thin smile that came back to her seemed forced. He did resent her spending time with Jake. Still, his reply remained cool, "Not at all, my dear. Not at all."

Caroline then escaped out the back door, and hurried through the trees toward her preplanned task.

* * * *

Mitchell closed the door to his office and picked up the phone. He wanted to check in with Ruby and see how their plan was progressing. Even though he'd only left a short while ago, he intended to be sure his housekeeper stayed on top of things this time. He had stressed his desire for urgency. He'd delayed long enough. Now was the time to act.

He wrinkled his nose in disgust as he thought back to the morning's activities. Ruby's services had not come free of charge this time. He'd seen right away that she was going to be stubborn, which wasn't a good sign. Surely she wasn't jealous of his plans for Caroline: he had never led her to believe there could be anything between the two of them. Well, no matter, she'd be out of his life soon enough.

"Why would you want my boy to do that?" she'd asked after he outlined his initial plan. "He could get in trouble with the law, and he's working hard to keep out of trouble."

Like hell he is, Mitchell thought. Ruby's son Gordon always seemed to be in one sort of scrap or another. He'd be the perfect person to help frame Jake. Gordon would set up the cache of stolen antiques in the playhouse and Mitchell would take care of the rest—with pleasure. The secluded little building was the perfect place for a burglar to stash his goods unseen—and if somehow Jake managed to have a little accident in the process of his crime, well, that would just be too bad.

"There's no chance he could get in trouble, Ruby," Mitchell reassured the woman with confidence, "because the whole point is that Stanton be caught stealing from the estate. Then we're rid of him."

"How come you're so eager to get rid of him?" the housekeeper asked suspiciously. "What's he done to you?"

"You know what he's done," Mitchell replied angrily, then immediately made an effort to cover up his venom. He had told Ruby the story a million times, but if necessary he must tell it again. His plan depended on her help. So he patiently explained how Jake's writing the estate history would make him a success in the literary world, while Mitchell toiled away running the estate for a meager salary and no recognition.

Finally, he'd convinced her—through coercion and a little physical persuasion—to call her son. Gordon, of course, would be thrilled with the prospect of making some easy money. That morning, Mitchell had made out a list of the items he was to take from the manor, along with a step-by-step timetable. Everything was in place.

"Ruby?" he said when she picked up the phone at his house. "Did you reach Gordon?"

"Yes, I was just leaving for his apartment. I didn't think I should have him here. I'll have him call you later."

"Excellent thinking," Mitchell responded, again thanking his lucky stars for her resourcefulness. He sincerely hoped he did not have to deal with her in the same manner he planned to deal with Jake. But if need be, he could. He would do anything to protect the reputation of the Lyndfield name. And nothing must stop him from having what he wanted—what *they* wanted—Caroline and the secrets about her mysterious time-travel. Unfortunately, one would mean little without the other.

* * * *

Jake rubbed his eyes and stared at the papers spread in front of him. As May had promised, Mitchell's notes provided a wealth of information. Evidently, the curator of Lyndfield had known for years of Evan Ludington and William Lyndfield's participation in satanic rituals and black magic—the reason for all the occult literature, more than likely. Mitchell had researched everything from obscure meetings of cultists to organized hedonistic rituals. But how they all tied together, Jake couldn't figure out without the diary or diaries. And whether or not their studies were somehow connected to Caroline's arrival here might be something they would never know. How could one explain the unexplainable?

He dialed the number at the manor. "Hello, Lyndfield Trust." May's voice crackled across the line.

"May, Jake here...is Johnston in today?"

"He just arrived. Why?"

"Oh, I'm just plotting again. Can you keep him busy? I want to check something out."

"I suppose. What are you up too?" she whispered.

"Another treasure hunt."

"Is Caroline with you?"

Jake laughed. "Hardly. Isn't she busy with her rounds right now?"

Something about the sudden silence on the other end of the line struck him at once. "May?"

"She should be there with you, Jake... She left here thirty minutes ago."

Tightness gripped Jake's heart. *If something had happened to her...* Then abruptly he realized she must have come up with the same idea he had. But treasure hunting could be dangerous. Especially if you planned on trespassing...

"I'll call you back, May." He slammed down the phone and headed out the front door.

* * * *

180

Caroline could not believe her luck. Ruby Henderson was just closing the back door when she peered through the trees at Mitchell's house. After no more than a couple of minutes, the woman's black Buick headed down the drive. Now all she had to do was pray the door wasn't locked.

Again, she was in luck. She pushed open the heavy back door and slipped quietly into the house. Probably there was no need for caution, but just to be safe… She made her way down the hall to the study where she and Mitchell had been when Jake arrived. Whatever she needed to find would surely be in that room.

Mitchell's house lost much of its foreboding in the daylight. It didn't seem nearly as claustrophobic as she'd thought the night before. She opened the door to his study and stepped into the room. Streams of the midday sun filtered through the curtains, casting threads of light across the furniture.

Now what, she wondered?

After a moment, she went to the desk. Clean and neat, it somehow reminded her of the man himself. Mitchell appeared such a proper man, a man who seemed to keep everything in its correct place. She still found it hard to believe he might be involved in underhandedness, especially in such a seemingly simple matter as withholding information. What did it matter to him if the truth were known about her father's experiments? What bearing could a hundred-year-old mystery possibly have on Mitchell Johnston's present? She opened the desk drawers one at a time, sifting through the contents carefully. Rows of files, pens and pencils, and papers of various kinds lined the insides—nothing out of the ordinary. The bottom drawer, however, was locked.

Figures, she thought with wry amusement. But how on earth was she to get it open? The carved ivory letter opener on top of the desk caught her eye. Well, if force was necessary, so be it. She picked up the instrument and began prying the drawer open. With a loud click, the lock gave way under her hand.

Inside the drawer, under a manila file, lay a very old, very large red leather volume. She knew at once it must be Evan's diary. As she removed the book from the drawer, a blast of frigid air hit her forcefully. She looked around. The room was empty and silent, the doors and windows shut against the outside. But suddenly, it was freezing. Caroline pressed the book to her heart, trying to warm herself, but the chill only cut deeper.

What would she find here? she wondered. *Did she even want to know the truth?*

For a long moment, she considered replacing the book in its

drawer and leaving empty-handed. She was here now, in this time; what did it really matter what had happened to her father? Caroline knew in her heart she had had nothing to do with his death. And the rest of the world would care little after all these years.

It's important, a thin voice whispered inside her. She turned and painfully studied the drawer. What if Mitchell missed it? What then? Would he know she had taken it? Or would he suspect May, or Jake?

She stood, frozen with indecision. The oppressive, almost evil heaviness of the atmosphere appeared. Combined with the chill, it made breathing suddenly difficult.

Choices. Always, there were choices... What if she made the wrong one?

Abruptly, she remembered the last time she'd been with Francis. He had asked her to act, but she waited, frozen with indecision. If only she had made a choice, the choice she wanted to make, he might not have died. Now of this might ever have happened. This was her second chance. She must take the risk...

Clutching the book to her breast like a prized jewel, Caroline fled the room, and then, the house.

He caught her just as she was backing out the door. "What do you have there, Miss Lyndfield?" he demanded in a deep voice.

"Oh!" She spun around, obviously startled. "Jake! You frightened me to death!"

"As well you should be. What the hell do you think you're doing?"

She stole a quick look around. "Not here. Let's get out of here before someone comes home."

He followed her into the cover of trees and then pointed to the book in her hands. "Looks like you found it."

Caroline gladly released her hold on the book and handed it to him. "I think so. You look."

They stopped walking and he opened the book to read the nameplate. "Bingo," he said. "This is it!" He planted a kiss on her cheek. "Good work, Watson."

Confused, she attempted a laugh. "I was frightened. I kept remembering our talk with May about second chances and taking risks."

"Those aren't the kind of risks you should take alone. We don't know what we're dealing with here, Caro. We're going by the feel of it alone, and it doesn't feel good." He peered seriously into her eyes to be sure she was paying attention. "Don't do that again."

"But..."

He put a hand on her shoulder. "Please..."

She smiled. "All right." They resumed their walk. "So now what?"

she asked him. "Mitchell is sure to find it missing."

"Not necessarily. I'll read it this afternoon then take it back before he gets home. The main thing we need to know is what the old geezer is up to. What's he protecting?"

Caroline stared longingly at the book and Jake gave her a hug. "I promise I won't keep anything from you. Okay?"

She nodded. "Okay...shall I tell May?"

"Too risky. Just finish out your day and keep Mitchell there as late as possible. Got it?"

"Got it," she smiled, enjoying the new terminology.

Jake gave her a quick kiss and watched her back as she headed toward the manor, awed once more at the bizarre chain of events that had brought her into his life. Love was really something...

* * * *

Jake closed the red leather book and slumped into the couch.

A long painful sigh escaped his lips. This was worse than he ever would have imagined. Somehow he felt he should have known these things. Something in William Lyndfield's recorded history should have hinted at the truth: his connection with Evan Ludington, a neurotic writer/scientist possessed with a desire to conquer the paranormal; Lyndfield's own obsession for power; his failure to marry again; his reclusive habits... All this should have triggered Jake's suspicions, and yet, nothing had. All he'd ever felt was his own sadness, his sense of loss. Maybe those feelings had blinded him to everything else.

He thought of hourglasses Caroline had shown them that morning. They had been the keys after all—keys to a malignant empire of drugs, hypnotism, rituals, lust... What a despicable web of evil had been woven here—and for what reason? William Lyndfield had everything money could buy. Wasn't that enough?

Jake wondered what he would tell Caroline. He didn't think he could bear to see her face, to feel her pain when she discovered her father had been more than just a child molester and a murderer. He had been the chalice of devil himself—and not once, but many times over. Evan had supplied his lusts...for blackmail, for experimentation, and, however ironic it might have been, for Caroline. In Evan's crazed mind, Jake believed, he'd really loved her—and had sought only to protect her from a father who might even stoop to using his own daughter to achieve lecherous satisfactions.

Still, he shuddered at the part Evan's 'protection' had played in Francis Monroe's—Jake's—own fate. No details, just the words on the faded paper: 'I have dealt with Monroe once and for all.... He will trouble us no more.'

In the end Evan had killed again, this time for himself however, to protect all he had built with William Lyndfield's money. The fear he might lose his power and position had been great enough that he'd let Caroline take the blame for this final violent act. Evidently he had thought such was a better fate than accepting the blame himself. And perhaps he had hoped some day to find a way to be with her again, wherever she had gone. Everything was recorded here, in his journal. They'd wanted to find answers, and now Jake had them all.

Almost all... He still didn't know exactly what had happened to Evan Ludington or how Caroline had come to be here, in this time and place? Evidently Evan had never found the answer to that question either, or if he did, he hadn't recorded it in this journal. So what forces of fate had catapulted a young woman over one hundred years forward in time? And more importantly still, could she stay?

CHAPTER 21

Man marks the earth with ruin.
Lord Byron

Mitchell checked his watch for the hundredth time that afternoon. Deciding upon a course of action might not always come easy to him, but once done, he wanted the plan to proceed with haste. Especially in this particular case...so much was at stake.

After Jake Stanton was out of the picture, Caroline would need more love and support than ever, so of course she would turn to Mitchell. He intended to see May was kept otherwise occupied. He glanced through his office door at the older woman, still bent over the ledger on her desk. She'd been acting rather strange all day, watching him closely, almost as if she expected to see some queer behavior. Did she suspect he was up to something? He hoped not; he'd grown accustomed to May's presence in his life. But he would do whatever was necessary to ensure that presence did not turn into interference.

The phone startled him with a shrill ring. He picked it up. Gordon. At last. "Just a minute," he told the young man on the other end of the line, and rose to close his office door.

"Well?"

Gordon had a nasal whining voice and tolerating the sound of almost caused Mitchell to change his mind. "It's all arranged. Ma told me what you want and I can do it. No problemo."

"When?" Mitchell asked with irritation, hating to have to call upon such scum.

"How 'bout tonight?"

Mitchell's estimation of Gordon grew. "Tonight? That soon?"

"Sure 'nough. I'm a man of action, ya know."

With a visibly brighter outlook on the day, Mitchell considered for a moment. Would he be able to set things up here that quickly? May would be leaving in about an hour and thanks to Henry McWilliams, she would be occupied for the evening. Caroline was downstairs: he could catch her alone. And he'd heard her telling May earlier Jake would be working at the gatehouse until late.

He opened the drawer of his desk. He had forgotten to bring the hourglass, but he'd brought the drugs—just in case. Alone, they should be enough to give the girl a nice long nap. Yes, he could do it...

"Excellent, Gordon," he said with satisfaction. "I'll make the arrangements that need to be made and then meet you here...say about

185

seven o'clock?

"Gotcha, man. An' you'll have my dough?"

"Of course...till tonight then...." Mitchell replaced the phone in its cradle and cheerfully considered his rival, soon to be no more.

* * * *

The hours passed liked slow molasses for Caroline. After only one day as a tour guide, she knew it wouldn't be the job for her. While Lyndfield Manor had been the home where she'd been raised, it couldn't be the place where she spent the rest of her life. Times had changed, and this place had changed with them. From what she could surmise, people didn't live in houses like this anymore. Oh, they certainly had curiosities about this, but maintaining a place like this would cost a fortune Caroline no longer had. The house felt different now, and too many painful memories filled every corner of it.

Caroline wanted—if by some miracle of God she was allowed to stay in this century—to start a new life—somewhere else, anywhere else, as long as she could be with Jake. She wanted work that would take her out into the world and allow her to give something back to it. It might take some time to discover just exactly where she fit into this world, but she would find it, she knew. Together with Jake—Francis— God willing. She had never considered herself a particularly religious person, but she offered up a multitude of silent prayers of gratitude now.

She was on her way up to May's office, so they could walk home together, when Mitchell waylaid her in the hallway. He put a finger to his lips and motioned silence. Curious, she followed him through the open door into her father's library.

"We need to talk," he told her gravely.

"About what?"

With an icy grip, he took her hand and squeezed it. "About last night. About you."

A cold dread crept over her, partly at his touch, partly at his words. Something had happened...but what? He hadn't been acting this way earlier. Had he discovered the missing journal already?

"I...I was just going home." She fought to keep the quiver from her voice.

"Tell May you're going to stay here and have a cup of coffee with me. To help me catalog some things."

"Can't it wait, Mitchell? I am a bit tired."

He squeezed her hand tighter and his bony fingers bit into hers like bars of steel. "This is important, Caroline, or I wouldn't ask. Please..."

Finally, she nodded in agreement. She *had* promised Jake she would keep Mitchell here as long as possible. This would give him some extra time to return the diary if he hadn't already. And nothing bad could come of it except she'd be delayed from finding out what Jake had learned from it. Maybe, just maybe, Mitchell had finally decided to confide in her. She might go home knowing more than she had this morning. Risk, again. She must take it.

She followed him upstairs just as May was closing the office door. "May," she said calmly, "I'm going to stay and help Mitchell for an hour or two. Will you tell Jake for me?"

The older woman looked surprised and stopped gathering her things for a moment. "Are you sure, honey? It's been a long day."

"Yes," Caroline replied firmly. "I promise I won't be late."

"Oh, by the way, May," Mitchell interjected. "You had a call from Henry McWilliams earlier. He wanted to have dinner with you. I'm sorry I forgot to mention it."

May looked pleased and reached for the phone. "I'll just give him a quick call," she said to Caroline. "Since you won't be in until later, my dear, I may as well see Henry. I've been missing him lately."

Mitchell tapped his foot impatiently on the floor. "Oh, he said you could meet him at the diner. He said you'd know where."

The older woman put down the phone and again turned to Caroline. "Are you sure you'll be all right then?"

"I'm sure. Just tell Jake I'll be a little late before you leave. All right?"

Still somewhat uncertain, May nodded and started down the stairs. She gave a sharp look in Mitchell's direction, but he had already returned to his office and was taking files from a cabinet. Caroline smiled at her with encouragement. "See you soon."

"Now..." Mitchell returned from his office with two cups steaming with coffee and a handful of files. "We can relax."

"Why don't you want May to know what we're discussing?"

They had taken seats side by side on the sofa. Caroline took a long sip of her coffee, almost too sweet with its cream and heavy-handed spoonful of sugar.

He fidgeted with the waist-pocket on his vest. "I didn't think you'd want her to know."

"To know what?"

"About last night?"

Caroline drew a breath and took another swig of the coffee, suddenly wishing it was something stronger. "What about last night?" she asked softly.

Mitchell had put the files on the coffee table in front of them, and moved nearer to her so their knees were just touching. "I felt like it was a beginning..."

His steady penetrating gaze bore into her eyes like an eternal night unrelieved by the merriment of stars. Caroline experienced an intense sense of discomfort, but fought to remain calm. Again, she drank from her coffee cup, using it as a small shield between herself and him. What on earth was he talking about?

"You and I, my dear...the future."

His words had begun to sound thick and distant, Caroline thought, and vaguely wondered why. They reminded her of something...what did they remind her of?

He stroked her hand, but his touch wasn't warm and soft; it burned like dry ice. She watched, unable to stop him, as he evenly caressed the skin just between her thumb and index finger. Her eyelids suddenly felt heavy as leaden blocks. Why was she so tired all of a sudden? Had the day taken more of a toll on her than she'd realized? She wanted desperately to stay awake, to hear what he had to say to her.

Caroline groped for a word to say to him, but nothing would come. Again, she reached for her coffee, but somehow, her hand misjudged the distance and the cup fell, shattering the mug and spilling the thick dark liquid like blood across the wood floor.

That was the last thing she remembered.

* * * *

"What the hell do you mean she stayed to work late with him. Fury rose in Jake's chest. When he'd asked her to keep him late, he hadn't meant this late. He'd been waiting all day. He'd read the journal twice before sneaking it back to Mitchell's. There's been plenty of time to do all that, and now he wanted her back here. He wanted to hold her, and then he wanted to sort through the pieces of all this insanity and come up with viable solutions—to what he knew in his heart was an unsolvable dilemma.

May appeared nonplussed by his reaction. "I really don't think there's anything to worry about Jake. She's a big girl, after all."

He paced back and forth. He'd wanted to spend this evening talking with the two of them, piecing things together, trying to figure out exactly what Mitchell Johnston was up to in all this; instead Caroline had stayed behind to cavort with the enemy while May went off on a casual date with Dr. Henry.

Jake debated as to whether he should tell May about his discovery of the journal. He wanted to know how much she thought he should tell Caroline, but he didn't want to spoil her evening by bringing it up now. May had a right to her moments of happiness just as much as he and Caroline did. He sensed she'd felt the strain of all this as much as the two of them had. She needed to relax for one evening. They could always discuss this later.

But then, once Caroline got home, she'd want to know what he'd found out. Well, he simply wouldn't tell her. Besides, he still needed time of his own to think all things over. For example, what was the right thing to do? What was his discovery going to mean to the estate funding? Granted, scandal attracted crowds, but devil worship and ritualistic murders...

Tying a scarf around her head, May re-entered the living room. "Well, I'm off," she told him. "I may be late so don't wait up." Appearing to notice his quietness for the first time, she asked, "Are you all right?"

"Great," Jake replied with barely a touch of sarcasm.

May's eyes penetrated him. Is something wrong?"

Jake drew a long breath and decided to let her go. "No.... I just thought the three of us—you, me and Caroline— had plans for the evening."

Lightly, May brushed his comment aside with a whisk of hand. "I know. I know. But that mystery's waited a hundred years to be solved, Jake. One more day won't matter. Besides, I suspect you and Caroline can find other things to keep you busy." With a quick wink back she headed out the door.

But as she left, Jake wondered if maybe one more day just might matter more than any of them knew.

* * * *

May fought a silent battle with herself as she left the gatehouse and headed toward her car. Jake wanted her to stay at home tonight. Something was on his mind. Maybe she shouldn't go out after all. She could always see Henry some other evening. She held the car keys in her hand and peered into the night, suddenly struck by lightheadedness. The world turned a fuzzy gray around her and she gripped the side of the car, struggling to maintain her balance. Something coursed through the air, close...some knowledge, truth. They were fighting to get to her, to tell her...she didn't know what. Then, through the trees, she saw the barest outline of the little green playhouse. But it wasn't really a playhouse at all, was it? It was a house of evil...

May shivered and turned to go back inside, deciding she must stay with Jake after all. "No..." A voice came to her from nowhere. A soft gentle voice that permeated her very being and warmed the core of her soul.

She looked around, but found she was still alone. She closed her eyes for a moment and pictured Jake and Caroline as they had been that morning, in love, their eyes filled only with each other. This was their battle. They must fight—and win—it themselves. May might have the links with the past, but she couldn't change it for them. If it could be

189

changed, in this time and place, they must do it themselves. Without her help or her interference.

She slid her key into the lock and whispered a prayer to the gods and the angels of the night. "See them through..." she prayed. "See them through this time."

* * * *

Mitchell labored with Caroline's body, amazed such a delicate creature could seem so heavy in an unconscious state. As he laid her across the sofa in his office, something clattered to the floor. He'd wondered why he'd been unable to find his that morning. Caroline must have seen it on the floor last night and slipped out with it, probably curious at another so like her own. She'd suspected something, then. Oh, well, no harm done. They were both in his possession now. If only he could unlock their secrets...

He pocketed the two glasses and then drew in a one last look at the girl's motionless form. He'd given her enough sleeping potion to last at least a few hours, and he'd be back to wake her hours before it wore off. Too bad she would be awakened by the chaos of Jake's accidental death. But of course Mitchell himself would be there for her...

A light tap at the outer office door arrested his thoughts. He left Caroline and hurried to answer it.

Gordon Henderson poked his shaggy blond head in the door. "Hey," he said cheerfully, "all set, partner?"

Mitchell bit back a sharp retort and a grimace and merely nodded. The young man looked exactly as Mitchell remembered him from five years ago, unkempt and dirty, like a common criminal. Mitchell couldn't think why he'd bothered with Ruby's son at the time he'd been in trouble for burglary, but now he was glad he had. Gordon's usefulness would prove itself tonight.

Mitchell retrieved a list from his desk and led Gordon downstairs. All was in place. He'd laid out the exact items they needed to move and figured it would take about two hours. He'd made certain Gordon parked off the estate and they would move the items with a dolly. They wouldn't need a lot, just enough to make it look like Jake was stealing. Luckily, because of his mention to the board Jake's removal of the diary from the library and its subsequent 'supposed' loss, this wouldn't come as a complete surprise.

Careful to leave the light on in his office so Jake would think he and Caroline were still working, Mitchell slipped down the hall. The only weak link in his plan was if Jake decided to come looking for Caroline. But, fairly certain the young man would not put in an appearance this time, Mitchell had decided to take that chance. And then, when it came time, Mitchell himself would make the call that would set the evening's events into action.

Now, it was time.

* * * *

Jake had just reached the limit of his tolerance level when the phone rang. He yanked it up. "Caroline?"

"Jake." It was Mitchell.

"Yeah, Mitchell, this is Jake. Put Caroline on."

"She's in the lady's room, Jake. She and I have discovered something quite interesting in some old files tonight. She asked me to give you a call and ask you to meet us at the playhouse."

A shiver ran down Jake's spine. "What's up?"

"She asked me not to say. She wants to surprise you. She said you'd understand when you got there."

Jake had a terrible sense of foreboding, and he wasn't sure why. Caroline would never lead him into anything dangerous. She loved him. He was sure of that. But where was she? Why hadn't she called him herself? And why did she want to meet at the playhouse, the one place she feared more than any other? Had they found something that convinced her to go there? Or had Mitchell done something to her? He'd kill him if he had.

"Jake," Mitchell's bland voice droned on, "Are you there?"

"Yeah, I'm here." *What the hell is going on,* Jake asked himself? "So you two will meet me at the playhouse then?"

"In about fifteen minutes. We'll just lock up here."

"Okay," he agreed, "see you there then."

Jake hung up the phone and went to the hall closet to get his jacket.

* * * *

Mitchell hung up the phone. He'd better hurry now. Jake would be at the playhouse in just a few minutes. All he need do was wait for the young man's arrival.

Gordon was on his way to lay the final evidence of the crime: Planting Caroline's diary back in Jake's room. In the end it would be Mitchell Johnston's word against Jake Stanton's. And, ironically enough, since Jake had been commissioned to write the words Mitchell always thought he himself would write, he felt confident his word would be accepted in the end. After all, Jake had stolen the diary—the librarian would testify to that.

Mitchell opened his desk drawer and withdrew the pistol the estate board had long-insisted he keep on hand. It would definitely be his word they listened to now, because Jake wasn't going to be around to refute it.

CHAPTER 22

The wrecks are all thy deed...
Lord Byron

Caroline slept, dreaming the dreams of her childhood. She knew she should be asleep, but try as she might, she couldn't seem to drop off. Tomorrow was her ninth birthday; she felt like she might burst with the thrill of it. She knew Aunt Jess planned to give her a new set of gardening tools and a seed catalog. Some girls might want china dolls in frilly lace dresses, but not Caroline. She didn't want to play ladies at tea parties. She wanted to grow things. She'd known this for as long as she could remember.

A crack split the night and she jumped from her bed and scurried to the window. She hated storms. This one roared like a terrifying monster, with particularly violent crashes and lights.

Something caught her eye in the trees, a quick movement, followed by a streak of white. It looked like...no, it couldn't be. The light flashed again, and this time she felt sure of it. But it couldn't be, could it? Her friend Rachel, led into the darkness by Evan Ludington. Why?

Caroline hated Evan Ludington. She shivered with the chill of him now, his foul breath, his cold fathomless eyes. She didn't know why, but she believed him to be an evil man, with some kind of terrible control over her father. She wished it could be just her and Father and Aunt Jess, like it had been when she was very small, right after her mother died. Before Evan came and began his terrible reign over them all.

Why was Evan taking her friend Rachel into the night? Rachel was only seven, the daughter of Mrs. Goldsmith, their housekeeper, and Caroline knew the little girl had no business walking out with Evan on a cold and rainy eve.

"I'll get her," she whispered to no one in particular, then grabbed her robe from the end of the bed and vaulted into the night, a small avenger with a mighty task.

* * * *

"Damn," Jake said aloud as he pulled the door of the gatehouse shut and looked around. "Where the hell did this storm come from?"

Rain hadn't started falling yet, but the sky looked as if it might explode at any minute. Thunder and lightening battled for supremacy of the night. A heavy stillness added its own oppression to the raging war. Jake felt insignificant as a sparrow caught in its might.

Why, he wondered once more, *did Caroline want them to meet at the playhouse?* She hated the place. Had she discovered some reason for her fear that she wanted to test immediately? But why had she wanted Mitchell there? Jake couldn't understand it, but he felt compelled to do as Mitchell had asked.

As he drew nearer, the little house took shape against the woods. The irony never failed to amaze him about the place, just a doll's house, after all, but such an awful sense of malevolency. Something evil. He'd hadn't been particularly aware of it before, at least not in the way Caroline was, but tonight its force struck him with malevolence as he approached.

The windows, curtained in pitch, seemed to hide frightening secrets of their own. Jake hoped Caroline or Mitchell had thought to bring a flashlight, because he hadn't. They weren't going to be able to see much in this light, and Jake didn't relish the idea of the three of them being shut up in there together if the storm got worse. Now, if it had been him and Caroline alone, that would be a different matter. He still couldn't quite get over the novelty of the two of them, the special power that had somehow brought them together. Even now, his body tingled at the thought of her.

Rain burst from the clouds just as Jake pushed open the door stepped inside. Thank God he hadn't gotten drenched beforehand. He could only hope Mitchell and Caroline had already arrived and missed the storm as well.

Right away he noticed the icy frost clinging to the still air like particles of some long-frozen world. The chill thrust its claws into him, thick and unnatural. The second thing he noticed was that, although Mitchell and Caroline did not seem to have arrived yet, the room wasn't empty. As his eyes adjusted to the dark, he made out shapes of furniture and other small items.

"What the hell?" he swore, immediately certain something was afoot.

Then a figure stepped from the corner and in another flash of lightning, Jake caught sight of a silver barrel pointed directly at him. The grim face above it belonged to Mitchell Johnston...

* * * *

Heavy rain caught Caroline about halfway to the playhouse. As the first drops pelted her body, she suddenly had a sense that she wasn't asleep after all, that tomorrow wasn't really her birthday. She wasn't exactly sure who or where she was. But all the same, something bad was about to happen, and she had to stop it.

The storm had drenched her by the time she reached the playhouse, yet she didn't rush in. Frightened as always, she stopped a few feet away and stared at the little building, knowing it would offer her no real shelter from the storm.

Rachel. Her friend Rachel had gone in there with Evan. Why had she gone out with him in the middle of the night? Rachel, usually so timid, that wasn't like her at all.

Caroline tried to force herself to move toward the house, knowing she must prevent whatever tragedy was about to happen there. But even as she took the first small step, she felt armies of fear gathering oppressively around her. She mustn't go in there. *They* would get her in there.

As she stepped back, she sensed an even greater fear. The fear that she if she did not go in, she would lose whatever or whomever she now needed to protect. If she let the evil win this time, there would not be another chance.

Slowly and with leaden steps, she moved forward. Her anxiety was still there, almost overpowering in its ferocity, but she kept inching ahead, unwilling to stop or be stopped by powers unseen.

* * * *

"Ah, Mitchell, I guess I should have suspected you were up to something." Despite the dreadful cold, Jake didn't feel particularly afraid. He felt like a character in a play, and this just happened to be the next scene. He must play it or ruin the show.

"Come closer," Mitchell rasped, his voice hollow and somehow strangely affected by the cold in the room so that it did not sound like his voice at all. "Pick up that sword on the table there."

Jake did as he was ordered and studied the long silver shaft of the sword. "One of Lyndfield's heirloom's? So what am I supposed to be doing, Mitchell? Stealing it?" He faced the older man like a hesitantly confident soldier. "You'll never get away with it."

Shrill laughter filled the room—Mitchell even sounded like the villain from some evil novel. For the first time Jake experienced a thread of apprehension. This whole setting seemed oddly out of time and place.

"Of course I'll get away with it," Mitchell said. "No one will be here to question the fact that you were robbing the estate."

"What about Caroline?" he asked. "And May?"

"They won't be able to prove you weren't. All the evidence will point toward you. And this is one time where Caroline's confused state of mind will be quite helpful."

Fire boiled through Jake's veins. "You'd use her like that?" He could just make out the thin slash of Mitchell's smile against his stark white face.

"Only temporarily. She'll forget you soon enough. With my help, of course."

Mitchell held up the two hourglasses so they caught a splinter of light and Jake's eye. So he must know their secret, after all.

"Don't count on it," Jake said with more confidence than he felt. "She's remembered me for longer than you think."

For an instant Mitchell appeared taken off-guard. "What does that mean?"

"I found Evan's diary, Mitchell. I know about his crazy time travel theories and William's hideous appetites. I also know who our Caroline Lyndfield really is."

Jake heard the click of the hammer as Mitchell pulled it back. Was this really going to happen? Was he really going to die—again—at the hands of a madman? Would fate be so cruel as that?

"Well," Mitchell droned glibly and without emotion in answer to Jake's unspoken questions, "That's all the more reason for you to die, then."

* * * *

Then quite suddenly, Caroline was in the room. The frozen hell of its wasteland hit her even before she opened the door. Here it was...this was what she had come here for. But then the cold brass of the doorknob somehow made contact with her hand and she knew she would go in. She must, mustn't she? What other choice was there?

The alternating light and dark of the storm allowed her a staccato picture of the interior. In the first flash, she saw the altar, with candles and an oddly-shaped star at its center. She could barely breathe, and she fought the night for what little air she could manage. She knew what else was there in the dark. How, she had no idea; but know she did.

The second flash lit her father's face, twisted and grotesque, not the face of the man she thought she knew and loved. This was a hard face, a face seeking only to satisfy itself. A face that found its pleasure in cruelty. Caroline tried to cry out to him but, suddenly mute, her voice would not come.

The third flash fell across Rachel's pale skin, as she lay in a trance-like sleep at the foot of the cold marble slab next to where her father stood. The night seemed to come alive with light then, and Caroline saw everything at once. The glint of her father's knife as it crept like a violent hand across her friend's slender neck, the river of red that gushed from Rachel and splattered on the floor like tea spilling from a broken vessel, her father as he bent over the child and took his ugly horrible pleasure on her still form.

Caroline's cry pierced the darkness like a wounded animal raging against its painful death. It burst from the core of her and permeated the room, and the night, and the darkness itself. As she looked toward her young friend again, this time she saw Nan, lying helpless beneath her father's rigid body. She saw Evan. She remembered another struggle. A struggle so terrible it had somehow thrust her out of time and place toward fulfilling an unbelievable destiny. The last thing she remembered was the anguish in her father's eyes as he reached out for her. She cried out for Francis.

Then the light flashed again, and Jake was there, standing only a few feet from her, her father's sword at his hand. She wondered if he had come here to fight the forces of evil with her?

She moved toward him as lightning flashed and then exploded with a thundering boom against the confines of the room, splitting the barriers between past and present and suddenly allowing Caroline a clear picture of what she must do in moment. She threw herself in front Jake even as he tried to push her away. The next flash came not from the sky, but from the corner of the playhouse. A small flash, followed by a loud pop, and at almost the same instant she felt the sting of pain in her arm. Looking down, she saw a streak of red. She felt no fear or pain, but almost relief. Everything was going to be all right.

Even as Jake lunged for Mitchell's gun, he noticed the flames from the last bolt of lightning, threatening to engulf the room, its occupants, and the Lyndfield treasures. Right now however, the antiques were the least of his concerns.

Somehow, Mitchell slipped beyond his grasp and grabbed Caroline. He pointed the revolver at Jake and waved him back like a man gone suddenly mad.

"I'll kill you. I'll kill her. But I'll kill you first."

"Give it up, Mitchell. You can't pull this off. Think of Caroline. She's wounded."

Briefly, Mitchell glanced down at the girl in his hold. Apparently satisfied she hadn't been seriously hurt, he backed toward the door.

Caroline's eyes sought Jake's in the now glowing darkness but she, like he had been earlier, seemed calm, as if she had conquered whatever demon had haunted her and was now at peace.

Gunfire filled the room again, but Jake out-maneuvered it.

Then Mitchell catapulted out the door, dragging Caroline with him.

Jake's gaze followed Mitchell's direction: he suddenly knew what lay ahead. Time to put his own demon to rest.

* * * *

Before Mitchell had yanked her outside, Caroline had caught a glimpse of the fear in Jake's eyes. She well understood his terror. Mitchell had chosen the one place to go that Jake—Francis— feared above all others: the river.

She struggled only mildly as he pushed her through the dense woods. Her arm stung wildly now and she did not have the strength to resist. Besides, she had a deep inner confidence that if she could face her demon, Jake would face his as well. That he must face it.

Demons of the dark forest winked at them through the trees and Mitchell, with rasping breaths, charted their tragic course as the rain beat them like pelts of steel. Caroline prayed there were angels there as well, hidden in the dark clouds perhaps, but carefully watching all the same. Watching, and waiting for the right moment to intervene on loving golden wings.

As they neared the rusted railroad trestle near the back of the estate, Mitchell slowed his pace. Suddenly, Mitchell plunged a hand deep into the pocket of his sweater. It emerged clasping an hourglass.

"Here's our escape, my dear," he told her with eyes half-crazed. "It's our only way." His fingers dug into her arm. "You must tell me now. I know you have the answers. How do these work?"

Caroline shuddered as she looked at the slender object. She knew now what Evan had used them for. To hypnotize her father's helpless victims. Rachel. Nan. And only God knew how many others. How could she have lived her whole life with a man so twisted? she wondered. Without suspecting a thing?

Mitchell squeezed her arm again and she grimaced at the pain. "Tell me, Caroline," he demanded. "You must tell me what you know. It's our only hope." He put his mouth close to her ear, yelling above the wind. His breath reminded her of Evan, the terrible Evan, who had used her, her father, perhaps even her aunt. Who had set all the evil in motion...?

"I don't know what you want from me," she replied, trying to maintain calm, trying to delay him long enough for Jake to gather his courage and help her.

"How did you do it?" Mitchell screamed. "How did you travel through time?"

"I don't know."

His nails bit into her skin. "You do. You must. You and I must do it now. We must get away from him. He wants to hurt you. Just like your father wanted to hurt you. Only I can protect you now."

Caroline shook her head, spitting out the strands of rain-soaked hair that had found their way into her mouth. "But I don't need *your* protection. I don't want to get away from Jake. I love him."

The sting of his slap surprised them both. She brought her hand quickly to her face, now both wet and burning. Mitchell jerked her out onto the old trestle and for a moment they both teetered there. Then, he got his balance and with the muzzle of the gun pointed against her neck, he carefully edged them out over the river.

"You will tell me," he said, "or we will go to our deaths together."

She could see Jake now. He wasn't far away. His pace was steady, but she sensed the hesitation in his gait.

She willed strength to him and concentrated all her love in that direction. If love could bring her across years to him, surely she could send him what he needed of it most.

Mitchell had stopped and was watching Jake as well. "Tell me, Caroline," he urged. "Hurry. We haven't much time."

"I don't know how it happened, Mitchell. I swear I don't."

He forced her to sit on the old steel ledge, and she did, glad of the unexpected respite from his anger and her own unsteady legs. He stared hard at the glass in his hand, as if willing it to offer some answer.

Then her eyes found Jake, taking his first shaky steps onto the trestle.

He'd never been so afraid of anything in his life. The wind, the rain, the cold—he knew them all. Knew them from a time and place reason told him he had no way of knowing, but know them he did. That night came back to him, a living, breathing reality. It had happened right here. Evan must have found it so easy—just one push. The gusting wind had carried him down quickly; the water sucked and pulled and finally covered him with heavy smothering arms. Then his world had gone black.

Jake's foot slipped a little on the slippery wet metal and he grabbed an overhead bar to steady himself. He gulped the night air like a dying man. But he wasn't. He wasn't a dying man. Not now. Not this man. Not this time. This time he would fight. He had to live. He had someone wonderful to live for.

"Let her go, Mitchell," he called out, feeling a ferocious power over the wind. "You don't want to hurt her. It's me you want."

He prayed his voice carried and sounded stronger than he had felt a moment before. His head still spun so badly he was sure he'd tumble from the rusty iron form any second. Bells rang a cacophony in his ears: his hands trembled like half-formed JELL-O. But at the end of this steel bridge was the one reason he had to live. The fear he must fight now was nothing compared to the life he would be forced to live without her. The life he had lived until now...

Though the distance, through the vicious and dark night, the pull of her love filled him courage. There was love, there was faith, there was hope. He would not let her down.

Mitchell lifted his eyes from something in his hand and waved the gun at Jake. "Get back. I'm warning you."

A shot ricocheted off the steel bar next to him.

Close. But not close enough. Jake took another step forward.

The water below churned murky and dark. Looking at it briefly, he not only remembered its chill, he experienced it all again, the way it had closed over his head and swallowed him down, down, down into his icy depths. That had been hell.

Sharply and with great effort, he forced his eyes back up to the two figures at the end of the trestle. He mustn't think about the past now. That had been then...this was another time, another place. Another chance.

"Mitchell," Jake said with sudden calm, "Please."

"She's mine, Stanton." The older man's arm tightened possessively around his captive and he moved another inch closer to the edge.

He's lost his mind, Jake thought, but Caroline, like himself, appeared calm and confident.

Now that the moment had come at last, it seemed they both were ready. They would not let fate be their enemy this time.

"Caroline, please." The night became suddenly still, and Jake heard the despair in Mitchell's voice as he begged the girl. "Please come with me."

She shook her head stubbornly.

Where does he think he can take her? Jake looked down at the raging water, his stomach queasy.

Then in a flash of light, he caught a glint of what Mitchell had in his hand. The hourglass...had he figured out how to send them back in time?

Jake remembered what he'd read about the glass in the diary. He still wasn't sure if he believed it completely, but he didn't want to risk not believing.

"Put it down, Mitchell. Drop it. It won't help you." He reached out a hand imploring. "It never helped Evan and it won't help you."

"But he knew its secrets. He must have."

"He did not," Jake yelled. "He was an evil man and he fed evil with evil. He didn't have the secrets to time travel. Neither does Caroline."

Mitchell's face crumbled in that instant.

Jake had inched close enough so that even in the darkness he could see how worn and aged the man looked. On his forehead, the red streak seemed to glow fiercely. *A mark of the devil,* Jake thought irrationally.

"Caroline..." Mitchell's voice broke off painfully and he stared into the girl at his side's face. "But you loved me, didn't you?"

With sad denial, Caroline tossed her slowly head from side to side. Jake was so close now he could have sworn he saw a tear fall from the man's eye. A tear, or was it only a raindrop?

Dismally, Mitchell let the hourglass slip from his hand and it fell, another silent teardrop, into the river below. Then he released Caroline's waist and stepped over the steel rim of the trestle, catapulting himself down into the pit of watery darkness below.

It was truly over now.

CHAPTER 23

But tell of days in goodness spent,
A mind at peace with all below.
A heart whose love is innocent.
Lord Byron

How they climbed off the trestle and back to the solid ground below remained a mystery to Caroline. She didn't know who shook more—Jake, or she.

The storm had evaporated and the plump shape of the moon peeked from behind a bright cloud like a timid child, with the world its calm parent. The night seemed strangely silent and free of its previous turmoil as they stood there arm in arm, safe at last. Safe, forever....

"Are you okay?" Jake asked. "How's your arm?"

For the first time in some while, she remembered her wound, but looking down, saw it had only been a graze, not even bleeding now. Her heart felt truly light as she nodded and went into his warm embrace. For a long time they remained motionless there, seeming to need the strength and reassurance from each other that all was well, and safe. That they were together and nothing could part them now.

"I think we won," Jake whispered at last.

She smiled up at him. "It's about time, isn't it?"

"I'll say..." He bent and claimed her lips. Another few minutes passed as each melted into the other's love.

Finally, Caroline stepped back and turned toward the river. "Somehow I feel sad for him," she said softly. "None of this was really his fault at all. He just got caught up in an old drama, I think."

Jake put an arm around her waist and shook his head in agreement. "He was only playing his part. And it could only come out this way."

Her eyes caressed his. "Do you think he was Evan? Come back from the dead?"

"I don't know, Caroline. I don't know what to think about Mitchell, or any of it really. I only know I believe. And you are here. Somehow."

As they walked slowly back toward the big house, the shrill sound of fire sirens cut like a high-pitched cry through the night. Jake held Caroline back with a touch and they paused and looked toward the now-smoldering playhouse.

"I'm glad it's gone," she told him harshly. "Now, I feel I truly belong here. Like it was the last link to my past. And now it's destroyed..."

"Caroline..." Jake squeezed her hand and looked lovingly into her eyes.

He sighed one of his long and lovely sighs, as if weighing carefully the words he wanted to say. The moonlight shone full on his face now, and she drew in the sight of it, her heart near bursting with love. Jake brought her hand up and pressed it to his cheek. His gaze bore into her.

"There's a lot they'll be asking of us. And there's a lot I haven't told you yet."

"About my father?"

He winced slightly and nodded. "I'm not sure where to begin.... He wasn't the person you thought he was."

Caroline stood firm, willing herself to be strong—and remember. "I think I know most of it," she told him softly. "It came back to me. In the playhouse."

Only mildly surprised, he hugged her tightly. "I love you..." He drew back and continued after a moment, "So you remembered what happened to your friend?"

"My friends..." Her voice broke slightly. "There was Rachel, too. Taken by my father for God knows what reason...some evil he believed in."

Jake nodded. "His obsession with power overcame him in the end. Your father thought he kept his wealth and stature because of the murder and the devil worship. I think he must have always had an abnormal desire for young girls. That's probably why he married your mother. She was young and she loved him. Later, Evan provided for his lusts and blackmailed him at the same time. He even convinced your father to will him most of the estate. Evan did it for you, mostly." Jake squeezed her hand. "I guess they argued when you disappeared. Somehow, your father blamed Evan for what happened to you in the end. I guess he loved you in his own way. I'm sorry."

Caroline's eyes remained sadly trained on the burning building in the distance. "I don't think either of them knew the meaning of that word—Love. At least I know I didn't kill him."

She let out a long sigh of her own, releasing as much anguish as she could in that one breath. "That was a long, long time ago, Jake, too long to be a part of either of our lives any longer. There's nothing I can do for my friends any more than I can do anything for my father. And what I needed to do for you, I think I've done that tonight."

Jake wrapped her once more in his loving arms, cradling her like the precious treasure that she was. "I'll say you have. You've done more than you needed."

He leaned close to her for a long time, and she could feel the warmth of his breath like feathery kisses against her neck. She wished they could stay here, just like this, forever, but she knew there was much to decide. And the hours before dawn were growing short.

Finally, he spoke. "So maybe there is one last thing we can do for your father."

She slid back in his arms a little, but his warmth stayed with her. "What?"

"We can protect your family name...let the past be the past."

"Your book?"

"There won't be any book, at least not the kind I had hoped to write, revealing all and finally putting the mystery of Caroline Lyndfield to rest." He grinned. "I'm thinking of a nice picture book...what do you think?"

Caroline looked toward the last remnants of the playhouse. "Why would you want to do that? You lost your life because of him. And Evan—"

Jake touched the tip of her nose with his finger. "That was fate, love. And that was then. I'm doing this for you.

"But what about Mitchell? We can't blame all this on him."

"We'll tell them he was trying to stop the theft in progress. He followed the guy to the river and slipped from the trestle." Jake paused for effect. "Then the burglar got away. It's simple."

Caroline thought it probably would be simple. May would be here soon, knowing in her all-knowing way that they needed her. She would help them without question. Questions, and answers, would come later. Mitchell's death would be ruled an accident of the storm, much as Francis' had once been.

Mitchell, the estate, it would all be protected. For an instant, Caroline wondered why they should bother. But almost immediately, she realized it was not the people themselves who were to be hated, but rather the evil which often gathered them in. It would do no good to harbor malice toward Mitchell, or Evan, or her father. That in itself would eat away at them and leave nothing but the bitter shells of the people they could become. The people who had hurt her, and Jake, and her childhood friends, were all gone now. The task of the present was to let them go, pray for their salvation, and pray some day humanity would find a way to overcome the malignant forces which always chaotically fought to find a way back into the world.

"Well," Jake whispered, "what do you think? Are you game?"

Wistfully, she returned his smile. So much still new to her in this life. Words, for instance. Caroline knew no matter how well she adjusted to this century, a part of her would always marvel at its difference from her own. But this was her place. She belonged in this time, and she belonged with Jake.

Where she did not belong was at Lyndfield. They must find a new horizon for themselves, and begin again. Together. Somehow, she knew it would all come about as it should. Life's ebbs and flows...

"I'm game," she replied and leaned into his hold. "Will we play this 'game' forever?"

Jake kissed the top of her head and laughed lightly. "You betcha," he told her. "And always."

As one, they walked toward the playhouse, where Caroline's life had ended...and then somehow started once more. Where tonight, her past, once and for all, became her present.